THE DIG

———

Also by Sheldon Russell

Empire (Inola, Okla., 1993)
The Savage Trail (New York, 1998)
Requiem at Dawn (New York, 2000)
Dreams to Dust: A Tale of the Oklahoma Land Rush
    (Norman, Okla., 2006)
The Yard Dog: A Mystery (New York, 2009)
The Insane Train (New York, 2010)
Dead Man's Tunnel (New York, 2012)

THE DIG

In Search of Coronado's Treasure

Sheldon Russell

UNIVERSITY OF OKLAHOMA PRESS : NORMAN

This book is published with the generous assistance of The McCasland Foundation, Duncan, Oklahoma.

Library of Congress Cataloging-in-Publication Data

Russell, Sheldon.
   The dig : in search of Coronado's treasure / Sheldon Russell.
     pages cm
   ISBN 978-0-8061-4360-6 (pbk. : alk. paper) 1. Coronado, Francisco Vásquez de, 1510-1554—Fiction. 2. Quests (Expeditions)—Fiction. 3. Excavations (Archaeology)—Kansas—Fiction. 4. Quivira (Legendary Place)—Fiction. 5. Historical fiction. I. Title.
   PS3568.U777D54 2013
   813'.54—dc23

2013001300

The paper in this book meets the guidelines for permanence and durability of the Committee on Production Guidelines for Book Longevity of the Council on Library Resources, Inc. ∞

In memory of
Kirk Bjornsgaard

Acknowledgments

A special thanks to my editors Kathleen Kelly and Emily Jerman for their guidance in writing this book; to copyeditor Jay Fultz for his insight and for his diligence in its preparation; to my agents, Michael and Susan Morgan Farris, for their loyalty and support; to the members of the reading committee, who gave of their time and wisdom; and to the University of Oklahoma Press staff.

And, of course, a personal thank you to my wife, Nancy, who steers me through the highs and lows of my work with a steady hand.

Author's Note

Coronado's expedition took place centuries ago, and much about his journey has been lost to time. Notes in the back of this book are provided to suggest the nature of the terrain and the distances he traversed, rather than to provide geographical specificity about his route. While based on research, the expedition narrative remains a work of fiction and not of history.

THE DIG

1

The day Dean Halsey called him into his office, Jim Hunt knew that trouble awaited. Halsey checked the peer evaluations and then looked over his glasses at Jim.

"Frankly, Mr. Hunt, we're disappointed in your progress."

The heat rose in Jim's neck. "I can do better, Dean Halsey. It's just that I had to take on a second job."

"We don't give out scholarships to just everyone here at the University of Oklahoma, Mr. Hunt. You're obviously intelligent and have the potential to become a first-rate archeologist."

Jim's mouth went dry. "Gloria has had a really hard time since the baby. She's just been so unhappy and then when she lost her job, I had to pick up the slack. I didn't have the time I needed to complete the work."

Dean Halsey slipped the evaluations back into the folder and clasped his hands in front of him. "There are plenty of talented students around who deserve a scholarship and will work hard for it. When we invest in someone, we expect a commitment."

"Things piled up," he said. "Gloria has been so dissatisfied, the baby, and the apartment is so small."

"The department makes it a practice not to get involved in the personal lives of students, but it's clear that your home life is in need of attention. Perhaps you should take care of that first.

Come back when you've worked things out, and we will reconsider an application."

Jim gathered up his backpack. "I've lost my scholarship, then?"

Dean Halsey stood and opened the file drawer, retrieving a paper. "I have here a letter from the park department. They are searching for someone to conduct a survey of dig sites in the area this fall. I'm prepared to recommend you for the position."

"The park department?"

"It's a staff-level position, but it would give you a chance to straighten out your life and get your finances in order. Perhaps you should consider it."

"It's not what I had planned, Dean Halsey."

"To continue as you are will only harm your opportunities for a career in archeology later."

Jim shifted his backpack to the other shoulder. "I don't know."

"There is one hitch," he said, handing Jim the letter. "The job requires field experience, an area in which you are decidedly lacking."

"I'd planned to do that after completing my program."

"Might I suggest you do some volunteer work in a dig to satisfy the requirement. There happens to be one scheduled at the Celf Historical Museum in Lyons, Kansas, this summer. With that experience, you should be able to get on at the park department without difficulty."

"That would mean no pay all summer."

"It's the best I can do. Think it over, Mr. Hunt, but don't wait too long."

Gloria shut the television off with the remote and looked up at him, her eyes flashing. "What do you mean no pay?"

"For field experience, and it's just for the summer," he said.

She tossed the remote aside, pulling her legs under her. Her ankles were thin and shapely, and she'd polished her toenails a deep red.

"You've lost your scholarship? How do you expect us to live?"

"I'll borrow a little to get us through the summer. I can live inexpensively at the dig. I can get by. Maybe my mother will take care of Sara so that you could take a part-time job. Then in the fall, I'll apply for the park department position. With Dean Halsey's recommendation, I'll be a shoo-in."

Gloria swung her legs around, dropping her face into her hands. Her ears peeked through her hair like white mice. She stood, jabbing her hands onto her waist and narrowing her eyes.

"You expect me to stay in this place all summer while you're out digging for bones or something?"

Sara cried from the back bedroom. She probably needed changing. Caught up in her soaps, Gloria sometimes forgot to change Sara's diaper.

"It's just for the summer," he said. "I can drive back on the weekends."

"And what if there are things *I* want to do?" she said, clamping her arms across her breasts. "Everything's always about you."

"I'm doing this for us," he said, "for you and Sara. Once I've finished my program, things will be better."

From in back, Sara cranked up full volume. He could tell by the way she shortened her sobs that she hadn't eaten.

Gloria turned her back to him. "I'm sick of waiting around. I'm sick of listening to you talk about archeology all the time, and I'm sick of listening to that kid cry."

Jim set his backpack on the table. "I'll check on Sara and then we'll talk."

The milk in Sara's bottle had soured, and her diaper sagged. He changed her, fixed a new bottle, and then picked her up. He hummed to her as he walked back and forth in the room, and when she'd quieted, he tucked her in. Not until she'd fallen asleep did he close the blinds and creep out.

The television and lights had been shut off. Moonlight shot through the window, a shaft of silver edging across the floor. He looked for Gloria in the kitchen and then in the bathroom. He checked the bedroom and found her closet door open, hangers scattered on the floor. His heart sank when he discovered the car missing from the driveway.

How long he waited in the darkness before falling asleep, he didn't know. But when he awoke, the sun was high in the morning sky, and Gloria had not returned. She did not return that day nor the next nor ever again.

———————

His mother listened quietly on the other end of the line, and said, "Maybe if you two had married, Jim."

"I don't think so."

"I'll come to get Sara and make arrangements for your things," she said. "You do what you have to do this summer."

"Are you sure?"

"She will be fine, Jim. I raised *you*, didn't I?"

After that, he called Dean Halsey, then packed his suitcase and bought a bus ticket to Wichita.

Not knowing what to expect in Lyons, he boarded the bus alone on a Monday morning. As it pulled out of town, he could see the university stadium and the apartment where he and Gloria had lived.

On the bus, he pondered Gloria's charge. Perhaps she was right about his preoccupation. He lived for archeology, was intent on pursuing the remnants of the Spanish conquistadors' grand pursuit four and half centuries ago.

2

Because Hernando de Alvarado was loyal, tireless, and when necessary appallingly brutal, Coronado relied on him for the most difficult of tasks.

Earlier, on his foray to Cicúique, Alvarado had captured an Indian, a large and powerful warrior. His hands and feet were chained, and he now clambered up the hill. Friar Juan Padilla followed behind them. Drawing his Toledo sword, Alvarado motioned for the Indian to drop onto his knees.

"Welcome back, Captain," Coronado said.

"I rejoice in being in your presence again, my general. I have brought a captive, a Pawnee. Though he can run like the wind, he could not outrun a Spanish horse. We call him the Turk because he's so big and ugly, as can be seen, and a danger to all.

"One must be careful in telling secrets in his company, because he's very crafty, and he knows our language, which he has learned by listening to his captors. We have captured his friend, Isopete, a Wichita and a man of slower wit, as is most readily seen."

"No man befriends Isopete," the Turk said, looking up at Coronado.

The Turk's voice, deep as a drum, summoned the attention of all present. He smelled of weeds and horse sweat. Black hair

7

fell about his shoulders, and his eyes snapped. Powerful arms bore against his chains, and a scar ran the length of his cheek. A tattoo of dots and lines encircled his throat like a necklace.

"And why have you brought this Turk to me in this manner?" Coronado asked.

The Turk said, "It is I who know of the golden cities, which can be found by few men, for the way is most difficult."

Alvarado dropped his sword on the Turk's shoulder and slid it into the soft skin of his neck. A drop of blood gathered on the point of the sword.

"Do not speak to the general without consent, Turk, or my sword will taste your flesh."

"You may speak the truth, if it pleases you to live," Coronado said.

The Turk glanced up at Alvarado, who withdrew his sword.

"The Turk speaks truth even now, for he fears the wrath of the Spanish warrior," he said.

"I beseech you then to speak only that and live out your years, Turk," Coronado said.

"I have been to the north and have seen this gold and silver, which gives great happiness, for it is more pleasurable than a woman's heat."

"Speak more of this gold and silver which turns the heads of men."

"Enough gold for a thousand men. The trees hang with bells of gold, their chimes sing in the wind, and the women cook in golden pots. Silver chains hang about their waists and from their hair. Even the birds have golden sand in their craws. Gold is left to lie about, because no one troubles to pick it up, though it drifts about the land like snow. I have seen this myself in wonder, though even I soon wearied of gold."

Coronado looked over at Alvarado. "Does a man who speaks only truth deserve the chains?"

"Such a man is uncommon, my general, even in Spain, and in a land such as this, most rare indeed. Servantes, a man most holy himself, did witness the Turk talking to the devil in a pitcher of water. Should not such a man be chained?"

Coronado turned to the Turk. "And so, Turk, you are in God's eyes a liar and collaborator with Satan, the sworn enemy of the church."

The Turk shook his head. "I am a holy Catholic, my general, as the *Requerimiento* commands. Each day I pray for my heathen soul and for the long life of the King of Spain. I pray for Captain Alvarado, and even for Servantes, though sometimes he drinks of the friars' wine."

Alvarado shrugged. "I have seen the evil in the Turk's eyes in the first light of day when it cannot be hidden. His conversion is false, as is his tale of gold, and I should have run him through with my pike many weeks ago so that I might have slept in peace at night."

"And where is this gold, Turk?" Coronado asked.

"Far away in the land of Quivira," the Turk said.

"Coronado will show what happens to liars. Alvarado, bring forth the heathen, the thief who dared steal from the cook's fire, so that his rectitude may be judged and witnessed by all."

"As you command, my general."

"Fetch also the hunting dogs, which hunger for justice, so that the perils of deception cannot be mistaken, or perhaps the Turk, as so many before him, has only dreamed of gold, and wishes now to make amends to Coronado and to his God."

The Turk shook his head. "The gold is not mistaken, my general, for I have seen it with my own eyes."

"Bring the thief to me," Coronado said.

Alvarado brought forward an old Indian tied at the end of a rope. Coronado removed his helmet, cradling it in the cup of his arm.

"And is this the man who dare steals from those who would bring him salvation?"

"The heathen is secured at the end of a rope, my general, for he is more stubborn than a friar and would have been throttled by less benevolent men many days past."

Friar Padilla looked up through his brows and shook his head.

"And does he speak only with his hands?" Coronado asked.

Alvarado shrugged. "Grunts and snorts, like those of swine."

Coronado walked around the old Indian, whose hide hung from his bones. His hand jerked with tremor, and blood oozed from the briar scratches on his legs. He smelled of dirt and sour.

"Ask then, Alvarado, if he is a thief as charged and steals food from those who would save his children from eternal damnation?"

The old man grunted and looked at his feet.

"He says that the general's own man ate the meat in the darkness of his tent."

"Tell him that to lie to Coronado insults the King of Spain, blasphemes the mother church, that he will be lost in the fires of hell from which no man escapes."

Friar Padilla said, "To lie is to break God's commandment, upon which all other commandments rest, for a liar is defiled by both man and God, and such a man will surely suffer the agonies of hell."

Coronado nodded. "Tell this man that the dogs will strip away his hide, that he will stand quivering and bleeding before God, that Satan will take his soul into the underworld forever."

When Alvarado had finished, the old Indian shuffled his feet. Locking his eyes on Coronado, he spat into the dirt.

Coronado's jaw rippled, and he motioned for Alvarado to bring the dogs forward. The curs lunged at their ropes, their hindquarters trembling, their front feet lifting off the ground.

When their ropes tangled, a fight ensued, the dogs snarling and slashing, their necks bloodied, and bits of fur floated about in the air. Kicked apart by their keepers, they slunk back, yelping and biting at their own wounds.

The old Indian's eyes widened, and his breath shortened. His knees buckled, and he grabbed at the rope to balance himself.

"Release him, then," Coronado said. "So that he may face the retribution that he, and no other, has chosen."

With a slash of his sword, Alvarado severed the Indian's restraint, and he dropped at Coronado's feet. The Indian lifted himself onto all fours. His belly hung slack from his ribs, and his arms trembled as he struggled to stand. The dogs howled and churned, and their keepers leaned into the ropes.

Coronado signaled to Alvarado, and with a flourish, Alvarado lifted his sword, releasing the dogs. At first they sniffed the ground, urinating and defecating as they stirred about. Then as if by command, they circled in twos. A white bitch, wide between the eyes and big as a cougar, assumed the lead. The pairs flowed in behind her, dust rising from their feet and drifting over the conquistadors.

The old man turned in a circle, his arms limp at his side. His forehead shined with sweat, and a ring of moisture spread across the front of his breechclout.

His breathing stopped when he'd made his decision to head for a stand of trees a hundred yards away at the top of the hill. Just as he broke into a run, four dogs split from the pack, two on a side, looping wide to cut him off.

He did not slow nor alter his course but ran hard for the trees. But even as he breached the hill, the first dog caught him in the buttocks. Setting its front feet, the dog thrashed its head. The second dog came from the side, striking him hard in the kidneys. The old man grunted and spilled forward into the dirt.

The pack moved in, tearing at his flesh, tugging him this way and that, dragging his body into the trees.

Coronado turned to the Turk. "The holy Padre Marcos de Niza spoke of gold and treasure in this land, but after many leagues, only clay huts and heathens have been found. Why should the Turk now swear he has seen what others have not? Why should Coronado follow the Turk into this faraway land called Quivira?"

"If the general sets me free, I will lead him there, as no other man can do. The people in this land drink from cups made of silver, and the women wash their hair in pots made of gold." Holding out his hands, he added, "To find such gold will bring great honor to Coronado."

"Honor for Viceroy Mendoza of New Spain," Coronado said.

The Turk lifted his arms above his head and said, "And for the greatest conquistador of all, Francisco Vázquez de Coronado, and for his army of noble warriors."

"If the Turk speaks the truth, there will be souls to be harvested for God's glory."

"And so many lost souls hastened to their salvation because of my general."

"And grace for the friars who pray daily for the heathens, holy men who mark the way to deliverance," Coronado said.

The Turk clasped his hands across his chest. "And for the glory of Francisco Coronado when he kneels before his Spanish god, for no other conquistador will have so many who follow his council."

Coronado turned, scanning the horizon. "You have seen the fate of liars, of those who betray and steal. Have you not, Turk?"

"The wisdom of the dogs is certain, my general, but the Turk fears not their judgment. Follow me, and I will lead you into the land of Quivira."

Coronado turned to Alvarado. "Return him to camp while I consider his words. Later, when I have discerned the truth of this matter, I will have him brought to me."

When they were gone, Coronado went to his tent, retrieving his wife's letter from his satchel. The letter, dated September 16, 1540, was even now nearly a year old. News traveled slowly in the great wilderness of the Americas, and had it not been for the arrival of the friars from New Spain, he might not have received the letter at all.

She loved him, she said, and missed him, though a busy life with friends kept her from weeping each day since his departure. And everyone, she said, had great faith in his finding and conquering the Seven Cities of Cibola, the seven cities of gold that Cabeza de Vaca had described so eloquently upon returning from his expedition. Though she had yet to hear from her dear husband, she knew that he would bring honor to the Catholic Church, to Viceroy Mendoza, and to her own father, the colonial treasurer, who had given 50,000 ducats of his own money to help finance the expedition.

These ducats concerned her greatly, since many of them had come from her father's treasure, but also she prayed daily that he would honor the other royal families' contributions, because for him to fail would most surely bring shame and dishonor on her father and on herself. She signed the letter: Doña Beatríz, your loving wife.

Coronado knew that by now Doña Beatríz had probably learned of his failures. He must redeem his honor, find the gold, save her from disgrace.

Putting the letter away, he went outside, pulled off his helmet, and let the breeze sweep his hair. He had grown thin and haggard from the journey, and his legs trembled from the torturous days on horseback.

He thought of Doña Beatríz's black hair and penetrating eyes, the way she held her chin high as if the whole world should fall prostrate at her feet.

But, so far, he'd found no seven cities of gold, only six cities of mud, sticks, and straw. He'd found no gold, only pueblo-dwelling Zuñi Indians who harvested melons and maize and struggled for survival in the bitter cold of a high desert. He'd found no gold, only poor savages who agreed to the *Requerimiento*, the order stating that God held dominion over the whole earth, though the Indians understood not a word of Spanish.

There was no gold, only the Indians at Tiguex who steamed their bodies in pits against the snow, and whose women copulated on all fours. There was no gold, not an ounce, not a trace, not a single clue as to where it might be.

Coronado watched Alvarado walk from the hill. Alvarado stopped at camp's edge, waiting for Coronado to speak. When he didn't, he said, "The Turk is secured and awaits your judgment, my general."

Coronado walked over to Alvarado, placing his hands on his shoulders. "The Turk is to be released, for no other can lead us to the gold."

"But we have seen no gold, my general. There is no proof. We would follow the word of this Turk into the wilderness?"

"Provide him a bath, or the dogs may have their day. Give him clothes and a mount. Tomorrow he leads us to the land of Quivira."

"And if he speaks not the truth, my general?"

"Then death by the dogs will be his mercy," Coronado said.

From the hilltop, he could see the Turk, who squatted on his haunches and looked out onto the prairie.

3

Coronado sat atop his mount and watched the band of conquistadors move out from the Tiguex pueblos. The Turk led the column. His black hair twisted in a single braid between his shoulders, and he wore a turquoise nugget about his neck. He turned and looked at the line of Spaniards behind him.

The Turk kicked his horse into a fast walk. The bay strutted and tugged at the bit, and the Turk leaned in, giving him his head.

Alvarado followed behind the Turk and bore Coronado's flag atop his pike. He rode his black steed, an animal worthy of his rank, and his helmet gleamed in the morning sun.

Friar Juan de Padilla walked beside him, carrying a small cross over his shoulder. Destined as kindling for the evening fire, the cross, cut fresh each morning, would be borne throughout the day by Padilla on foot. No hardship, no matter its discomfort, discouraged Padilla, nor caused him to waver in his mission to catechize the Indians and salvage their lost souls. Even now, dust covered his robe and gathered in his beard, and by evening only his eyes and his smile would shine from beneath his coat of grime.

The counter walked beside him, that soldier assigned to count steps in order that leagues traveled could be calculated and recorded in the journals at day's end. Later, completed maps would be transported back to Viceroy Mendoza for future expeditions, and, of course, for the raising of additional funds.

Even the heartiest of counters soon broke under the monotony of this duty. Coronado, always in need of effective discipline, discovered that such an assignment served as excellent punishment for the miscreants among them.

The column drew out behind as far as the eye could see, over two hundred and fifty Spanish conquistadors, noblemen all, but with little military training or experience with hardships.

Even so, many had proven themselves resilient and worthy soldiers on the trail. All were mounted on good stock, save the sixty crossbow men, who marched as a unit on foot. Their bows, too stout for any man's arm, could only be cocked with a goat-foot lever, requiring a man's full weight. Such a task proved impossible on horseback, and so, like the friars, they marched afoot in the dust.

The other eight hundred and fifty men who followed, Indians for the most, had been rounded up along the way by Coronado. Though hearty warriors, the Indians' loyalty could not be trusted when things turned sour.

Somewhere days behind the column, the animals and herdsmen trudged along. Such were the sizes of these herds, supplying the needs of the army, that they fell ever farther behind each day.

Watching the Turk as they moved into the valley, Coronado was full of doubt. His jaw rippled, and his stomach tightened. He stood in his saddle and scanned the eastern horizon.

Riding up beside the Turk, he said, "Tell me more of this gold, Turk. The distances in this place are without end, and the heat is great. Perhaps we are disposed to suffer and die at your hand."

The Turk hooked his leg over his horse's neck. "The way is stony and rough, my general, and Quivira lies many leagues away. The land is large, but it abounds with gold. Still, without a leader who has gone before, all men are known to suffer misfortune."

"But you have made this journey to Quivira and still live?"

"Yes, my general, because I have seen this here. Without knowledge of the way, men suffer great hardships. The winds, which never fail, drive men to madness, and shamans, those of wisdom, tell of old people who have never known the rain nor have seen the green grass."

"But the gold awaits as you have sworn?" Coronado asked.

"The gold awaits as I have said, my general. Even though in this land, the serpents bring death and the water tastes bitter, the way is known by the Turk, and he will deliver the conquistadors. Though the gold is rich, the land sings with beauty and lives in the heart. Such a place cannot be forgotten."

"But the *gold* is there?"

"The gold is forever, my general."

Coronado looked back at Alvarado, who dozed on his horse.

He turned to the Turk. "How many leagues to this land of Quivira?"

The Turk held up his ten fingers and shook his head. "More than can be counted, my general, and the conquistadors move as the tortoise. My general's beard will be white and his legs bowed like an old squaw is before he first sees Quivira."

"This may be so," Coronado said. "But it is in our numbers that we are safe."

"And in your horses, my general, and in your swords of steel."

"Without these things you would boil us in your pots, Turk."

Friar Padilla looked up through his dust-covered brows at the Turk and shifted his cross to the other shoulder.

"It's God who protects the Spaniards," he said. "He leads us through the wilderness with the light of His righteousness. Only the heathens need fear the things of this world."

The Turk said, "The one who walks speaks the truth, as the Turk speaks the truth. Does the Spanish god not ride on a bay such as this? Does he not guide the conquistador to Quivira? Is he not real, because the Turk has seen him against the morning sun with his crossbow and Toledo sword? Does not the Turk and the Spanish god as one lead the conquistador? What then does the general fear?"

Coronado listened to the Turk's words. "And there is gold as you have said?" he asked again.

"And fish in the streams as big as men, and great kings, and towers with golden bells that ring with the rising of the sun, and the women . . ."

"The women?" Coronado asked.

"The women are most worrisome, my general."

"Worrisome? What is meant, worrisome, Turk?"

"Everywhere they follow begging for sexual favors. Day and night they beg, but it is never enough."

"Is this so?" Coronado asked.

"Humph," said Friar Padilla. "There is much work to be done in Quivira."

4

---

riar Padilla's final mission in the Lyons area was on Jim's mind as he approached the Franciscan monastery. Throwing his suitcase over the fence, he worked his way under the gate of the Saint Francis of Assisi Cemetery. He never could pass up a burial ground, and it took more than a lock and a "no trespassing" sign to deter him now.

Brushing the dirt from his elbows, he reached back for his suitcase, glancing about to make certain that no one had spotted him. High on the hill stood a mausoleum with marble façade and wrought-iron gate. It commanded the grounds and held sway over the simple wooden crosses below. Cemetery roses languished in the heat, and bees, their legs laden with pollen, labored off into the blue.

Something inexplicable drew him in, perhaps the serenity and calm of the grounds. One might call it spiritual, even superstitious, but in this place the past reached out to him. Perhaps that's why he spent his days digging through the remnants of the dead. Contrary to Hollywood's portrayal, archeology offered little adventure, or prestige, even less money, and could be tedious, exacting work.

He'd labored alone throughout his studies, secluded in dank archives and libraries, picking through old documents and relics until he reeked with the stink of antiquity. But he'd loved it. Had Gloria been happy, things would have worked out.

He'd hitched his way from Wichita and walked the final miles to Lyons. Now, nearly there, he missed Sara even more. But the walk had suited him, had postponed the challenge ahead, a challenge he resisted for yet one more moment.

A squirrel darted across his upward path, and Jim jumped. He stopped at the turn of the path to rest and to take in the view. From this height, he could see the Lyons wheat elevator on the horizon and the red tile roof of the Franciscan monastery below. The trees, planted there against the winds that bore down night and day from the southwest, marked the desolate landscape with dots of green.

A drive twisted into the countryside beyond the monastery and terminated at the steps of an imposing manor. Greek columns reached skyward, and marble gargoyles peered down from them. Stained glass adorned the myriad windows and shimmered in the sunlight, but the colossal doors were closed, shut tight against the outside world. With all its majesty, the mansion, a curiosity in the midst of the prairie, had a singular beauty, akin to that of a painting hung in the starkness of a white room.

The final climb to the mausoleum turned steep and rocky, and when his foot skidded from under him, he came down hard, tearing his jeans and skinning his knee. "Damn it," he said, blowing on the scrape.

He leaned against the mausoleum gate. Secured with a lock, it failed to give. He peered through the bars and could see steps descending into the darkness. A cool breeze rose up. Bits and pieces of tile, loosened from the ceiling above, lay scattered on the floor.

He wondered who must lie within. Were their deaths common? Did they slip away or die in pain? Who closed the door upon them that dark funeral day?

"What a schmaltz," he said, shaking his head at the whole pretentious layout.

He retrieved his shaving mirror from his bag, located the sun, and directed the shaft of light through the bars. He could just make out an immense iron door at the back of the mausoleum, its brass handle green with age. Heat-forged hinges supported its massive weight.

An ancient grave perhaps, containing generations of dead—yet another example of the human predilection to bury one upon the other? Who knew?

He heard and registered the sounds of steps, but too late. The blow slammed across his shoulders, and he reeled, his mirror clattering away. He dropped to his knees and shook his head against the brain fog. An arm, thick as a tree trunk, encircled his neck.

He struggled to break the hold. He could smell his attacker's breath, feel the heat of his body. Jim's yell soon faded to a whimper as he starved for oxygen. His blood churned, and black dots formed before his eyes under someone's relentless hold. The taste of tin flooded his mouth, and his arms and legs flopped out of control. Drool strung from his lips, and darkness descended. He grew still, his chin lowering against his chest.

5

Jim shook away the fog and lifted himself up. The sun beamed high overhead, and the air smelled heavily of roses. The mausoleum on the hill shimmered under the white heat of noon. Gnats worked at the crack in his lip, and his head thumped with each beat of his heart.

He brushed the dirt from his luggage and turned to orient himself. His head spun, and nausea swept over him. Someone had dumped him alongside the road like a worn-out couch, but at least his bag had been tossed out with him.

The drone of locusts rose from the grassland, broken only by the distant caw of a crow. Shortly, he spotted a bridge and worked his way down to the stream that rambled into its shadows. He scooped the cool water onto his face and wiped the smell of fish and mud away with his shirttail. His lip had swollen to the size of his thumb. Not since the eighth grade had he been in a fight. Then, as now, his lip had taken the brunt of his assailant's anger. A late bloomer, Jim had grown to over six feet and now enjoyed considerable strength, particularly in his arms, a genetic contribution from his father, who had been a locally renowned athlete. But for Jim, physical prowess had come too late for developing swagger. He'd already turned his passion and energy to his studies. Still, women, who often wearied of men's bluster, could find his modesty endearing.

He closed his eyes and leaned back on a bridge timber, releasing the tension from his shoulders. The stream reminded him of his childhood on his grandfather's farm. In a place just such as this, he'd discovered an Indian arrow point. He didn't know whether the find itself, or his grandfather's enthusiasm, accounted for his love of archeology. But in that moment he knew how he wanted to spend the rest of his life.

In college his fascination with archeology grew. Other students partied away their weekends while he pored over books on Mesoamerica, Cortez, and Coronado, or dug through the archives for some obscure clue to the past.

Everyone agreed that his contribution to archeology would be important, that Jim Hunt would bring honor to his professors and glory to the profession. But all had failed to account for Gloria, the one drawback in an otherwise exemplary career.

And now he sat under a bridge in the middle of nowhere with a busted lip and a sore neck. He took a last look back before climbing the embankment and striking out the remaining distance to Lyons.

He soon spotted the Rice County Sheriff's car parked in front of the pool hall. Jim thought once to file a complaint about the assault. Of course, some might say he'd been trespassing on private property, not exactly blameless himself. Still, being choked into oblivion struck him as harsh consequences for merely trespassing in a cemetery.

In the end, the condition of the patrol car dissuaded him from pursuing justice. The bumper, having been torn from its mooring, stuck out at a right angle to the body proper. Cancer spots had metastasized in all four fender wells, and the emergency lights, coated with a layer of bugs, had been wired with baling wire to the top of the car. On the best of days, nothing suggested the triumph of good over evil.

So he moved on. In due course his lip would heal, and the sting of injustice would subside. There would be a hell of a lot less trouble in the end.

Little claim could be made for Lyons's cultural evolution, manifested by a farmers co-op, a Dairy Queen, and a shoe and boot repair shop. A few other businesses, surrounded by empty store-fronts, clung to life. The grain elevator rose at the edge of town, and silence reigned. The ever-present wind blew dust down the streets.

A blond brick building squatted on a rise at the south end of the town, a two-story bunker with a flight of steps leading to the doors. Bars covered the windows. Old elms, their leaves curled and yellowed, spread about the grounds. Ancient farm machinery lurked behind the chain-link fence like rusty old dinosaurs. Jim knew that he had found the Celf Historical Museum.

He set down his bag and paused for a moment, took a deep breath, and entered.

The familiar smells of mold and glue and paper hung in the air. Mounted heads with glassy eyes stared down at him from the walls: whitetail deer, coyotes, buffalo, a cougar poised to attack. Cases upon cases of flint points lined the walls, those everyday Indian tools that had littered the plains like aluminum beer cans.

"No bags allowed in the museum, sir."

Jim jumped at the voice. "Oh, damn," he said. "You scared the life out of me."

She covered her mouth with her hand. "I'm sorry. I didn't mean to startle you, but no cameras or bags are allowed in the museum."

She smiled at him. Her jeans hung in a slide about her hips, and she posted her hand on her waist.

Jim rubbed the tingle from his hands. "I'm a bit gun-shy, I guess."

"Could you sign in, please? Oh, the pen," she said, reaching into her pocket. "I've run off with it again."

He could smell her perfume, lilac or gardenia, or something like that. She'd double-tied blue strings in her white running shoes, and her shoulder-length hair, the color of clover honey, had bleached light from the sun. She was tall, and her brown eyes locked onto his without hesitation. Her mouth curved in a slight but permanent pout. Her facial features were not beautiful, but when combined, their effect was both inviting and rather intimidating.

"I'm not a visitor, actually. My name's Jim Hunt. I'm an archeologist, a student of archeology, I should say, from Oklahoma City."

"Eva Manor," she said.

"Are you the curator?"

"That would be Earl Celf. He's in the basement doing heaven knows what with a woolly mammal. I man the desk and make certain people sign in. I also help construct displays, order books for the store, and clean the bathrooms from time to time. Now will you please sign in? Our funding depends on it."

He signed the register and handed her back the pen. She tucked it into her pocket.

"I don't mean to be presumptuous, but are you okay?" she asked.

"Okay?"

"Well, there's this," she said, pointing to her lip.

"Oh, that. A little accident at the Saint Francis Cemetery."

"You didn't go into the cemetery?"

Picking up his bag, he hung it on his shoulder. "I did, but then I've never been attacked in a cemetery before. It's usually rather quiet."

"That probably would've been Mitch Keeper, Evan Kingston's right-hand man."

Jim shifted his bag to the other shoulder. "And Kingston would be?"

"The owner of the mansion. The cemetery belongs to the monks. Your bag, I'll put it behind the desk. You can pick it up when you leave."

"So, who's buried in the mausoleum?" he asked, handing her the bag.

Eva shrugged. "Some say it's Kingston's wife. Who knows for sure?"

"Odd, isn't it?"

"Kingston is a very private person."

"And a wealthy one by the looks of it," he said.

"What is it you are doing in Lyons?" she asked.

"I'm here for the museum's summer dig."

"We use volunteers, Mr. Hunt. Our museum could hardly afford professionals."

"I *am* a volunteer."

"But won't you find us amateurish and provincial?"

"I'll try to be a team player, Ms. Manor."

"Yes. Well, it's called the Milton site, likely a Wichita camp," she said. "There's been a couple of flint points and an old pot brought in by the locals, along with some rusty iron."

She leaned in close, and he could smell her perfume again.

"There's no pay, you know, and we're not digging for King Tut's tomb."

The door opened, and an old couple came in. The man wore overalls and a sweat-stained ball cap. A two-day stubble sprouted from his face, and fence pliers protruded from his back pocket. The woman, her hips sprawled and uneven, waddled along behind him. Blue veins knotted down her legs, and ringlets of hair stuck to the perspiration glistening on her neck.

Eva directed them to the register and then to the genealogy room.

"The new computer in the genealogy library is our most popular feature in the museum," she said. "The less people have, the more certain they are to have descended from royalty."

Jim nodded. "Laying claim to the past is easy and proving the negative is difficult."

"May I ask why someone with your knowledge volunteers for a dig in Lyons?"

"It's rather a long story. Look, Ms. Manor, I'm a volunteer. All I need is a summer's dig experience and an inexpensive place to stay."

She looked up at him. "We ask questions of all our volunteers, Mr. Hunt. Mr. Celf and I have put a great deal of effort into this museum."

"I promise to abide by your rules and not to interfere," he said.

"I wouldn't mention the thing at the cemetery, not if you're interested in a smooth start," she said.

"No, I won't."

"Follow me then, Mr. Hunt," she said. "It's time you met Earl."

6

Earl Celf snored away, his feet propped up on the split-log table in the soddy display in the basement. A wisp of hair, having lost its hold on his balding head, drooped over an ear.

Eva called out his name. Earl tipped backwards in the rocking chair and threw his arms in the air.

"Good god," he said, clambering to his feet.

"I've a Jim Hunt here to see you, Earl."

"Well, what's keeping you?" he asked, pushing the strand of hair back into place.

Secured by both belt and suspenders, Earl's pants drooped in folds atop his shoes, and his shirt buttons strained under the weight of his belly. A spot of gravy had congealed on his shirt, and his glasses had turned gray with dust. A liver spot, the shape of a thumb, marked his forehead, and he smelled of mushrooms and old newspapers. His teeth were the color of peach pits, and he'd missed a patch of whiskers sprouting from the folds of his double chin.

"Mr. Hunt is here for the summer dig," Eva said.

Jim reached out to shake his hand. Earl hesitated and then reciprocated. His fingers drooped into Jim's hand.

"The dig doesn't start for another week," he said, hitching up his pants.

"I thought I might do some preliminary work since I arrived a little early," Jim said. "I understand it's a Wichita campsite?"

"We draw our conclusions *after* a dig, not *before*, Mr. Hunt. In any case, no one is allowed in a site without supervision. There's only one boss on a dig."

"Of course. I only meant . . ."

Eva found a chair, dropping her hands in her lap and placing her feet to the side.

"Mr. Hunt is an archeologist, or nearly so, out of Oklahoma City. He's come to Lyons for personal reasons it seems."

Earl slid his suspender back onto his shoulder with his thumb.

"We've no money to pay for digging Indian pots," he said. "Such funds would have to come out of the genealogy account, and the patrons wouldn't stand for it."

Earl paced then, clasping his hands behind his back as he gathered up his customary speech.

"People out here came in on the Santa Fe Trail when this country had nothing but heat, misery, and savages. They scrubbed out a living where others couldn't have lasted a day. They did it by helping each other when the going got tough. No one expected pay for it. They did it out of the kindness of their hearts. Course, times change, don't they?

"They had grit, you see, and they passed it on through the generations one after another. It's what gives Lyons folks special ties to the past. This community still respects and admires its ancestors, remembers who they were and what they did, unlike most city folks I know."

He hiked his foot onto the step of the soddy display.

"We're a tough lot, and we're proud. Our ancestors didn't take to being led around by the nose, and we don't either. We built this museum without a dime of government money. We figure to do the dig the same way."

"I'm a volunteer, Mr. Celf. I'm assuming that's without pay."

"Take this museum," he said, lifting his palms up. "I turned this old hulk into one of the finest institutions in the state. Gave

her over to the council debt-free. She's a tribute to those who
came before. There's not a man in Lyons wouldn't tell you the
same."

He hesitated. "A volunteer, you say?"

"I'm here to get field experience," Jim said. "It's a requirement for park service employment. In other words, I can't get
my job without it."

Earl bit off the end of a cigar and stuck it halfway into his
mouth. A drop of sweat rolled off his bald head and raced down
his neck. He dabbed at the top of his head with a handkerchief
and leaned in, peering through his glasses at Jim.

"What happened to your lip, boy? You been fighting down at
the pool hall?"

Jim touched his mouth. "Oh, that. Just an accident. It's
nothing."

Earl hooked his thumbs under his suspenders and rocked
back on his heels.

"So you're out to get your fingernails dirty, are you?"

"I'll do what's asked of me," Jim said. "Of course, if there's
any way I could help in the meantime, I'd be pleased to do so."

"Long as you understand who's in charge."

"I'm here to learn."

Eva stood. "Mr. Hunt doesn't have actual field experience,
Earl. Perhaps we should wait."

"You know how to establish a site?"

"Yes, sir. I think so."

Earl studied the end of his cigar. "I suppose it wouldn't hurt
to get a start before the others arrive. Nothing I hate worse than
volunteers standing around with nothing to do like a bunch of
ducks quacking for bread."

"Yes, sir. I can see where that might be a problem."

Earl checked his watch. "I'm running late for a council meeting. Mayor Sims wants to name Fifth Street after her grandson,
Freddie. Freddie Street, for Christ's sake. Anyway, maybe you
could locate the particulars on that site, but I don't want you doing no excavation, not without me there."

"I understand," Jim said.

"Eva here might show you where the Milton place is."

"Well, I don't know," Eva said. "I'm rather busy, and it's the weekend."

"Old Man Milton can show you where those boys of his found the points and potsherds. They tried to hustle a chunk of farm machinery while they were at it. Didn't get by with that, I can tell you. Anyway, you can take it from there."

"I will need a little equipment—string, stakes, hand tools," Jim said.

"I got a dig kit. Now you be damn careful out there, Hunt. Those digs are hard to come by, and I don't need anyone screwing it up. That ol' bastard Milton could change his mind in a heartbeat about us being out there."

"I'll be careful."

Eva stood. "By the way, Earl, Mr. Hunt is in need of a place to stay. I'm thinking he might use the museum workshop. There's a cot, even a shower of sorts."

"Town's full of rooms," Earl said. "Lyons doesn't have a big tourist season, you know."

"Stufflebaum has his hands full with the displays," Eva said. "We need some janitorial help, unless Mr. Hunt feels cleaning up is beneath his education."

"Sounds fair to me," Jim said.

"Well, I don't know. Can't provide room and board for every volunteer that shows up for summer fun. Guess you could do some sweeping up, that sort of thing."

Earl put his hat on and adjusted it over his eyes.

"Well then, if it's all right with Stufflebaum, that's settled. I'm off to Freddie Street, God help me. Now if Stufflebaum objects to you being in his shop, you'll just have to make other arrangements. You understand?"

"Yes, sir."

"And I don't want any messes left behind when you move out."

"No, sir."

Earl turned at the top of the stairs. "And that site's damn close to Kingston property. Don't you go straying off the Milton farm. Mitch Keeper's not someone a city boy should go poking with a stick."

Jim's lip cracked. "That's what I hear."

Eva dropped the extra workshop keys into Jim's hand.

"The shop is in the back next to the fence. Stufflebaum's gone to the city for a load of plywood to make the new pottery display. He probably won't be back until late."

Jim picked up his bag. "If there's anything I can do."

"Do your work and let us do ours, Mr. Hunt. We'll get along fine."

"I'll remember that," he said. "And who is this Stufflebaum?"

"Our taxidermist and handyman. Without Stufflebaum this place would have fallen apart years ago. He's a little off-center, but don't underestimate him."

"No. I won't."

"There are supplies in the shop cabinet—cleaners, toiletries, that sort of thing. You can use the phone, providing you don't make long-distance calls."

"I'm looking forward to seeing the Milton site. I'm wondering when we might go?"

"Tomorrow is Saturday," she said. "It's my day off, but if we are to get a head start, I don't see that there's much choice in the matter. I'll pick you up in the morning, early."

"Fine. My enthusiasm gets ahead of me, and I forget that archeology is just a job for some people," he said.

After Eva left, Jim slumped into a chair and closed his eyes. He seemed to be taking a tiny step in the direction of his interest in southwestern archeology. In graduate school his research on Spanish expeditionary routes into the Americas had made the conquistadors come alive in his mind.

7

At the base of the trail, the Turk cut north, following the valley for passage through the foothills. They could hear the distant rush of a river. The sound grew louder as they rode on, and the smell of spray and fish filled the air.

A rock wall loomed before them, and they turned east. Soon they stood on the shore of a rolling river. The water churned through the rocks. It smelled of snow, and droplets of icy water gathered on their faces.

Alvarado walked to the bank of the river and studied the currents.

"Spring has come," he said. "The waters are swift and cold and traversing the river would be most difficult. Both horses and men could be lost in its current."

Coronado looked up the river and then down.

"We must hasten on to Quivira," he said. "Many days may pass before the waters subside."

Alvarado moved down the bank, and his feet sank into the mud. He cleaned the muck from his boots with a stick and tossed it into the water. It soon drifted from sight.

"The river turns south, and the steepness of the shore is less difficult. But how many leagues must one travel before the waters slow? All the while, the column moves farther from the land of Quivira."

Coronado dismounted and climbed down to the river's edge, sticking his hand into the rushing water. An ache crawled up his fingers and pooled under his arm.

"The horses might stall and drown in such cold," he said.

Alvarado turned to the Turk. "And how is it the Turk, who has passed this way before, did not know of this?"

The Turk slid from his mount and squatted on the bank. Spray gathered on his shoulders and glistened under the sun.

"It is so that the Turk has crossed this river many times in his journey to Quivira. It is so that the river may be swift and cold, but the bottom is sound. This the Turk knows."

"You have set a trap for the conquistadors, Turk, though one from which you'll not escape. This I swear by the saints."

"No, Captain. The sun warms early in the mountains and takes no counsel of the Turk. Only the Spanish god could have made it so. It is He who makes the waters flow and no other."

Isopete, who had been waiting within hearing distance, stepped forward. "The Turk has led the conquistadors to their end," he said.

"What does this Isopete say?" Coronado asked the Turk.

"That no man, not even the Turk, whose wisdom is great, can know the mountain river's flow."

Turning to Isopete, the Turk said, "Take your leave, Squaw. The general sickens of your lies."

Isopete muttered something to himself and shot a look over his shoulder at the Turk.

Coronado said, "Perhaps the Turk sees clearly the way of God's will, though it be our misfortune. Both Spaniards and heathens have little say in the warmth or cold of the sun."

Alvarado mounted his horse and looked down the column of men. "If it's God's will, then what does the general order?"

Coronado took up his horse and studied the river. "Get a line and tie it to the Turk, who knows well the river's bottom, so that he may traverse the waters and secure a lead rope for the others to follow."

The Turk looked at him. "But, General, a warrior such as I cannot swim, since in my land, where it seldom rains, there is no need for such talent."

Coronado drew his sword and examined its tip. "But then the river is shallow and with a sound bottom, as you have said."

The Turk looked at Coronado and then at Alvarado. "Yes, so it is, my general."

"Cast the Turk a line," Alvarado said. "And we shall see."

The Turk stepped into the icy waters, while Isopete, charged with feeding out the line, sat on a rock high above the river.

The Turk glanced over his shoulder at Friar Padilla. "Perhaps the river changes course, and the bottom no longer touches my feet," he said, calling back.

Friar Padilla lifted the cross, casting its shadow onto the river. "This you do in His name and for the glory of the king of Spain. God protects His sheep."

Higher up on the riverbank, Coronado's tent had been pitched so that he might view the proceedings while soaking a carbuncle that had developed on his hind side.

Alvarado had ridden downstream to check the grade of the banks and now worked his way back. The soldiers, taking advantage of the delay, rested in the shade or washed their feet at the river's edge. All waited for the Turk, who now edged into the river.

Rocks cropped from the river floor, narrowing and speeding the flow into a torrent. Water gathered under the Turk's chin and tugged at his legs. Shivering, he pulled for more slack. But when he stepped forward, the river swirled higher. He choked on water and called for more slack from Isopete.

Suddenly, the bottom fell away. Held taut by the line, the Turk was drawn down by the current. He fought his way up once again. Gasping for air, he broke the surface and pulled at the line. From his perch on the other side, Isopete watched on.

The Turk, drawn down into the river for the second time, struggled against the current, arms limp, lungs ablaze, the waters sucking him ever farther into the darkness.

From the rear, Alvarado galloped up next to Isopete.

"Let out the slack, you imbecile," he shouted. "You're drowning the Turk, the one who leads to the gold."

Alvarado, dropping from his mount, shoved Isopete aside and took over the line. Isopete raised his arms over his head.

The Turk spiraled upwards from the bottom of the river. He spewed water and slapped his way to the other side.

———————

Later, when safely across the river, Coronado summoned Isopete and the Turk to his tent. Water dripped from the Turk's braid, and a bruise darkened on his chin.

The Turk glared at Isopete and cursed him under his breath. Isopete spit on the ground, and crossed his arms over his chest. With his sword drawn, Alvarado stepped between them.

"So, Turk, your memory has failed," Coronado said. "The river bottom is not as remembered from your last journey to Quivira?"

"Isopete did not slacken the line," he said. "Had I a weapon, he would know my vengeance."

Coronado looped his scabbard about his waist. "Is this true, Isopete, that your lack of vigilance at the line could have cost the Turk his life and the conquistadors the gold they seek?"

Isopete muttered something in his native tongue.

"What does he say, Turk?"

"That the morning sun blinded him, my general, and that he could not see the Turk at the bottom of the river."

"Perhaps Isopete speaks the truth," Coronado said.

"He knows not the truth nor his own father," the Turk said.

"Dissension between you is disagreeable to those who must listen on this most difficult journey. I shall have it cease or, heaven bless me, I'll put you both to the sword. Is this clear?"

The Turk folded his arms over his chest and leveled his gaze on Isopete. "Yes, my general. Isopete will not lie again nor fall blind in the morning sun. This I swear with my life."

8

Dissension did not agree with the mild-mannered Jim. He hoped he was not off to a bad start with Eva. After all, they were on the same quest. He opened the workshop door and peered into the darkness. He ran his hand along the wall and flipped the switch. A single bulb flooded the room with light. He jumped back, gooseflesh racing down his arms.

"Jeezus," he said.

A coyote with empty eye sockets gaped at him from the corner of the room. Its skinless skull glistened with grease, and its jaw hung slack in a tongue-less smirk. Next to the coyote, a squirrel lifted its front paws as if in prayer, while its hide hung like a winter coat on the nail behind.

Jim turned, his mouth open, and scanned the room, which was crowded with a variety of dead creatures—armadillos, skunks, porcupines, a deer the size of a quarter horse—all in various stages of dismemberment. They seemed to peer at him with glassy eyes, indifferent to his presence.

A diamondback was coiled to strike from the worktable. The snake's pink mouth gaped wide, its fangs cocked at a rat intent on escape. With its tail looped over its back, the rat raced for freedom, peering over its shoulder with eyes wide and wet, while a rabbit chewed a stalk of grass and watched on, oblivious to the dowel pin extending from its own anus.

Other stilled creatures glowered and snarled from their perches on the walls. Birds lifted their wings in permanent flight or forever regurgitated food into the uplifted mouths of their nestlings. Jim rubbed at the tension that had gathered in his shoulders.

A shower stall with its door missing sat in the corner of the room. A bar of soap melted over the drain, and a black beetle, big as a water turtle, paddled its way across the floor of the shower. The stool, in best prison style, squatted in the open like some misbegotten shrine, its tank cracked, and the pipes beneath green from the leakage. Electrical tape had secured the broken lid, and an old *Readers' Digest*, abandoned by the last user, lay open on the floor.

Taxidermy tools, heaped on any available surface, included saws, scalpels, and skinning knives. There were fleshing beams, artist brushes, and pallets of paints on the workbench. Boxes of salt and drums of borax had been stacked in the corner next to the john. Stretching boards leaned against the wall, and on the shelf above the workbench, jars of glass eyes and stacks of ear liners had been stored. The slight stench of decomposing flesh permeated the room.

"Nice," Jim said.

Pages from the *Lyons Daily News* covered the old army cot that had been pushed into the corner. Underneath the cot, Jim found a set of elk antlers, an empty pizza box, and a pair of flip-flops that had aged to the color of mustard.

Jim, exhausted and grimy, sat on the edge of the cot and pulled off his shoes. He needed a shower and hoped that the monstrous beetle wouldn't drag him into the underworld. Still, one couldn't go all summer without a shower, so in the end, he took his chances.

Turning out the light, he lay down on the cot. Moonlight cast through the transom above the door, and a thousand glass eyes seemed to wink in the darkness. He rubbed at the soreness in his neck. In the distance a train pulled a hill, its whistle rising and falling.

He didn't think about Gloria so much now, not every waking moment. But in the quiet times like this, times when sleep and memories rolled in like a tide, the pain returned.

The moon rose above the shed, and the wind rattled a piece of tin on the roof. Free of Gloria, he could now do what he had to do. With luck, he'd be on his way in a matter of weeks and could return to his studies. He had only one job as he saw it: get the experience and then get the hell out of Lyons.

———————

Sometime in the night, his eyes popped open, his heart raced. Something was screeching from out of the darkness. He sat upright in bed, his heart chugging in his ears. And when something or someone touched his arm, he kicked off his covers and bolted out of bed, determined not to be the victim of yet one more assailant.

The light came on, and he struggled to focus through the confusion.

"Here now," a voice said. "You can't be kicking my cat around."

A man stood in the doorway, his arms full of sacks.

"What?"

"My cat can't fly, Mister."

"Who are you?" Jim asked.

"Might ask you the same, seeing as how you're sleeping on my cot."

Jim rubbed at his face. "You must be Stufflebaum?"

"But then I still don't know who you are, do I?"

"Oh, yeah. Jim Hunt. I'm here for the summer dig. Earl said I could stay in the workshop in trade for a little work."

"Ain't no such thing as a *little* work," he said.

Stufflebaum set his sacks on the workbench. He reminded Jim of a spider, all legs and arms, and he had the skin of a catfish, an odd mixture of yellows and greens and whites. His pants hung slack in the rear and were hitched up with a leather belt. Too long for his waist, the belt doubled back through a loop to keep it out of the way. He'd buttoned his shirt to the top, and strawberry hair, uncut and unkempt, hung over his collar in strands. He wore a mustache, thin and wiry like a seal's, and his eyes, the color of worn denim, looked as if they'd been picked from the taxidermy jar.

"Did you say cat?" Jim asked.

"That's right. Precious."

Jim lifted his brows. "Precious?"

"Like a jewel, you might say."

"Is she part cougar or what?"

"Oh, she didn't mean nothing. Just mistook you for a long-tail rat, that's all."

"I'm six-feet two and don't look the slightest like a rat."

Stufflebaum fished through his sacks and came up with a beer, tossing it over to Jim.

"Precious is cockeyed, you might say. One eye shoots up this away, the other down yonder. Precious can't see shit, daylight or dark."

"Precious attacks people?"

"Precious attacks pretty much everything so as not to take any chances. Bill Massey's German shepherd wandered in here by mistake one day. Took me and Earl both to get Precious pried loose." Taking a swig of beer, he wiped off his mustache and looked at the floor in thought. "That dog didn't have a patch of hair no bigger than a postage stamp left on him anywhere."

Jim popped his can and took a deep drink. His hands steadied, and he looked around the room again.

"Now don't you worry about Precious," Stufflebaum said. "Just let her know you ain't no long-tail rat. She's got ears like a desert fox, and once she's got you figured, why, you're as safe as that coyote over there."

"About the cot," Jim said. "I'm sure there's a room in town."

Stufflebaum finished off his beer and crumpled up the can.

"Like ol' Precious, I just didn't expect a stranger sleeping in my shop. You want to stay here, that's fine with me. Course, come Monday I start early before the heat gets up. You can live with that, I got no problem."

Looking at his watch, Stufflebaum tossed his beer can in the trash.

"Well, I'm running late, and Earl don't pay overtime. There's coffee in the cupboard there, and a cafe down the street for biscuits and gravy. And don't you worry about Precious. She's sleeping by now, I figure, or hunting for long-tails down in the supply room. Want me to catch the light?"

"Sure. Okay."

"Good night, then."

"Yeah," Jim said. "I hope you're right."

How long Jim lay awake listening for Precious in the darkness, he couldn't be sure. But the night sounds waned, and the moonlight faded from the transom before he fell asleep.

9

The morning sun reflected as a red ball in the window of Hanson's Shoe and Boot Repair. Jim combed his hair in the reflection before moving on to find the cafe.

A small anteroom resembling an outhouse had been constructed over the entrance of The Westerner Cafe as a windbreak. It now hung from its moorings, causing the door to drag on the sidewalk. A handwritten menu was posted on the window, along with an announcement for the local quilting club, stating that the club's meeting would be held in the library at seven on Monday night.

Jim entered, and an overhead bell clanged. The cook peeked under the serving window. A Victorian bar covered the entire east wall, presumably taken from some grand hotel that must have existed in Lyons during better times. Its huge mirror, dingy with dust, and its cracked walnut columns signified its age. The bar itself, made of marble and brass, had dulled with years of use and now supported a television set, tuned to the weather with the sound turned down.

A wood carving, a replica of an Indian head nickel, sat on the opposite end of the bar. Incongruously, the carved face wore sunglasses, and its nose had been broken off, perhaps in a riotous bar fight during more dangerous times.

Jim waited for the waitress, who turned out to be the cook. He'd rolled his sleeves to the elbows, and he wore a food-spattered apron.

The cook pulled his receipt book and pencil out of his pocket. His fingernails had eroded to the quick from dishwater and soap. He leaned over the table, giving Jim a whiff of onions.

Jim ordered two eggs over easy.

The cook tucked the book back in his hip pocket. "You with that survey crew out on Ten?"

"I'm here for the dig."

"The dig?"

"You know, archeological stuff out on the Milton place."

The cook grinned over at the old couple sitting by the door, who had been watching ever since Jim had entered.

"I got a storm cave you could dig."

"Thanks, anyway," Jim said.

The cook nodded. "Never know when the next fool will turn up, do you?"

Jim sipped on his coffee, which tasted faintly of bleach. The couple had finished their meal and continued watching him from across the room.

"Say," the old man said, pushing back his hat. "Ain't you the guy at the museum yesterday?"

"Yeah, that's me."

"Thought you looked familiar. Don't let ol' Henry pull your leg. He kids everybody that way, but he can cook up a mean egg."

"I can forgive a lot for a good egg."

"I'm Pete. Me and Auntie been tracing back our ancestors up to Earl's museum computer."

Jim sipped at his coffee and then chanced the question.

"And what have you found?"

"Churchill," he said.

"Churchill?"

"Winston."

"No?"

"On my daddy's side. A cousin to my great granddaddy on Winston's mother's side. American, you know?"

"I think I'd heard that."

"Yes, sir. And it turns out Auntie's goddang near related to the queen herself—not exactly the queen herself but a distant cousin of the queen herself. It ain't all entirely clear yet."

"That's remarkable," Jim said, looking over at Auntie, who worked at wiping egg off her chin with a napkin.

"Course, I'd rather be related to Winston than any queen. Winston's a goddang war hero, you know."

"Among other things," Jim said, "including a master of the English language."

"Shot them Krauts to hell, didn't he?" he said.

Jim checked the service window for his eggs. "Well, glad you're enjoying your research. Maybe I'll see you up there sometime."

"Oh, sure. Me and Auntie's up there near every day. That genealogy's interesting stuff. Hadn't been for Earl coming up with that library, I'd gone to my grave thinking I'm no more than just another dirt farmer. Here I am related to Winston Churchill the whole of the time. Who would've thought?"

"Well, we can learn much from the past," Jim said, looking at his watch.

Pete started to leave and then stopped. "They got a ham and bean special in here—cornbread, too. Damn good."

"Thanks. I'll keep it in mind," Jim said, turning to his breakfast.

When Jim started to leave, a man entered. As he ducked under the door, he brushed past Jim.

"Watch it," he said.

Jim stepped into the windbreak behind him. It still smelled of sweat and tobacco. When he looked back, the man was sitting at a table, giving his order to the cook.

Jim struck out for the museum. Though he enjoyed people for the most part, they had a way of complicating his life. He decided it might be better to limit his eating at the cafe. The fewer people he knew, the better. With luck he could be out of Lyons soon and be drawing his government salary by summer's end.

———

Eva waited on the steps of the museum. She waved at him and pointed to her car, which she'd parked under the shade of a tree. She fell in beside him, and he could feel the warmth of her arm against his.

"I'm late," he said.

"It gets hot early around here," she said. "We need to be on our way."

She'd tied her hair up in a bandanna and wore denim shorts with a pink top.

"I'll need a few things—compass, notebook, a steel rod and a hammer to place a corner marker," he said.

"I've put Earl's dig kit in the car," she said. "Will you be laying out the site today?"

"Not today. If we can get it located and a reference point set, we'll be doing well."

"I thought you didn't have field experience?"

"Contrary to popular belief, you can learn a lot from books," he said.

As they pulled down the road, Eva opened her window. Her scent drifted in on the wind. He glanced at her legs, tanned and trim like a runner's legs, but with a small half-moon scar on one knee.

"I've packed a lunch," she said. "I didn't know how long this would take."

He hooked his elbow out the window. "I'd forgotten about lunch," he said. "I'm not so good at creature comforts, I'm afraid."

"Like all men," she said.

"How far to the Milton place?"

"It lies behind Kingston and is cut off from the main road by the estate itself. The only way in and out is over the river."

"We're going to swim a river?"

"Well, I hope not. There's a low-water bridge that's passable when the river isn't up."

"Why doesn't Kingston let them cross his land?"

Eva shrugged and pushed back hair that had strayed from the bandanna. "Some say Kingston is trying to freeze Milton out, so he can buy up his place."

"Is this Milton guy interested in archeology?"

"Hardly," she said, turning off onto a dirt road. "His boys brought in those artifacts to sell. Earl gave them money for access to the site."

"His personal money?"

"Earl lives on the edge of town on a small tract. Never had much, kind of a trader. He's always buying or selling something— junk, cars, hogs, doesn't matter what—and in his spare time, he pokes around for Indian points, pots, that sort of thing. I guess you could call him an amateur archeologist."

"A hobbyist?"

"Over the years, he's educated himself, particularly about the Wichita Indian culture. And then he built the museum, eventually turning it over to the city council."

"How did he come into money?"

Eva glanced over at him. "Is Earl's business part of your research as well?"

"Just a question. I understand questions are expected around here."

"Touché," she said. "Earl's thrifty, some say to a fault. In fact, some say tight. I must admit it came as a surprise when Milton took the money from him."

"Surprise?"

"They've never gotten along. Rumor has it that Earl turned Milton in for moonshining and that Milton never forgave him. The Milton place is hardscrabble land, and the old man is a bit of a throwback. He doesn't want anything to do with anybody. He must have needed the money badly to take it from Earl."

She paused. "The Miltons have always seen it hard. I went to elementary school with his boys, but as soon as they could, they dropped out."

He watched Eva as she maneuvered the road. She reached for a bottle of water from the cooler in the backseat. Where her tan ended, whiteness plunged beneath the blue denim shorts. Quickly, he turned to study the sunflowers speeding by his window.

She tipped the water, and a droplet raced off her full lip and down her chin. "How were your quarters?" she asked.

Jim lifted his brows. "I spent the night with a dead coyote and a cockeyed cat. Other than that, spectacular."

Just then the road made a sharp turn and dropped into a valley, its floor dominated by a wide and meandering river. An aged cottonwood soared from the bank, marking the low-water crossing.

They got out and checked things over. A few inches of water flowed over a concrete base that had been poured directly onto the riverbed. It provided a hard surface for the wheels and little more.

Jim clutched the dash when they pulled in and looked over at Eva. The water lapped and gurgled around the tires as they moved into the river's expanse. His stomach tightened and did not ease until they had climbed the opposite bank.

"Pull up, would you?" Jim asked.

Eva edged over to the side of the road and shut off the car, waiting as Jim studied the river valley.

Chert rock jutted from the prairie floor like broken glass, and yellow flowers peeped here and there from their cracked beds. Dry gulches wormed and looped through the landscape, their banks cutting though the chapters of time. Hills swept down from the horizon like the steps of an ancient temple, each layer a record of passing eons. To look at them one could see the world emerge from its beginnings and climb into the bright sunlight of the day.

Eva rocked the steering wheel and waited. Finally, she asked, "Are you okay?"

"Sometimes it's almost as if I can feel them," he said, rubbing his face.

She let the wheel straighten in her hands as she studied him.

"Feel what?"

"Most folks live their lives in the present, believing that's all there is."

"But not you?"

"In my head, I can't always tell. It's like different movies playing in a theatre. Where is the reality?"

"Perhaps you have an overactive imagination," she said.

Jim rolled up his window. "You don't like me, do you?"

Her eyes locked on his. "I don't know you," she said.

"Then why the rub?"

"You are contemptuous of us, Mr. Hunt, and of this whole dig thing. It's quite clear you don't want to be here. How do you expect us to feel?"

"Maybe you don't know as much as you think."

Eva started the car and pointed down the road. "The cutoff is just there. Do you want to go on or not?"

He paused before answering. "Yes," he said. "I want to go on."

10

The car pulled into the Milton yard, and the chickens squawked and scrambled for cover under the lilac bushes. A dog lay against the foundation of the house, its hind legs stuck in the air.

John Milton and his two boys waited on the front porch of the two-room shack. The old man had one foot on the railing and a high-powered rifle within reaching distance of his right hand. He pushed his hat back on his head and stuck a toothpick in his mouth.

One of his two boys, his shirt covered with field dust, leaned against the doorway. His nose and the tops of his ears had peeled from sunburn. The other boy sat in the rocking chair, his legs crossed and his hands locked behind his head. His hair, sun-bleached to copper, hung over his eyes, and he had a quarter-sized hole in the bottom of his boot.

John Milton drew his leg down from the railing and crossed his arms over his chest. "Eva," he said.

"Mr. Milton. This is Jim Hunt. He's come to help us this summer."

"It's a sad day when folk have to wade the river to get to the Milton place. Kingston's closed the road, you know, and got us locked up until we can't breathe no more."

"We came to check out the site," Eva said. "Thought you might show us where Dub and Luke found those relics."

"Over to the back side," he said, pointing his chin. "Next to Kingston."

"We're anxious to get started."

"Don't go crossing onto Kingston land. He's hired on Mitch Keeper to patrol his place, and everybody knows Keeper's crazy. Course, he's not crazy enough to come on Milton property. I can drop a deer quarter-mile away with this rifle, and he knows it well enough."

"We'll not trespass," Eva said.

"Dub here will show you where they found them pots. You can't drive all the way. It gets rough in them canyons."

Eva glanced at Jim. "We'd like to establish the site today. Get some idea how big it might be, that sort of thing."

"Well, them pots were just laying top of the ground, broken up like they were. I wouldn't paid no mind hadn't been for Dub here. He thought Earl might buy them for his museum. For once, turned out he knew what he was talking about. Course, I should have known I could have made more money selling beer cans than what Earl Celf pays."

Dub grinned and looked up from the rocking chair.

"We think it might be a Wichita site," Eva said.

Old Man Milton nodded. "My daddy always said Indians lived up and down this here valley, and why wouldn't they? Hell, there's caves everywhere. They're cooler in the summer and warmer in the winter. And there's water year-round in that spring up there. Guess they didn't have that bastard Kingston to worry about, or Mitch Keeper neither for that matter."

"The site has the potential to add a lot to our understanding of the Wichita culture," Jim said.

"Seems a fool thing for grown folks to do," Milton said. "Wasn't for Kingston crippling my operation, I wouldn't have nothing to do with it myself. Can't get the truck over that low-water pass. She breaks through, and it's hell getting her out. Can't get my trailer in or out neither, even in the dry season."

Milton lifted his shoulders as if prepared to fight. "Hell, they poured that low-water back in the thirties during Roosevelt's

WPA, claiming not enough bedrock for a real bridge. No one ever used it except for riding horseback or driving cattle across. They poured that concrete with too much sand, cheap bastards, and now the river's nearly eat it up. And when she rains, ain't nothing to do but wait her out."

Flipping his toothpick onto the dog's belly, Milton looked across his place and shook his head. "It's a short walk as the crow flies. If Kingston had any decency, he'd let us through and that would be that."

"Why won't he?" Jim asked.

"Why don't the sun come up in the west? He tried to buy me out once, but he don't have enough money, does he. I'd have to cut across no more than a corner, but he won't have it."

"Have you talked to the law?" Jim asked.

"Oh, sure, government's always helpful, ain't they. They raised my property taxes two years in a row, because of the value going up on the Kingston estate, they said. 'Raise *his* taxes, you bastards,' I says. 'I'm still selling three-dollar wheat, that is when I can get it to town.' "

"We appreciate the opportunity to excavate the site," Eva said. "With luck we should be finished by the end of summer. There's strict regulations in place for the volunteers, and we'll recover any damages to the topsoil."

Milton studied the dog, which had just dug a hole under the porch. Circling twice, the dog flopped down in the hole, dirt stacked on the end of his nose, and looked up at the old man.

"Well, it ain't much, 'less you need it. Earl Celf has always been a tight ol' fool."

"We should be on our way before the dark catches us," Eva said.

"Dub, run them up to the canyon and then get on back. We got that north forty to work this afternoon."

———————

They waited until Dub had disappeared over the hill before unloading the car. Earl's dig kit, an old army toolbox, had been stocked with everything that Jim would need.

By the time they reached the canyon, the breeze had faded. Clouds like giant cotton balls cast brief moments of shade.

"Look," Eva said, pointing to a piece of rusted iron half-buried in the creek bank. It had gathered debris from spring floods. "Pieces of farm machinery. We find it all over."

"The floodwater must move pretty fast through here," he said.

As they got closer, Jim could see the source of the creek high up on Kingston property. The creek seeped down from the hillside, stole over the border, and spread onto the Milton place.

Jim knelt where the land opened onto a plateau. Eva found shade under a cottonwood, pulling her legs into her arms.

"I think this is it," he said.

"Have you found something?"

He took out a notebook and pencil. "See how the vegetation is greener here than the adjacent land?"

"Maybe," she said.

"And the contour looks as if it has been disturbed at some point."

"I don't know. It all looks the same to me."

He drew in the perimeters of the plain in his notebook and recorded the symbols for the various landmarks: the rock Eva sat on, the cottonwood, the grove of wild grapevine growing in the ravine to the north.

The sun rose hot overhead, and the locusts serenaded them from the recesses of the canyon. Clouds rolled and climbed into the blue, and the faint smell of dust and moisture rode in on the currents.

Jim worked while Eva searched out the small cave tucked back in the grapevines. At some point in the past, a portion of the ceiling had fallen in but had since stabilized. Water trickled from a fissure and gathered into a crystalline pool in the rocks. She drank with cupped hands, splashing the icy water on her face and the back of her neck. She rejoined Jim, who had just finished his schemata.

"Okay," she said. "Now what do you want me to do?"

"This is about midpoint," he said, pushing his pencil into the ground. "You walk to the left to where the plain ends. I'll walk to the right and then we'll come back to this point. We'll work forward until we've scanned the entire area."

"What are we looking for, exactly?" she asked.

"The obvious things, of course—potsherds, points, flint chips— but keep your eye out for sinks or depressions, too. They can be an indication of a garbage pit or grave site. Pieces of charcoal can signal an ancient campfire, and bones are always important. Watch for anything angular, or straight, anything contrary to the natural lay of the land. It will be most likely man-made."

For hours they combed the area, back and forth like chickens scratching in the dirt. Clouds fomented in the heat and gathered on the horizon.

"I've found something," Eva said.

"What is it?"

"Charcoal, I think."

Jim studied the black splotches in the ground. "We've got us a campsite. You keep looking. I'll flag these finds and record them in the field notebook."

By the time they'd finished the search, Jim had discovered a handful of flint chips near the old cottonwood and potsherds in a sink on the far western perimeter of the site.

Eva sat in the shade, waiting for him. She had one shoe off to massage her foot. Dirt clung to her knees and to her elbows, and the knot of her blouse had given way.

Once inside the cave, they ate their lunch in silence. Outside, the sky darkened, and a few drops of rain splattered to the ground. Within moments a deluge swept and hissed outside the cave entrance. Soon, water coursed from higher ground, filling the ravines and plummeting into the canyon below.

Jim walked to the opening and looked out at the site flags that now bowed under the wind and rain. He turned, and lightning stilled the world in blue, silhouetting Eva's figure against the wall of the ancient cave. Thunder pealed behind him and rumbled down the canyon.

"We'll never get out now," he said. "I'm afraid you're stuck with me for the night."

"Yes," she said, looking up at him. "I know."

The signs of the site had aroused hope that demanded results, something real.

Jim was half asleep as the theatre in his head projected shadowy images on the cave's wall. Barely visible helmet tops were marching in a timeless quest.

11

Coronado donned his sword and his helmet and ordered Alvarado to fetch the Turk.

The Turk and Alvarado came and waited for Coronado to speak. Coronado paced, stopping in front of the Turk. "I am displeased that the Turk has seen fit to lead us through many useless turns. The heat is great, and my men are fatigued. We have suffered much, and still there is no gold."

"The Turk suffers as does the general, though he knows in his heart that the gold awaits."

"So the Turk proclaims, but the conquistadors who follow believe his story to be hollow. Though I, myself, believe him, it is uncertain that those who are disposed to kill the Turk can much longer be dissuaded."

"The gold is untold, as is the silver, though not so much as the gold."

"And is the gold in coin, or does it lie loose upon the ground?"

The Turk crossed his arms over his chest. "Golden plates, as full as the moon, are left untended. Statues of gold of great weight still lie where struck. The children drink from golden goblets, and golden masks adorn the doors of each tent. Buried in caches are gold and silver chains and turquoise as large as a warrior's shield."

Coronado nodded. The rumor of such treasure had refused to die in New Spain.

"And did such fortune fall from the sky into the land of Quivira?"

"In my time, the gold has always been so. Perhaps the people dug it from the mother earth."

"So, great mines abound in this land, or are golden nuggets washed up by the streams? Or perhaps the people took the gold from those of less valor?"

"The gold has always been so, my general, like the wind and the clouds."

Alvarado warned: "And the Turk has seen the wrath of the dogs, has he not?"

The Turk's eyes widened. "The Turk prays to the Spanish god for his salvation, and he fears the underworld where men burn forever. He fears also the general's dogs and the king of Spain. When Coronado returns to his land with the treasures of Quivira, the Spanish god will rejoice, and the king will kneel at his feet."

The Turk paused. "But beware Isopete, whose heart is black, and who sulks in his tent. He persuades with smiles, while planning the end of his enemies."

Coronado rubbed at the carbuncle on his backside, which had worsened with the long hours in the saddle. "Then these things will not be forgotten by any man, though the way ahead be difficult, for truth rides with us, Turk. And when we have come to the gold, the Turk shall be received by kings as the great warrior who has shown Coronado the way."

The Turk said, "Isopete is an old squaw who fears much, while the Turk leads with great courage, as the general has witnessed this day."

"Why does Isopete despise the Turk so?" Coronado asked.

The Turk snorted. "He has been shamed as a hunter and scout."

"A small dishonor to cause such fury," Alvarado said.

"Isopete is low-born, and his woman sleeps in any man's tent."

"In the Turk's tent as well?" Alvarado asked.

"The Turk's tent is dark on moonless nights," he said.

As the conquistadors moved out, the sun rose hot overhead, and by noon their helmets blistered their ears. Sweat gathered beneath their breastplates, and their swords burned welts on their legs. Mosquitoes whined in their ears and dined at their veins.

Coronado gave the order to remove, and all sighed with relief. The soldiers tied shirts or scarves over their heads and drank from cupped hands at a tepid stream.

Trapped by the heat of the valley, the breeze faded and then stilled. The men grumbled at the journey that lay before them, and they gathered in groups. Only Alvarado stood alone, his shoulders squared and his jaw set.

The Turk headed due east and now waited in the shade for the lumbering column.

At dusk Coronado drew up, raising his arm to signal the day's end. The Turk, Alvarado, and Coronado walked to the edge of a bluff that looked onto a land stretching into infinity, a land void of character, so vast and barren as to shrivel the spirit.

"It has no end nor way," Alvarado said. "I fear harm follows us."

The Turk pointed eastward. "The gold lies beyond the horizon, my captain, where the morning sun rises."

"But how many leagues?" Alvarado asked.

The Turk dropped his head. When he looked up, he said, "The way is stony and rough, and the sun burns in the sky. The conquistadors, who move as the turtle, will suffer much. I fear no man shall see the gold before his beard has grown white."

Coronado glanced over at Alvarado. "And what would the Turk have Coronado do?"

"The lizard wags from its nose to its tail. The longer the lizard, the slower its wag. Such is the way of the conquistador."

Coronado knelt and looked out on the wilderness. Doña Beatríz's fortune, as well as the viceroy's, lay in his care.

He knew in his heart the gold to be out there, for those having witnessed it were many. Friars, under oath of the Virgin Mary, had proclaimed it so. How could he now doubt it?

And no man, having witnessed the might of the conquistadors, would risk betrayal and the wrath of the hounds, not even a man such as the Turk.

———

The next morning Coronado summoned his officers. Alvarado, standing front and center, watched on as Coronado paced the line of men, his hands clasped behind his back.

"Today, I command that one-half of Coronado's army shall return to the Tiguex pueblos," he said, clearing his throat. "Our numbers are too great and do now slow the march to Quivira."

Alvarado stepped forward. "But what of the herds we have left behind, my general? What shall sustain those who go forward into this desolate land?"

"Coronado has taken council of the Turk, who knows this way, as his ancestors before him. The land ahead is plentiful with game, so, like the Indians, we shall take of its bounty and leave behind that which is not required. Relieved of this burden, the conquistadors will soon reap the treasures of Quivira."

"But, my general, our numbers protect us. Without them, and without the herds which provide our sustenance, we will most surely perish from starvation and the heathens' arrows."

Coronado's eyes locked on Alvarado. "The treasure is at hand, as the Turk has said, and the bitterness of winter awaits. None know of its time nor of its severity. With our ranks lightened, we shall advance quickly to Quivira, secure the treasure, and return to the safety of Tiguex before the onset of the winter."

"But, my general . . ."

Coronado held up his hand. "Captain Alvarado, the decision requires not debate."

———

As the Turk predicted, the pace of the column quickened with the reduction in force. But each day the horizon extended before them without end, and within the week, the food had dwindled. The Turk found water, though bitter with salts,

which sent the men scrambling into the weeds. Soon, like ba-
boons, they squatted openly, scrubbing their bottoms with hand-
fuls of bunchgrass.

The stench, high on the wind, brought hoards of stinkbugs
into camp, where they rolled exotic balls into their storage holes
in the ground.

Camps, fireless and cold, did little to warm them against the
frigid nights. As the day's heat bled away into the thin sky, the
men shivered beneath their blankets and cursed their hunger.
Each day they moved ever farther into the plains, but without
game, save for the occasional wormy rabbit. All the men knew
they soon would perish from starvation, and their bones would
be scattered across the plains.

Each night Coronado called forth the Turk to his tent. How
far to the gold? How soon to find the game he had promised?
Where did the lowland end?

And each night the Turk pointed eastward, repeating his
mantra: The band of conquistadors is yet too large, my general.
Their numbers are slow like the tortoise. The gold is still many
leagues away.

The Turk shook his head. "Send more men back to the mountains, my general. The animals can hear the conquistador coming even before he breaks onto the horizon."

"But our weapons are great," Coronado said.

"Yet the Indian is swift and stealthy and eats more often."

"I have halved the conquistadors, Turk. Would you halve
them yet again?"

"Yes, my general. Halve them again, before I become a grandfather in my own land."

12

Without Eva's presence, Jim might have imagined he was on a boy's adventure, scouting for splendor, much as the Spanish conquistadors had. The rain passed and he walked to the canyon to see if they could get back to the car. There they would be out of the weather until the low-water bridge became passable once again. But what had been a dry arroyo a few hours before had been transformed by a torrent.

Eva spread cedar branches on the floor and covered them with her windbreaker.

"It's roaring full," he said, ducking into the cave.

"We can build a fire outside," she said. "Enough to dry out. By morning we should be able to cross. These arroyos empty as quickly as they flood. We've drinking water and the cave for shelter, if the weather turns ugly."

The rain eased, and he gathered what dry wood he could find to build a small fire at the mouth of the cave. Eva sat down on a log and hooked her hat over a limb. Jim took his place next to her. She smelled of rain and wood smoke, and he could see the small half-moon scar on her knee.

Darkness closed in, and overhead the sky bloomed with stars. He banked the fire and walked to where the light bled into the darkness.

She dried her hair with her shirttail, looking up at him. "So what do you think of the site?"

"It's Woodlands, without a doubt. Whether it adds new information is another question."

"What's the next step?"

"In the morning we establish true north, then break the site into sections. Next time out, we can dig a test trench to expose the stratification to determine whether or not things have been disturbed. It's called stratigraphy. The process works well if nothing has been disordered, but that's a rare event. Time has a way of changing things."

"What do you think we'll find?"

"I think it's going to be abundant in artifacts. How far back they will go is anyone's guess. Erosion is pretty serious in these canyons. It could complicate matters. Once an artifact is removed from its strata, a great deal of information is lost forever. And then, of course, there's Earl."

"Earl?"

"You said that he's educated himself about the Wichita culture, and that's good. But he knows less than he thinks he knows about excavation. You see, excavation is a destructive act in itself. Without careful procedures in place, all can be lost. Discovery is one thing; understanding is another."

He paused and continued: "Amateurs can be the archeologists' nemeses. The rush to discover can destroy the source. It can kill the goose that lays the golden artifact. In the end, archeology is all about patience. Amateurs rarely have it, and the public has even less. In this case, things could be especially difficult."

"Because?"

"The site belongs to Earl, given that he paid for it. State laws on this are virtually nonexistent. Also it's his town and his museum. I'm just a guest, a volunteer."

"We've had a few digs in the past," she said. "They gave out pretty fast."

"The Wichita lived in a soft world—straw huts, wooden utensils, hide clothing," he said. "It's rare for that to survive. Of course there are flint points and potsherds that often make it through."

Eva dug her toes into the sand and thought about what he'd said.

"That could happen with Earl. He collects indiscriminately. For as long as I've known him, he's gathered and hoarded whatever he could find. Sometimes the things he collects don't even make sense. Pete told me that he saw Earl carry off boxes of old magazines someone had set out for the trash."

"That would be the Pete of Winston Churchill fame?"

"The same."

"Collecting and hoarding are different activities, different motivations," he said.

"Earl's house and outbuildings are packed with everything imaginable, most of it useless. You'd think he'd no longer need to drag junk home."

"Hoarding is rarely about money," he said. "It's about having, or more accurately, about not having. It's about security and possession and control."

"Earl saw it hard most of his life. Maybe that's what drives him."

Jim added more wood to the fire. "Is there someone who will be worrying about you not getting back tonight?" he asked.

"Not really."

"No family?"

She shook her head and gathered up a strand of hair that clung to her cheek. "Both of my parents died young. I'm an orphan, I guess you'd say."

"Oh, sorry," he said.

"It's all right. My father drank, you see."

"Look, I didn't mean to pry."

"Sooner or later someone in Lyons will tell you anyway. It's a small town. I wouldn't want you to think that he always drank because that wasn't the case. At one time, no better father existed. I thought he could do anything, and do it better than anyone else. He started going to the bar for a few drinks before coming home. Things worsened, you know. I can still hear the slam of that door in the middle of the night."

Jim picked burrs out of his sock and tossed them onto the fire. "I hope my daughter will remember the good things about me, too," he said.

She pushed back her hair. "You're married?"

"No. We'd planned to get married, but it didn't work out."

"What's your daughter's name?"

"Sara. She's staying with my mother for the summer."

Eva drew her knees into her arms. "In the end, my father failed us in every way. What he couldn't do, my mother did for him. She paid the fines, located the lost car on Monday mornings, washed the filth from his clothes, and juggled the bills. When he lost his job, *she* got one. And then one day she just gave up, I think."

Eva's face hardened. "I don't intend to let that happen to me."

"No brothers or sisters?" he asked.

She shook her head. "You?"

"A brother, Jesse. He's in computers out in California. He has two kids, both in braces. He's balding prematurely and has a wife who has put on five pounds a year every year since they've been married. We talk on the phone occasionally, very occasionally, because Jesse thinks that archeology is a plot to undermine modern technology and all progress in the Western world. Our phone conversations tend to be brief and heated."

Thunder rumbled in the distance, and a cool breeze swept in from the north. The fire sputtered and then brightened with new life. Light danced in Eva's eyes.

"Well," she said, stretching her arms over her head. "I'm exhausted."

"You sleep inside," he said. "I'll sleep out here."

At daylight, they set about finishing the layout and gathering up their equipment. By the time they got back to the car, the sun pitched high overhead. When they drove past the Milton place, they spotted Dub in the vegetable garden. He pushed back his hat and watched them round the corner.

Eva declared the low-water bridge passable, even though the water had deepened by several inches from the time of their first crossing. Jim gripped the dash as they pulled into the rushing water.

Halfway over the crossing, the rear tires lost traction, whining and spinning in the water, and the back of the car drifted sideways. Eva spun the steering wheel to bring it about. The tires caught, and she leaned back against the seat. Neither spoke until they were once again on the highway headed back to Lyons.

Eva pulled into the museum parking lot and waited as Jim unloaded his things.

"Thanks for sacrificing your weekend," he said. "I could never have found the site myself."

Eva nodded. "About last night. I had no business discussing my personal life that way. I'm not usually so forthcoming."

"Forget it," he said.

"I just want it clear that my interests are strictly professional."

"It's clear," he said. "I'll see you tomorrow."

He watched her pull out of the parking lot and onto the street. Just as she turned the corner, she glanced back at him for the briefest moment.

13

Stufflebaum poured himself a cup of coffee. "You dead?" he asked.

Jim rubbed at his eyes and then looked around for Precious, who slept at his feet, a length of toilet paper wrapped about her neck.

"More or less," he said.

"Ain't never stuffed a human being before. Make a hell of an exhibit, though."

"Maybe some other day, Stufflebaum."

"Looks like Precious signed a peace treaty," he said.

"Temporary cease-fire would be my guess."

Stufflebaum leaned over the coffee pot like a praying mantis and poured coffee for Jim into a cracked cup.

"Could make you into a caveman," he said, grinning. "You know—big club, beard, knuckles dragging the ground. Hell, I could add on three inches down where it counts and fill it with plaster of paris. Wouldn't cost that much."

"If it's all the same to you, I prefer being a live specimen, even if it means inferior accoutrements."

"Coffee okay?"

Jim took a sip. "Excellent, for an embalmer."

"Don't get used to it, but I figure anybody spending the night in this shop deserves a little morning pampering."

Jim looked over at Precious, who had turned to her morning bath. "Cat and mouse games have taken on a whole new meaning for me, that's for sure."

Stufflebaum checked his belt, drawing it up.

"Got to take the old pottery display over to Earl's. Thought you might give me a hand. Get back, I'll show you the cleaning routine."

"You're keeping the old display?"

"If there's ever a call for junk, Earl's going to be king of the mountain. We'll bring the display out the basement door. Meet you there."

———

Once the display had been loaded, they lumbered off in Stufflebaum's International pickup. Blue smoke seeped through the floorboard and through the litter of Styrofoam cups and newspapers, long since yellowed with age. Stufflebaum's bony elbow had worn the paint from the door, and the turning signal clicker swung by a loose wire under the dash.

"Nice truck," Jim said, rolling down the window.

Stufflebaum turned onto the main road and dropped her into high. The truck bucked and loped and then leveled out.

"Two hundred thousand without an overhaul. Course, she couldn't pull your dick out of a lard bucket, either," he said.

At the Boot and Shoe, they hooked a left and headed for the outskirts of Lyons. When they turned into Earl Celf's acreage, Jim sat back in amazement.

The house, an old two-story Victorian, sat smack in the middle of the largest assemblage of junk Jim had ever seen. Whatever Earl could salvage had been hauled and stacked into a series of refuse mountains. Everything had been placed into piles that ran the length of the property.

A threshing machine and a rack of scrap pipe sat just off the drive. Behind that, wringer washing machines, milk separators, fruit jars, and wood stoves had been stacked into rows. Beyond that, he could see posts, honeybee houses, refrigerators, a coal forge, and an Indian teepee with the hide missing.

Prefab buildings, many of them leaning precariously on foundations of cinder block, encircled the acreage like a frontier stockade. Filled to capacity, they threatened to collapse under their burdens.

"My god," Jim said.

"Earl's kingdom," Stufflebaum said, pulling up. "Earl sees treasure at every turn. Don't think he doesn't know what he has. He can go to a cardboard box buried under three tons of shit and pull out the exact magazine with the exact date he's wanting."

"How long has he had this obsession?"

"Since his mother dropped him on his head, you might say. There, that's where he wants this thing dumped," Stufflebaum said, pointing.

"What's Earl going to do with an old pottery display?"

Stufflebaum shut off the truck. "Hell's bells, boy," he said, pretending to hook his thumbs under his suspenders. "Folks come out here on the Santa Fe Trail made do with what they had. A man never knows when he'll need something. One day you're sitting in your house, and the phone rings. By god if it ain't the president looking for a pottery display. What do you say then? 'No sir, Mr. President, I had one, but I threw it away.' Hell no. That ain't the way they did it on the trail, and by god, that ain't the way Earl Celf's going to do it either."

Jim studied Stufflebaum, whose expression mimicked exactly that of Earl Celf.

"Are there any sane people in Lyons?"

"Yes sir," he said. "You're looking at him."

———

Back at the museum, Stufflebaum took Jim on a cleaning tour, pointing out where the supplies were kept and explaining to him that Earl conducted an inspection each Monday morning.

"The women's is generally clean anyway," he said, "if they don't plug the toilet with one of them sanitary things or write their phone numbers on the mirror with lipstick. The men don't aim so well. Figure on scrubbing the walls at least three feet up, waist-high, you might say. Course, I wouldn't do no heavy cleaning until Sunday night."

Jim pointed to a locked door. "What's this?"

"Museum storage. Earl keeps his artifacts in there."

"You been in the inner sanctum?"

Stufflebaum pushed his strawberry hair under his cap and checked the notch on his belt.

"I been everywhere one time or another 'cause ain't no one but me knows how to use a goddang tool. It looks just like that acreage of his out there, except more so."

"I'd like a look sometime."

"Earl keeps the key," he said, checking his watch. "Got to get started on that new display. Thanks for the help."

———

Jim swept the basement, taking special care to clean the new soddy exhibit. After that he stocked the bathrooms and carried out the trash.

When finished, he found Eva in the museum shop counting out change for the register. She dropped her hand on her throat. A small silver cross rested just where her sunburn faded away into the whiteness of her breasts.

"Do you know when we might get back out to the Milton site?" he asked.

Eva lowered her gaze on him. "I do have a job, you know."

"A site is a fragile thing. The sooner we get it under control the better."

"The Milton site has been there a rather long time."

"It's just that . . ."

Eva closed the cash drawer. "Is there more you needed?"

"Well, now that you asked, I thought I might do some work with the museum storage, make myself useful. Artifacts often get misplaced over time or don't get catalogued. There can be important information lost."

"Especially where amateurs are involved?"

"That's not what I said, exactly."

"You'll have to check with Earl about that. He's at the soddy exhibit."

———————

Earl Celf sat in the soddy display rocking chair reading the morning paper. He checked his shirt pocket, which contained a plastic penholder from The Westerner Cafe, three ink pens, and a tire-pressure gauge.

Taking out a pen, he peered over the top of his glasses as Jim approached. Jim noticed that the liver spot on Earl's forehead actually looked more like an engorged penis than a thumb.

When Jim greeted him, Earl leaned forward and dug at his leg as if something alive had just crawled into his pants.

"Well, by god, Lyons has a Freddie Street," he said. "Now Old Man Bernard is set on naming Fourth Street Pinkie, after his granddaughter. What the hell is the world coming to, that's what I want to know? Folks come in here on the trail wouldn't be naming no streets Freddie and Pinkie for Christ's sake."

"Times change, Earl."

Earl studied Jim as if it were the first time he'd seen him. "You get that site located?"

"Yes sir. Looks interesting."

"Wichita, ain't it?"

"Have to wait and see what the evidence turns up," Jim said.

"Well, the Wichita lived here, you know, and not the goddang Eskimo."

"Some things can only be learned from field experience."

"Goddamn right," Earl said, rolling up his paper. "And what you're likely to find is Old Man Milton squelching on the deal. His people didn't come in on the trail and can't be trusted. They rode in on the train, all fat and easy after the heavy lifting been done. Knowing Milton, he'll likely be asking more money to build a bridge across that river of his, or to put his idiot sons on the council—then we could have North and South Idiot Streets, I suppose."

Taking a chance, Jim pulled up a chair. When Earl didn't protest, he sat down in it.

"You get the cleaning done?" Earl asked.

"I see you have a storage room where you keep your artifacts."

"Ran out of display room."

"Has anyone taken a systematic look at it?"

"I looked at it when I put it in there."

"Sometimes things get lost in storage, things that could be important."

"Ain't nothing lost down there," he said. "It's all in storage."

Jim put on his best serious face.

"And without people like you, it could have been lost forever, Earl, but sometimes things get overlooked, stuck away in a drawer, things that could be important, maybe even worth money, you know, for the museum, and all the time it's just sitting there in storage."

Earl hooked his suspender over his shoulder.

"What's found is found and ain't lost no more," he said.

"Happens all the time, Earl, and I'd like to make certain it's you gets the credit for important finds and not your successor."

"I don't want nobody poking around in my storage. Is that clear?"

"Yes, sir. I guess it is."

"I got things in order down there, and I want them left that way."

"I got it. Sorry to be a nuisance, Earl."

"You keeping them bathrooms in shape?"

"Mint clean."

"Don't go throwing them toilet paper boxes away, you hear?"

———————

Just as Jim finished the upstairs sweeping, Pete and Auntie came out of the genealogy library.

It took a moment for Pete to remember Jim. He pushed back his ball cap.

"Hey, Auntie, it's that guy from the cafe."

Auntie, refusing eye contact, examined her fingernails, which had been chewed into the quick.

"Hello, Pete," Jim said.

"Turns out like I thought," he said. "Auntie is related to the queen sure enough. Course we can't prove it until we get into the records."

"That a fact?"

Pete went on about Henry, the cook, who was envious of his relation to Winston Churchill, not to mention of Auntie's relation to royalty.

Jim headed out. "Nice seeing you again, Pete."

"Say, they got the ham and bean special tonight at The Westerner. Two ninety-five and all you can stand."

"Have a good day, Pete." He went down the stairs, stopping at the bottom. "I wouldn't let that thing about Churchill bother me a bit, if I were you, Pete. No matter what folks say, Winston made a hell of a Kraut killer."

Pete looked over at Auntie and then down at Jim. "What things would folks be saying?"

"It's just a ridiculous rumor," Jim said, waving. "Not to be taken seriously."

14

J im couldn't settle down to his reading. Even Precious had abandoned her quest for the largest long-tail and lay docile at the foot of his cot. From time to time she gazed up at him and swung her tail to the beat of an unheard tune.

He counted Stufflebaum's handiwork—fourteen stuffed creatures in all, if he counted the rat and snake as one piece.

He slipped on his shoes and got up. "What the hell, Precious," he said. "There are worse things than ham and beans at The Westerner Cafe."

Pete and Auntie looked up when he came in, but neither spoke nor acknowledged his entrance. Auntie dipped her head and pulled loose her skirt, which had gathered in a wad under her ample thigh. Pete busied himself blowing the heat from his spoon of beans.

Jim ordered the special, with beer, then read the local *Auction and Trade Guide* while he waited. Within moments Henry arrived with a bowl of beans the size of a Chevy hubcap. In addition he laid out side orders of stone-ground cornbread, onions and cucumbers marinated in white vinegar, two jalapeno peppers, and a longneck bottle of Bud.

Jim scooted back his chair and studied the lethal dose of grub. "Where's the rest of the harvest crew, Henry?"

"Don't worry," Henry said. "If you don't make it through the night, your body will last longer than a Pharaoh mummy's."

He pointed: "Takes a hell of a bowl of beans to shut Pete up over there, and he ain't said a word all evening, not even about how he can use a computer and how he's related to Winston Churchill, not even how he's so much better than the rest of us peasant commoners."

Pete glanced over with his brow furrowed.

Jim said, "Guess I'd brag myself being related to a war hero like Winston Churchill."

He ordered a second beer to put out the fire and sipped on it as he worked the crossword puzzle in the *Auction and Trade*.

He left a sizeable tip for Henry's warm service and had headed outside when a man blocked the door in front of him. Jim recognized the eggplant scar across his cheek and the distinct odor of tobacco and onion. They had met before.

As he stepped aside to let him pass, the man caught him with his shoulder. "Look where you're going," he said, curling his lip.

"Sorry," Jim said.

Outside, Jim paused to watch through the window as the man pulled up a chair. He had creases in the back of his neck as deep as a hippo's, and his biceps were pumped like a weight lifter's. The man glanced up, looking straight at Jim, his stare lethal and ominous.

Jim paused at the shoe repair shop, glancing over his shoulder. The sun settled onto the horizon, and the evening grew cool. He rubbed at his arms and had turned to go when a noise came from between the buildings ahead.

He pressed himself against the wall and edged forward until he could see into the alley. A trash can had been turned on its side, its contents scattered about, and he could smell the garbage in the evening air.

He recognized at once the man from the cafe: Mitch Keeper, Kingston's guard at the cemetery. Keeper had his head down, his hands buried in his pockets. Why did he wait in the alley now? What did he want from him?

Whatever the reason, Jim had no intentions of falling victim to Keeper again. Surprise now on *his* side, he stepped out. Keeper stood, and Jim rammed his elbow into his nose. Keeper grunted, and air rushed from his lungs. Red spots gathered in his nostrils, breached his lip, and spread into the cracks of his teeth.

Determined to finish the job before Keeper could recover, Jim slammed his fist under Keeper's ear. His eyes rolled white, and he wilted onto his knees. Then Jim delivered the coup de grace, and Keeper's teeth clacked like craps dice.

But Jim's victory ended abruptly when a white light exploded in his head, and the world wound down to a stop.

———————

Jim awoke with his face shoved into the hood of a car and his hands cuffed behind his back. His pockets were turned inside out. One eye no longer worked.

"What's going on?" he moaned, his cheek crumpled against the car.

A round-faced man spun him about. His badge hung crooked on his shirt, and a spot of ink had bled through his pocket.

He pushed Jim's head back with his forearm and spoke into his face. His hands smelled of grease and cigarettes, and his eyes, bloodshot with drink, narrowed in determination.

"Sheriff Nabson, Rice County Sheriff's Office. You're under arrest."

"For what?"

"Assault and battery for a start."

The sheriff opened Jim's wallet. Dumping the contents onto the hood of the patrol car, he checked his driver's license.

"Jim Hunt," he said. "Well, let's add vagrancy to that charge, Jim Hunt. You ain't got enough here for a night's room in our fair town."

"I'm staying at the museum."

Scooping up Jim's things, he dumped them into his hat.

"Now that's one I ain't heard before."

"I'm an archeologist."

"And I'm an alien waiting for the Starship," he said.

"But you can call the museum and confirm it."

Opening the door to the patrol car, the sheriff said, "Get in."

Jim climbed into the backseat. All feeling in his hands had disappeared from the cuffs, and his head thumped with each beat of his heart. A Coke can, stuffed with cigarette butts, lay on the floorboard, and the sour of vomit permeated the seat. The wire barrier between him and Sheriff Nabson bellied out where previous passengers had, no doubt, tried to escape.

The sheriff pumped the accelerator a couple of times. When the engine started, the smell of gas seeped through the floorboard.

"I can explain if you'll give me a chance," Jim said.

Sheriff Nabson looked in the rearview mirror. "You just broke Mitch Keeper's nose, you dumb bastard. There ain't no explaining that in a hundred years."

"He lay for me, Sheriff. Why? Or doesn't the law care?"

"This ain't the city, Hunt. Things can turn personal mighty fast around here."

"I'm an outsider, and I'm screwed?"

"That pretty much sums it up," he said.

"Some things are worth it," Jim said, leaning back against the seat.

As Sheriff Nabson pulled into the back of the fire station, he turned.

"Maybe so, but then you ain't seen our accommodations yet, have you?"

The jail consisted of a single cage at the back of the fire truck stall, smelling of sewage, diesel fuel, and cigarettes. A light bulb, covered with flyspecks, hung above the cage. The cot, no more than a metal slab, had been braced and welded to the cage itself. What passed for a mattress, now ringed with unidentifiable fluids, smelled like an old clothes hamper. The sheriff took an orange jumpsuit and flip-flops out of a metal locker and handed them to Jim.

"Is that really necessary, Sheriff?"

"Put them on," he said. "An orange suit makes a good target."

Jim put on the jumpsuit while Sheriff Nabson smoked a cigarette.

Nabson slammed home the door and checked the lock.

"Look, Sheriff, don't I at least get a phone call?"

"And who would you be calling?"

Jim rubbed at his head, now caked with blood.

"Eva Manor, for one."

"And her number would be?"

"I don't know."

"You don't know?"

"I'd have to look it up."

Nabson adjusted his trousers at the crotch. "You got no business bothering citizens you don't even know."

"How long will I be in here?"

"Until you get bailed out, but then it ain't likely anyone in Lyons is going to bail out a crazy man who broke Mitch Keeper's nose?"

"How long, Sheriff?"

Sheriff Nabson walked to the door and paused.

"I'd say about thirty days."

"I can't stay in here thirty days."

"Sure you can. Look at it this way, Hunt, for thirty days you don't have to worry about Mitch Keeper. How bad is that?"

Jim sank back into the cot and studied the rock walls beyond the bars. For him, thirty days in a cage was a lifetime. An archeologist had to be in the open, the only place to study the stratification of rock, which told a larger story backward from top to bottom, from the present into the past.

15

With the others gone, Coronado's remaining force mustered in half the time and traveled twice the leagues on a given day. The men responded both to commands and intent in a moment's notice. No longer did orders mire in translation and error. No longer did camp require an hour of daylight to assemble and another to disassemble.

But his force, having dwindled to only a few, now grew anxious. In the past, Coronado rolled over his enemies with little resistance. He quelled opposition with the size of his force, with the speed of his awesome horses, the swiftness of his reprisal. Now his crossbow men had left. His horses, little more than bags of bones, had shrunk in number. Reprisals rested with the enemy.

Determined to walk, as dictated by his order, Friar Padilla had fallen farther behind each day. He would arrive in camp after the others slept, say his vespers, and collapse by the fire.

In the mornings, Friar Padilla rose before the others, to get a head start. But soon the column would pass him by. He would often wave and smile, his teeth shining through his dusty beard.

The earth soon opened onto a rugged and numbing plain, and the men could see the friar from afar, a black speck trudging along in the distance and into the heat of the noon sun.

Coronado's confidence waned, spurring him to talk to the Turk, who rode with assurance in a due eastward course. Even Alvarado, a skillful soldier in his own right, gave credence to the Turk's knowledge of the land, while holding in reserve his own suspicions.

Isopete, a man given to brooding, complained of the Turk's attentions from Coronado. Isopete sneered and growled with each of the Turk's decisions, crossing his arms with such predictability that the men fell to mocking him, strutting about with their arms locked.

Soon, all mocking faded as the prospect of starvation grew more dire. Even small rodents were food for the conquistadors, who, at sight, beat them senseless with their pikes.

Desperate, Coronado summoned his marksmen and dispatched them in three directions for game. A week passed, and none had returned. On the eighth day, a soldier entered the camp so weak from hunger he could not speak above a whisper. His hair bristled with burrs, and the bones in his heels shone through. His eyes darted about as he struggled to focus on Coronado, who knelt next to him at the fire.

"And what fate has befallen your comrades?" Coronado asked.

"We were lost, my general, in the most grievous way. We circled from morning until night. One way seemed as another. One direction the same as all with no landmark to show the way. Our footsteps in the grass faded behind us. We shot arrows in the earth to follow home, but our bows broke, and our arms failed. We were lost as if at sea. By God's grace am I here this day."

The Turk, squatting at the edge of camp, held his horse's reins. Each night he tended his horse in solitude, grazing him under the moonlight. Now he listened and watched, his eyes locked on the returned soldier at Coronado's feet.

"And the others were disposed to suffer and die?" Coronado asked.

"Without food and water, no hope remained. They came to their appointed times. Ramirez prayed that his soul rest in hell, rather than in this forsaken place, and he wept for his wife."

"And how is it that only you have returned unharmed?" Coronado asked.

"By God's grace alone," he said, "and no other. I fear we shall all perish, for there is nothing beyond even the horizon. The Spaniards' bones will bleach in the sun, and they will be remembered by no man. They will be lost to eternity, of this I am certain."

After the soldier had been removed, Coronado paced, his hands locked behind his back. Lines drew in his face, and the carbuncle, having opened, pained him greatly.

He approached the Turk, who still waited in the shadows of the camp.

"Our hunters have failed, Turk. The game has fled, and the green water stinks and teems with vermin. Our horses collapse from poor pasturage. Each day worsens into another and yet there is no Quivira."

The Turk swung up on his mount. His legs did not quiver from lack of sustenance nor did fear tell in his eyes.

"The Spaniard does not know his way in this land. The Turk must lead, though it burdens him. He knows where the buffalo flow like a river. If Coronado would follow the Turk, who is a most trusted guide, he, too, shall see them. A few leagues more, and the land darkens with their bounty. The Turk sees this land even now in his dreams. Follow him, and you, too, shall see. The meat is sweeter than the Spaniard's goat and gives warriors much strength."

"So have we done for many leagues," Coronado said. "Still we die from privation. How much longer must Coronado wait?"

The Turk pointed to the horizon. "Soon, Coronado shall look upon the great beasts of the plains."

"And what of Quivira?"

The Turk mounted his horse. "And Quivira also, my general, as I have sworn."

16

For two more days the column marched eastward into the lowlands. Desperate, the Spaniards boiled prickly pear for sustenance, having witnessed this practice among the Indians, but by morning, their ignorance of the flora became sorely evident. Sick unto death, they moaned throughout the camp, their intestines rushing and their mouths foaming.

Some hemorrhaged, heaving blood and bile at the edge of camp. Blood seeped from under their fingernails and leaked from their tear ducts. One man died at the watering hole, where in great thirst, he drank tainted water, even after repeated warnings from the others.

Weakened and despondent, the men recovered but slowly, and were found to be useless during this time.

On the tenth day, Coronado rose from his bed in distress, having not heard from the ill-fated hunting parties. He walked to where the horses were staked for pasturage, and to where Friar Padilla, who had grown ever weaker from his ordeal afoot, had failed to rise before the dawn.

Coronado observed a darkening cloud on the horizon. He called out in alarm to the others, realizing only then that dust accompanied a great gathering of buffalo flowing onto the plain, so vast their number that no individual animal could be discerned from another. The beasts moved as a mass ebbing and flowing over the land. Their sound rose up as thunder, and the smells of fat, heat, and dust rode in on the wind. All of the prairie fell silent. Birds vanished from the sky, and the camp horses danced and tugged at their ropes.

Coronado called out once again, and the conquistadors, struck silent, gathered at his side. The Turk stood with his horse saddled and readied, while Friar Padilla, believing it to be intercession of the divine, fell to his knees in prayer.

Alvarado rode out for a better view, returning to report that the herd now grew greater than could be known. "There is no end," he said, sweeping his hand. "They flow to the ocean like a great river. I took leave for fear of being swallowed up in their midst."

"Mount your horses," Coronado ordered. "You as well, Friar Padilla. Litany must await its time, for tonight we shall taste the savory flesh of the buffalo as the Turk has promised."

Once mounted, the men turned to the Turk, who said, "The wise hunter takes those of the least effort from so many cows."

"We shall shoot them from afar," Coronado said.

The Turk shook his head. "They run in fear at the least sounds and cannot be stopped. With the warrior's stealth, they can be taken for many days to follow and know not even that they are hunted."

"The crossbow guards are no longer with us," Coronado said. "And without our guns, there is only the pike, a weapon long and cumbersome from the horse."

The men agreed to the pikes, and they formed and rode downwind toward the herd. As each man approached, he fell silent, taken into his own thoughts. Just ahead, a dozen bulls gathered in advance of the herd, their great heads swinging as they grazed, their black eyes shining in the sun. Now and again they paused to bellow or paw dust over their backs. Some bulls mounted others, their quarters humping in a mock breeding ritual, their great muscles quivering. Even the smallest of them towered five hands over the largest Spanish horse.

Dismounting, the men received their instructions from the Turk, who pointed first to the east and then to the west with deliberate ceremony.

"Circle out to the sun," he said in a whisper. "Bring the bulls forward, but with patience. Wait for the Turk to rise up and turn them aside, then set your pikes here," he said, pointing under his arm. "Be silent even so, and move on with disinterest, as does the wolf, who takes his prey without notice. In this manner, the cows turn to their grazing. Once distressed, all will be lost to the hunter, because no man or horse can then turn them aside."

The men shook their heads in agreement.

"And if a conquistador should falter?" Friar Padilla asked.

"He must die with his tongue clenched between his teeth," the Turk said.

Coronado led men to the east in accordance with the Turk's instructions, and Alvarado to the west. They moved with indifference, pausing to let their mounts graze before pressing ahead once again. The bulls lifted their heads to snort, or to sling slobbers onto their backs, or to plop into the grass, all the while suffering the conquistadors' presence, even at so close range.

When the Spaniards were upon them, the bulls drew together and loped toward the Turk. The men spurred their horses forward and lifted their pikes onto their shoulders. The pace of the hunters quickened, and from out of the grass the Turk stood, his arms open. The bulls cut away, dust billowing up from their hooves, and bore eastward, exposing their flanks to the conquistadors.

Blowing and snorting, the bulls broke into a hard run, their speeds like that of the jackrabbit, but they soon tired, as the Turk had predicted, and the conquistadors advanced upon them.

Pedro Sebastian, the youngest and most daring of them, stood tall in his stirrups and launched his pike. Falling short, it spiked deep into the earth and in the path of his horse's stride. The pike entered Sebastian's chest, propelling him from his saddle, and exited at the base of his neck. Impaled, poor Sebastian flailed about, his helmet clattering away, and his cry rose up.

The Turk leaped onto his horse and reined about. Coronado turned to see the herd gathering and drifting at the sound of

Sebastian's cry, as they might at the birth of a storm. He dug his
spurs deep into his horse's side and called out for the others to
flee. Throwing their pikes aside, the men raced behind Coronado, though the direction was unfortunate, for soon all were
soon swept into the maelstrom. Alvarado and his men were also
drawn into the eye of the rampage.

Coronado's party, including the unconquerable friar, were
swept along at the ridge of a great ravine. Fifty meters deep, it
rent the prairie in an open slash, and the buffalo plunged into
the abyss. The air soon reeked of blood and death from the car-
nage below.

The western flank, led by Alvarado, being unaware of the
danger ahead, rode full stride toward the ravine. Coronado cut
hard to the perimeter, signaling his men to follow. All did as
commanded except Friar Padilla, who turned westward toward
Alvarado.

While Coronado and his party escaped unharmed, though
greatly frightened, Alvarado and the others spilled over the edge
of the chasm, which now churned with dying buffalo.

Coronado, mourning the loss of his men, stood at the edge of
the ravine. The Turk, having come from the rear, dropped from
his horse at Coronado's side.

"It is as I said, my general, meat for a thousand warriors, and
the flesh is like no other."

Coronado's legs trembled, and his boot, having been torn
away, revealed a deep bruise on his leg.

"Where have you been, Turk, while the conquistadors die
from your counsel?"

"The Turk rides against the stream, my general, and the buffalo part as water from a rock."

Servantes pointed and cried out, "Look! See what arises from
the dead."

Friar Padilla crawled from out of the ravine, his garb torn and
covered with blood. He carried Captain Alvarado, whose clothes
had been torn from him, and whose face had been badly damaged from hooves.

The men rejoiced, clapping and dancing about. Friar Padilla
wrested the captain onto the ground and fell to his knees in prayer.

"How does Captain Alvarado live while all others perish?" Coronado asked.

"The divine hand of God," Alvarado said. "And the valor of Friar Padilla."

That night the conquistadors built a great fire, and all feasted on the savory flesh of the buffalo. The Turk, adorned in buffalo horns, paraded about the camp for all to see and admire, and as the night wore on, and a full moon rose, the men returned again and again to partake from the bounty of the bloody ravine.

17

Jim bolted upright on the cot, his heart thudding in his chest. The vision lingered in his head: the famished plain, the shaggy beasts with their hooves beating toward him. Somewhere a door rattled. Jim turned, rubbing the sleep from his face. The overhead light burned hot as the morning sun streamed in through the firehouse door. The beating continued deep in his brain.

Nabson opened the cell door and tossed in his clothes. "Get dressed, Hunt. You've been bailed."

Before Jim could ask anything, Nabson slammed the door and walked away. To keep his head from igniting, Jim leaned against the bars while he changed. His clothes still smelled of Henry's cafe, and a splotch of blood soaked the front of his shirt.

He found Sheriff Nabson in his office, his feet propped up on his desk. Pete and Auntie sat on a bench near the door. Pete, his fingers locked in his lap, nodded to Jim, while Auntie fumbled through her purse in search of something.

"Sign here," Nabson said.

"Who bailed me?" Jim asked.

"These people here."

Jim glanced over at Pete, who flashed him a smile.

"You see that court date there, Hunt?" Nabson asked.

"Yes."

"Fail to show up, I'll be coming for you with a warrant, you understand?"

"I understand."

"Don't leave the county. You don't show for that date, the bail is forfeited."

"Right."

"You do see how it would be?"

"I get the picture, Sheriff."

Outside, Pete hooked his arm through Auntie's as she negotiated the steps.

Jim said, "Look, I know this must put you at odds with the powers around here, but I'm grateful." He massaged the side of his head. "But why, Pete?"

"Winston," he said.

"Winston?"

"For not telling Henry about . . . I mean, being related to Winston Churchill's all I got, you see. If Henry ever found out about that rumor, I'd have nothing at all. Thank you for keeping it to yourself like that."

"Look, Pete, what I said about Churchill . . ."

"Me and Auntie got to go," he said. "You watch out for Keeper. He's a mean one, and he's got Evan Kingston's money behind him."

———

Jim found Stufflebaum in the shop with both hands in a opossum's belly. Precious lay on the bench, sound asleep, with all four feet in the air.

Stufflebaum held up his bloody hands and said, "Why, if it ain't Jim Hunt come home."

"You sure that thing's dead?"

Turning back to his work, Stufflebaum said, "It ain't complained yet, but then that's why I like taxidermy. I rarely get a complaint. Anyway, it's been in the deep freeze for six months."

"Anyone ever tell you how unpleasant that is, Stufflebaum?"

"Unlike that lovely eye of yours, I guess," he said.

Jim touched the swollen lid, which now resembled a keyhole. "Just a little accident," he said.

"I hear Mitch Keeper had a mishap hisself," he said. "What have you done to rile up such as him?"

"That's just it. I'm not sure. Anyway, how could you know about that already?"

"Pete and Auntie," he said. "They were in first thing to tell me what happened."

"I thought it might be kept quiet for a little while."

"Oh, it will be," he said, turning the opossum on its side, "until it comes out in Monday's paper. The county court docket is what keeps the coffee klatches alive out here."

The opossum seemed to look at Jim with glassy eyes, and for a moment he thought he saw its tongue move.

"Does anyone ever just keep quiet in this town?" he asked.

"The only thing quiet in this town is this here opossum, least till he thaws."

"Keeper waylaid me in the alley. I didn't have much choice."

"Keeper's a human error, that's certain, but he's not someone to go punching in the nose. Anybody ever tell you that picking enemies isn't your strong suit?"

Jim watched Stufflebaum comb out the opossum's fur. "Where do you get all these animals?"

Stufflebaum held the opossum up by its hind legs, turning it this way and that as he studied it.

"Roadkill, mostly. Sometime I hunt 'em down on the river. Here and there, you know."

"Then you freeze them?"

"It's best they stay frozen until I'm ready, as you might guess. Then I work out their brains with a wire, salt them up for cure, and sprinkle in a little borax to keep out the bugs. When they're good and dry, I stuff them with excelsior and do them up with a baseball stitch. They'll still be grinning when you and me is dust."

Jim sat down on his bunk and eased off his shoes.

"I'm going to clean up. If the shower monster takes me, you can have my things, Stufflebaum."

"Shower monster?"

"That fiend living in the shower. It's as big as that opossum."

Dumping a jar of glass eyes onto the counter, Stufflebaum sorted through them. "There, gray with a touch of red ought do just fine.

"Not to worry," he said, "so long as you shower before sundown."

"It's a vampire?"

"Just nocturnal," he said.

Thunder bumped in the dawn hours, and Jim rolled onto his side. In the dim light of morning, he could see Precious curled against the opossum.

Once up, he headed for the museum to do his chores before the public arrived. He wondered what Earl might do about the Keeper fracas if he heard about it and figured it most likely wouldn't be good.

On the way out of the shop, he patted Precious on the head. She turned on her side, drooping a leg over the opossum's neck, and commenced purring.

Clouds, their bellies heavy with moisture, drifted overhead, and the deep roll of thunder promised a rain.

Even at this early hour, he found the basement door unlocked. Perhaps someone had left it open. Halfway up the stairs, he noticed the storage door ajar. The light had been left on, and he could see Earl Celf, his glasses dropped down on his nose, sitting at the workbench absorbed in sorting through a box. Jim hurried back up the stairs, careful not to disturb him.

He tracked down Eva when he'd finished his chores and found her shelving new books in the souvenir shop. Her midriff peeked from under her blouse as she lifted onto her toes.

"Well," she said. "Who let you out?"

"Oh, you've heard, too, I guess?"

"Me and half of the town. Your disregard for the museum's reputation, not to mention mine, is a bit disconcerting, Jim."

"I had little choice, you know. I came upon Mitch Keeper lurking in the alley like some kind of thug."

"Funny thing," she said. "I've lived here my whole life and never spent a single night in the county jail."

"I doubt you've been attacked by Keeper, either," he said.

"Earl's going to have a stroke. Just what do you plan to tell him?"

"I don't know. How about the truth?"

She pulled out her cash box and tucked it under her arm.

"I'm certain you find all this entertaining, but this museum and this job happen to be important to me. Now, if you'll excuse me, I have work to do."

That afternoon Jim spent his time in the research library gathering information on the hunting practices of the Wichita. When he checked his watch, he had just enough time before the museum closed to examine the Wichita display. Often, museum displays were more romantic than realistic, and he needed a visual image as close to reality as possible before beginning the dig.

He found the display, a reconstructed camp and garden, located on the second floor. He compared the construction against his notes. The camp and hut were surprisingly authentic in their detail. Had it not been for the department-store mannequins with their Caucasian features, the whole thing could have passed muster. For the purpose of display, Stufflebaum's notion of stuffing a human or two might not be such a bad idea.

"Mr. Hunt," Earl said from behind him.

"Oh, Earl. I'm studying the Wichita display. Are you wanting to close?"

"I've been to the workshop looking for you. We need to talk. Come with me."

Jim followed him to the soddy where Earl took up his chair. He rolled a fresh cigar into his mouth and tossed the wrapper onto the floor. He bobbed his foot as he gathered up his speech. Mud had caked in the heels of his shoes, and burrs were buried in the frizz of his cuffs. The penis birthmark on his forehead had darkened even more with sunburn.

Earl cleared his throat and reached into his back pocket to retrieve the *Lyons Daily News*, which he'd rolled into a tube. "Know what's in this here paper, Hunt?"

"No, I'm afraid I don't know."

Earl shifted his cigar to the other side of his mouth and narrowed his eyes. "This is the sort of behavior that I don't tolerate, see. It's contrary to everything this museum is about."

"Look, Earl, Keeper started this little feud for whatever reason. I just evened up the score."

"That's the attitude that landed you in the county jail in the first place. A man like Keeper's apt to finish things ahead of even, if you get my drift."

"This guy assaulted me and dumped me on the road like a sack of trash and then he set out to waylay me in the alley. I have a thing about that."

Earl stood and ran his hand over his balding head. A wisp of hair lifted skyward on a current of static electricity.

"My advice is that you pack your bags and go home while you can."

"Running isn't my style."

"How about brawling? Is that your style? Brawling ain't something the citizens of this town understand. It ain't something I understand."

"Keeper chose the strategy, Earl, not me."

"My obligation to you is over, if I ever had one. I suppose you can stay in town if you're fool enough, but you can't stay here. I'm council chair and have a reputation to maintain. It isn't good for the museum either, so you can just pack your things and get on your way."

Jim's heart sank. "I need that field experience. I could be a lot of help to the project."

Earl laced his fingers over the top of his belly and looked at Jim through dust-covered glasses. "It's something you should have thought about before brawling with Keeper."

"Without that field experience, I can't break into a decent position, and I'm in need of a decent position."

Earl removed the cigar and spit tobacco on the floor. "Fact is, there isn't going to be a dig."

"What do you mean?"

"I've cancelled the Milton project."

"What? But why?"

Earl turned his back. His britches hung from his suspenders like billowing curtains on a drapery rod, and his shirt, too spare for his ample belly, gathered in a wad between his shoulders.

"Short of funds, and what's left can be better spent on the genealogy library; besides, it's not that promising a site. I don't need more pots, and I sure don't need more arrow points. I don't need volunteers breaking citizens' noses, and I damn sure don't need a mutiny of the city council."

"It's a rich site, Earl. Eva and I found artifacts even while we were laying the thing out. You can't close it down."

Earl turned. Digging a kitchen match from the bottom of his pocket, he struck it on the porch railing. Lighting another cigar, he looked at Jim through the cloud of smoke.

"I just did," he said.

———————

Jim stared at the spot Earl had stood. He'd spent everything he had getting here. "Damn it," he said, picking up Earl's cigar wrapper.

As he headed to the basement, lightning flickered, snapping and cracking, and thunder rumbled out onto the prairie. Rain fell and then deepened, drumming against the windows of the museum.

Maybe he could change Earl's mind. Maybe things would work out. He couldn't just leave. And what about Sheriff Nabson? What about the court date?

He leaned against the door of the storage room, rubbing the weariness from his neck. The door gave way under his shoulder, and he stepped back, staring into the darkness. Earl must have failed to lock up. He turned on the light and gently closed the door behind him.

The room overflowed with wood stoves, ironware, hand tools, cream separators, corn shuckers, and a dozen kind of kerosene lanterns. A two-headed stuffed calf stood in the corner, dust hanging from all four of its eyebrows. There were lard crocks, school photos, and an entire quart of rattlesnake rattles.

Old magazines, books, and territorial documents lined the east wall. Next to that, old letters, diaries, and ledgers from every agency in the county had been stacked in piles. The water fountain, buried under a stack of children's drawings, and an old hand-operated gasoline pump, blocked the only back exit.

Earl's most extensive accumulation consisted of Native American relics: buffalo-rib grassing needles, shell-tempered pots, elk-teeth necklaces, and Bois d'Arc wooden bows, not to mention a vast collection of war points, scrapers, and stone mauls. Nothing had been marked, cataloged, or stored in any systematic way.

A path no wider than a man's shoulders wound through the debris and terminated at the worktable, where a box with a hand-drawn map in it had "Milton Site" printed on its top.

Jim glanced at the door and listened for a moment before picking though the items. He counted ten war points—six agate and four Alibates. A cardboard box next to it contained an additional eight scrapers, all in good condition, and a chert lance with a fractured tang.

At the bottom, he found a piece of rusty iron, a crumpled lump the size of a man's fist and surprisingly porous. He held it to the light and could identify vestiges of pattern and form, but it lacked the uniformity of modern manufacturing.

He scratched his head and put it back. Whatever the material, it couldn't have come from the Wichita. With enough time and resources, he might be able to track it down. Unfortunately, he no longer had the luxury of either.

As he made his way across the compound, the sky opened and rain poured down. His shoes filled with water, and his scalp tingled as lightning crackled overhead in a high-voltage cosmic game of Russian roulette.

Stufflebaum had left the shop. At least Jim didn't have to explain. He'd explained enough for one day. Precious, engaged in a spit bath, ignored him as Jim gathered up his belongings. He found an umbrella behind the door with one rib bent and with a glob of plaster of paris stuck to its top.

He took a last look back. Bizarre as his stay had been in this menagerie, he had somehow grown accustomed to it. Not once in his tenure here, had there been a cross word between him and the other inhabitants.

He considered his choices as he pried open the umbrella. He could hitchhike out tonight, leave this town behind, take his chances on the warrant not being executed, but then Sheriff Nabson didn't strike him as the forgiving sort.

Just then a car swung through the compound gate, its headlights illuminating the sheets of rain. A black Fleetwood Cadillac pulled alongside him, its wipers thumping against the downpour. The driver cracked the window and held his hand up against the rain.

"Jim Hunt?"

"Yes, I'm Jim Hunt."

"Would you come with me, Mr. Hunt?"

Positioning his umbrella against the wind, Jim took a better look.

"And who are you?"

"Evan Kingston," the man said. "Please do get in."

18

Evan Kingston opened the passenger window wider.

"I've been meaning to talk to you, Mr. Hunt. Perhaps you'd care to come to dinner?"

"Excuse me?"

"Of course, if now is not a good time, we could make other arrangements."

Jim stooped down for a better look. Evan Kingston, balding and pale, made a slight figure behind the wheel of the Cadillac. Dressed in suit and tie, he could have been the local pharmacist or shoe salesman rather than Lyons's most powerful citizen.

"And why would you want to talk to me?"

Kingston slipped off his glasses to wipe away the fog on the lenses. His intense black eyes locked on Jim.

"This thing between you and Mitch Keeper," he said, putting his glasses back on. "It would be in your interest to discuss the matter."

Jim looked back at the shop and then at the museum. The only other engagement he had would be a wet night in the park.

"It just so happens that I'm free this evening, Mr. Kingston. I'd be delighted to join you for dinner."

"Then please get in. I'm sure you'll find your visit to the Kingston estate interesting."

The umbrella refused to collapse. After three tries, Jim abandoned it on the sidewalk and tossed his case in the backseat. The car smelled of leather and money, and the dash lights glowed like a miniature city skyline.

As they turned down Main and headed out on the highway, the rain deepened. The windshield wipers slogged against the deluge, and Kingston fell silent while he concentrated on the road. Jim recognized the cemetery fence that he'd crawled under that day, the mausoleum now lost from sight in the torrent.

They pulled into the garage of the estate, and Kingston relaxed. "Forgive me for ignoring you, Mr. Hunt. It must be obvious that I'm unaccustomed to driving. We can enter through here. I'll fix us a brandy and order our dinners while you dry off."

Jim followed him down the line of cars to the side entrance. With the exception of a single all-terrain, the other cars were all high-end sedans of one sort or another. The all-terrain, brawny enough for a safari or warfare, had mud splattered down its length.

"Are you a hunter, Mr. Kingston?"

"It's neither a passion I have nor one that I understand, frankly. Killing wild animals in the modern world is an irrational act."

"An uncommon position to take in this neighborhood, I should think," Jim said.

"It's true, of course, that hunting has always been a part of our human history but then we also dragged women about by the hair. Neanderthals, while predatory as a matter of survival, have failed to pass the evolutionary test. The need for hunting has been negated by grocery stores and packaged meat."

"Of course I find myself surrounded by those who still enjoy such barbarism, killing animals for no apparent reason other than it's in their power to do so. Perhaps the predatory gene is recessive and comes out with the help of high-powered weapons and mash whiskey."

It sounded like a prepared speech to Jim. "But what's the purpose of the all-terrain?"

"I fancied myself a geologist in an earlier life and never quite lost my taste for exploration. With this vehicle, there's no place on the estate that is inaccessible."

"A geologist?"

"We'll talk in the study, Mr. Hunt. The dressing room is just there. If you need dry clothes, I'm sure we can accommodate."

—————

Jim found Kingston in his study coaxing a small blaze in the fireplace. The room, clad in mahogany panels and strewn with leather chairs and plush couches, made for a stark contrast with Stufflebaum's workshop. Jim's feet disappeared into the opulent wool carpeting. Rain drove against the leaded windows, and the aroma of smoke escaped from the fireplace.

Kingston said, "There. Did you find everything you needed?"

"It's rather obvious, I suppose, but your home is magnificent."

Kingston adjusted his glasses and looked about the study.

"Thank you. I subscribed to the maxim that living well is the best revenge."

"In my case just living is the best revenge," Jim said.

Jim surveyed the titles in the library—works of Shakespeare, Dickens, and Chaucer. He slid out a volume of *The Canterbury Tales,* leafing through the Prologue, which he'd memorized in his undergraduate days. The gilt-edged book lacked the patina of use.

"Brandy, Mr. Hunt?"

"Yes, please."

Jim inhaled the brandy's perfume, a coalescence of fruit, earth, and sunshine. He sipped and waited as the glow soothed away the day's frustrations.

Kingston poked the fire, and it blazed into life, embers soaring up the chimney.

"I've ordered a chowder," he said. "I hope you don't mind?"

"Wonderful. Chowder is hard to come by at The Westerner."

"There are some disadvantages in living so far from the city. Good food is one of them."

Kingston paced in front of the fire, his hands locked behind his back.

Jim steeled himself.

"Mr. Hunt, I've been informed that you and my employee, Mitch Keeper, have had, shall we say, a misunderstanding."

"We *could* say that, Mr. Kingston. Mitch Keeper attacked me from behind, choked me into a coma, and left me for dead in the

road. He made the decision to try it again for no apparent reason. In response, I broke his nose."

Kingston sipped his brandy. Flames from the fire danced in
his glasses.

"You must know that Mitch Keeper is not the type of man
one should provoke?"

"Mitch Keeper is a bully," he said.

"More brandy, Mr. Hunt?"

"No, thanks. It loosens my tongue, as you can tell."

"I acknowledge the less attractive aspects of Keeper's nature.
In truth, they're why I hired him."

"I don't understand how my problem is your problem, Mr.
Kingston."

"I've put together a considerable fortune in my life, Mr. Hunt,
in all modesty, and there is no shortage of scoundrels prepared
to relieve me of it. My own disposition is one of basic good will
and does not serve me well with less savory characters. So I hire
the Mitch Keepers of the world."

"Beware the Hun, Mr. Kingston."

"I admit that I underestimated Mitch's penchant for physical
violence, and I would like to apologize to you for any discomfort
it may have caused."

"Mr. Kingston, I'm curious by nature, too curious. In this instance, curiosity superseded my good judgment. The mausoleum
tempted me, such a grand structure sitting alone out here in the
prairie. I couldn't resist, but I had no business trespassing."

"Thank you for your honesty, Mr. Hunt."

"I would gladly have left without an altercation had I been presented the opportunity. But that doesn't excuse my behavior."

Kingston's silhouette looked frail and bent against the firelight.

"Of course, you're not the first to be curious about the mausoleum," he said. "It's a favorite target of the local mischief makers.
In fact, that is the reason for hiring Mitch Keeper. The Franciscans are wonderful people but not the best of security guards.

Kingston changed tack. "You see, I came here many years
ago as a young geologist looking for oil deposits. No one else had
taken an interest in the area, and for good reason as it turned
out. There's more oil in the crankcase of my Cadillac than lies
under this land.

"My new bride came with me. Broke and disappointed, we left, but not before developing a fondness for the area. I swore that if I ever succeeded, I would return and build a mansion on this hill. Within a few years I had made my fortune in the southern plains, not in oil, but in natural gas."

"And you returned?"

"My wife died unexpectedly. The mausoleum is for her. I wanted something fitting. I intend to join her there soon enough. Of course, I didn't anticipate the attention such a monument would draw."

"I had no intention of desecrating your wife's tomb. No one appreciates the sanctity of memoriam more than an archeologist."

Kingston turned, holding his hands to the fire to warm them.

"I would like to propose that this conflict between you and Mitch be resolved without further incident."

"That would be up to him."

"I have explained to Mitch that he may have been overly exuberant in executing his duties. He has agreed to withdraw from the quarrel."

"I have assault and battery charges filed against me."

"That can be taken care of, Mr. Hunt, if you will settle the disagreement quietly."

Lightning sputtered in the distance. Thunder bumped and died away in a growl.

"I'm a stranger here. It strikes me that I might come out on the losing end of a court hearing."

Kingston poured himself another brandy. "So we have an agreement to let this thing pass?"

"If it's mutual."

"I'm reclusive by nature, Mr. Hunt, and prefer to live my life quietly. The locals feed on this sort of gossip, and my private business soon becomes public fare. You can see why I would prefer to stop it before it escalates."

"Consider it a truce then, Mr. Kingston. My pride will heal in time."

The dinner cart arrived with steaming bowls of chowder, French bread, and slabs of cold butter. Kingston ladled the bowls himself, and they ate as the rain whispered against the windows.

Jim pushed back his bowl. "Superb. Thank you for inviting me."

"I'm glad you enjoyed it, Mr. Hunt. Would you care for something sweet?"

"No, thank you. I'm quite content."

"Well then, tell me about this Milton site. I understand you will be starting the dig soon."

"There's been a change in plans."

Kingston looked up. "Oh?"

"Earl Celf has cancelled the dig."

Kingston's brow knitted, and he drummed his fingers on the table.

"And why so?"

Jim shrugged. "Because of lack of funds, he said, though a week ago that didn't seem to be a problem."

"I understood the site to be promising."

"There are plenty of surface artifacts, all suggesting a significant campsite."

Kingston searched out a box of cigars, offering one to Jim, who declined.

Kingston rolled the cigar under his nose before lighting it. "You'll be leaving soon, then?"

"I hope you've not wasted a dinner."

"Certainly not. I've enjoyed chatting with someone of your education and interests, Mr. Hunt."

"I'm disappointed it's cancelled, actually. I needed the field experience to complete my qualifications."

"I'm sure you must be, but there's little chance of starting a dig soon in any case. With the river up, there's no ingress or egress except over . . ."

"Over Kingston property," Jim said.

"You know that I've been pressured to open a road over my land?"

"I know Milton is unhappy, and he has a rifle the size of a howitzer."

"You must think it selfish of me not to permit it?"

Jim walked to the window but could see nothing through the driving rain.

"It's your land, Mr. Kingston."

"I made Milton a handsome offer when I bought this place, but he refused it." Kingston's eyes narrowed. "Unfortunately, it's too late now. I can't allow a road to be built through hallowed ground. We all make our choices, and we live with the consequences. Mr. Milton made his."

"Thank you for dinner, Mr. Kingston. Perhaps you or someone else could drive me back to town?"

"But on this rainy night? No, I insist that you stay. There are plenty of guest rooms. Surely the morning would be soon enough."

"Well, I don't know."

"After all, I'm the one who dragged you out on such a night. The least I can do is offer you a bed."

"If you insist then."

"Take the room at the top of the stairs. I've business to attend to early, so I won't see you in the morning. I'll leave orders for the cook to drive you. If we do not meet again, good luck to you, Mr. Hunt."

"Good night, Mr. Kingston."

Jim lay staring into the blackness of the vaulted ceiling of his bedroom. Outside, the storm raged, and the windows rattled against the wind. Unable to sleep, he tossed and turned in the luxury of his bed. Now that the business with the sheriff would be handled by Kingston, he could return to the city, find work of some sort, and wait for another opportunity. Little enough remained for him here now.

The rumble of the storm faded in the early hours, and the night grew quiet. Jim got out of bed and stood at the window. With the first light, the mausoleum emerged from the darkness. Framed by his window, it drew in close and surreal in the morning mist. He stood motionless, captivated by its forbidding presence.

Then for the briefest instant, he imagined a light move somewhere behind the stained glass window. He put his blanket about his shoulders and shivered, waiting for the dawn.

19

The minute Jim slid into the backseat of the limousine he knew he'd made a mistake. An eggplant scar plunged below Mitch Keeper's ear, and his hair curled on the back of his head like the wig on a cheap doll. He smelled of tobacco, rancid and distinct, and he had skin white as a cadaver's.

Jim didn't say anything nor did Keeper as they drove from the Kingston estate. Jim could see the mausoleum out of the passenger window. Each wall sported a stained-glass window no larger than a book and, in the front, a marble façade the color of cream glowed in the morning light. A carved angel over the door, its wings outstretched, secured the remains of Evan Kingston's wife.

At the bottom of the hill, the monks, looking like a flock of crows, worked at the monastery garden. They neither looked up nor acknowledged the presence of the car as it sped past.

Mitch Keeper hooked his arm up on the back of the seat as he drove. He wore a sword, with shield, tattooed on his bicep and had a silver ring on his little finger.

"Where?" he asked, turning his head.

Jim got a long take at Mitch Keeper's face, his brows thick and black against his white skin, his nose bearing the marks from Jim's elbow, and his eyes, sunken and inert. They looked like a dead man's eyes.

"Where?" he asked again.

"I'm not sure," Jim said.

"Nobody said nothing about driving you around all day. Decide or get out."

"The Westerner."

Once there, Keeper opened Jim's door and waited. His jaw rippled, and his breathing quickened. The eggplant scar wrenched his mouth askew, and his white cheeks had turned rosy with heat.

Keeper stepped in front of him when he got out. "The reason you ain't dead is because of Kingston," he said. "But one day Kingston ain't going be there. One day it's just going to be me and you."

Rocks and gravel spun onto the sidewalk as he sped away, and the black smoke from the car's exhaust drifted down Main.

When The Westerner door opened behind him, Jim jumped. For a moment he didn't recognize the lanky figure as being that of Stufflebaum, who hailed him: "Here I thought you bolted and without even saying goodbye."

"How are you?" Jim asked.

"Been listening to Pete and Auntie talk about their ancestors. Pete's taken to smoking cigars and speaking with a British accent, and Auntie walks around with a handkerchief in her hand, trailing it here and there like she's the queen herself. It's enough to make a man sick."

"Whatever Pete and Auntie do is fine with me," Jim said.

"Where the hell you been?"

"The Kingston estate."

"Did you see Churchill there?"

"I'm serious."

"Let's go back to the shop. You can lie to me while I'm having a beer."

————

At the workshop, Stufflebaum was incredulous: "You're telling me you spent the night at the Kingston estate?"

"I had dinner with Kingston."

"Sure, and I had dinner with Auntie's queen."

"Kingston doesn't want things to go any further between Keeper and me. Says he can fix it with the sheriff."

"I'd say that's likely, if he's a mind to. Come on, I've got some brews in the fridge. You can tell me about how next week you'll be having lunch in the Oval Office."

Stufflebaum swung open the workshop door, and Jim spotted Precious on the bench. Her eyes were fixed, and one paw, with claws extended, struck high above her head. Her ears lay flat against her skull, and her tongue, the color of blood, stuck out between her teeth.

"My god, Stufflebaum, what have you done?"

"Stuffed her. Precious and the hair dryer took a fiery dive into that bucket of brine there."

"And you had to stuff her?"

"In right good shape, considering, though I still can't shake the stink of singed fur. Seemed a shame to waste a good specimen, and I have gotten kind of used to having her around."

Jim shook his head and pulled at a beer. "I hope I never get sick around you."

Stufflebaum wiped beer from his mustache, sat down, and drooped one leg over the other. "So why did you pack up in such a hurry, Hunt, aside from wanting to hang out with Kingston and Churchill, I mean?"

"Earl didn't fancy having one of his volunteers being in jail. Then he cancelled the dig and invited me to pack my bags. I shouldn't be here even now."

"That don't sound like Earl. He's never happier then when all them volunteers are sucking up."

"Said he didn't have the funds and that the dig wasn't all that good anyway."

"Earl's been after that site for some time, though he'd never admit it. Don't make a lot of sense to me, but I'm just the handyman." Stufflebaum crumpled up his can and shot a basket across the shop.

"At least you have a job," Jim said.

Stufflebaum opened another beer, offering it to Jim.

"No, thanks. I need to stay alert, so I don't wind up like Precious."

"Never work when I'm drinking," he said.

"Don't you get enough of this place during the week, Stufflebaum?"

"Been trying to track down Earl and give him a heads-up. Word's out that there's a coup in progress down at the city council. Earl's objection to naming streets after the councilmen's grandkids has made him unpopular, you might say."

"Earl's not popular on the best of days."

"He signs my paycheck, and he likes my work. It's enough to make *me* loyal."

"You been out to his house?"

"Sure. Car's gone, too. Earl never takes that old heap out of town, and he's not at the pool hall either."

"Maybe he's buried under that pile of junk out there."

"Or maybe he's hobnobbing with Kingston like other uppity folks I know."

"Listen, you mind if I clean up?" Jim asked. "I should break the news to Eva about the dig."

"I don't mind you being clean hardly at all, Hunt," he said.

He found Eva's house only a few blocks from the museum, a modest bungalow with porch swing and potted plants. Eva answered the door with flour on her hands and nose.

"There's something I need to tell you," he said. "May I come in?"

Eva stepped aside. "I'm in the kitchen. You want hot chocolate?"

As they waited for the water to heat, he told her about the dig and Kingston and his trip to town with Keeper. Finally, he told her that he had no choice but to go back home and look for work.

"Listen," he said. "Maybe I didn't handle things so well. I know I'm a guest here, but I don't like being pushed. So, I pushed back. What I'm trying to say is that I'm sorry about screwing things up."

Eva filled their cups and sat down at the table.

"Maybe neither one of us handled things well. I get a little too focused sometimes."

"Yeah, me too," he said.

"It's just that we've worked hard to put this museum together, and it's always a struggle to get funding. A public brawl doesn't help so much."

"I know. I'm sorry, Eva."

"But I don't understand why he cancelled the dig. It doesn't make sense. Earl wanted that site."

"He said lack of funds."

"As far as I know the dig had funds," she said. "And what's Kingston's interest in all this?"

Jim dropped in two marshmallows and watched them melt into a brown puddle.

"I don't know, but he indicated surprise that the dig had been cancelled.

"There is one other thing I should mention," he said.

Eva folded her hands on the table. "Oh?"

"I broke into the museum storage, not exactly broke in, since Earl failed to lock it. But I sort of took advantage."

"That fails the felony test, I should think."

"I saw something in there that I can't shake."

"What do you mean?"

"Earl had been going through the artifacts that the Miltons brought to the museum. He had them all laid out on his bench, the usual stuff, points, things like that."

"And?"

"I found a wad of rusty iron."

"Farm machinery," she said. "A piece comes off a plow and is turned under. Years later someone finds it. Convinced that it must be an artifact, they bring it in, not realizing that Indians didn't have metal. It happens all the time."

"That's just it. This piece lacked the uniformity of machined metal. It's not Native American, and I doubt it's industrial either." Jim slid the last of melted marshmallow into his mouth.

Eva picked up their cups and set them in the sink. "That doesn't add up."

"Wish I could get a better look at it."

Eva shrugged. "That's easy."

"What do you mean?"

"I have a key," she said.

———————

Eva slipped the key into the storage-room lock, and the tumblers rolled over with an oiled click. She reached for the light switch, and Jim took hold of her arm.

"Maybe we shouldn't turn on the lights," he said, whispering.

"No windows."

"Oh. Let there be light!"

She closed the door behind them. The artifacts still lay spread out across Earl's workbench.

Jim took the piece of iron from the box and turned it in his hands. "This is it," he said.

Eva examined it. "You're right. It doesn't look like it's been machined. What do you think it is?"

He studied it for several moments. "Do you remember where we crossed the canyon below the Milton site that day?"

"Yes."

"And do you remember that old piece of iron buried in the mud?"

"Yes, I guess."

"Well, I don't know *what* this is, but I think I know *where* it came from."

Eva leaned over his shoulder for a closer look, and he could feel her warmth.

"I can't see that it amounts to much in any case," she said.

"I know it doesn't look like anything, but that's the point. What is it? I need another go at that site," he said.

"Earl's not going to allow that," she said. "With all this rain, you could never get over the low-water access in a car anyway."

He scraped at the rust and could see the semblance of design and pattern beneath.

"There is one way," he said.

Eva's eyes narrowed. "You're not thinking about crossing Kingston's land?"

"It's a straight shot over."

"Didn't you just get out of a scrape with Mitch Keeper and Sheriff Nabson, or am I thinking about someone else?"

"A person could wait until late, slip through the cemetery and be back before daylight. No one would ever know."

"You'd risk your neck for another look at that site?"

"It's not all that risky, and what could it hurt?"

She folded her arms across her chest. "And you're going on this little mission by yourself, I suppose?"

Jim shrugged. "I figure to."

"You don't think I would go, do you?" she asked.

He looked up at her. "The short answer: not in a million years."

"We'll park my car at the bridge," she said, "and walk in from there."

20

———

By three in the morning, darkness had descended over the cemetery. Jim and Eva could just see the outline of the monastery in the darkness as they crept through the crosses.

At the top of the hill, they dropped down to listen. The moon broke for a moment and lit the mausoleum in its ivory glow.

"Where from here?" Jim asked, whispering.

Eva pointed. "That way."

Stealing under the back fence of the cemetery like thieves, they worked their way through the blackness and into the valley.

"I'm going to use the flashlight now," he said.

"Okay, but be careful, Jim."

He panned the area with his light.

"Look," he said. "There's been a lot of disturbance here, like an old sink or something. See how it shifts from the strata above it?"

"Come on," she said. "I'll feel a lot better when we get this done."

He helped her up, and they headed due west. Soon they came upon a fence with "no trespassing" signs posted every few feet.

"This has to be it," he said.

A creek dropped beneath the fence and spread out into a wide meander. He turned off his light, scooted underneath the fence, and then held the wire up for Eva.

"I think the canyon is just over there," he said.

No sooner had he spoken when something moved in the darkness.

Eva grabbed his arm. "Oh, god," she said. "Someone's out there."

Jim clicked on his light, and eyes, red as coals, stared back from the darkness.

"Oh my gosh," Eva said. "It's Old Man Milton's dog."

The old dog loped forward, weaving between their legs and thumping them with its bony tail.

"For a minute I thought I smelled Mitch Keeper," he said.

"Enough with the jokes," Eva said. "I've had about all the fun I can stand for one night."

"Come on," he said. "The canyon can't be far now."

Jim found the piece of iron lodged in the bank, just as he remembered it. Eva held the flashlight while he worked the piece loose with his pocketknife. He held it under the light.

"I'll be damned," he said. "Look at this."

"What is it?"

"Bone. Maybe a femur, but it's in bad shape."

"Indian," she said. "Graves are common around here."

"But the iron is in the same strata?"

"Hard to tell. Maybe the site has shifted."

"Possible," he said. "Lots of water comes down this canyon."

"Are you going to take the iron back?"

"Yes. At the least, it's a hell of a coincidence." He turned the piece in his hand. "I have this feeling, you know. It's almost as if I've been here before."

"That's because you *have*," she said.

They shooed Milton's dog into the darkness and headed back to the cemetery. At the fence, Jim pulled Eva down beside him.

"Wait," he said, under his breath. "I think I saw lights."

"Where?"

"There, by the mausoleum."

Eva took hold of his arm, and he could feel her trembling.

"But who would be at the mausoleum this time of night—besides us, I mean?"

"I think that's Kingston's all-terrain," he said.

"Really? Kingston visits the mausoleum in the middle of the night? That's too bizarre, Jim."

"How are we going to get back?" he asked. "There's no way of knowing how long he'll be there, and it's the only way out."

"Well, there's the river," Eva said. "We could wade it. But the bottom can be unpredictable, especially in high water. The only safe way over is the low-water access, and even that's not certain."

"Come on," he said. "It's a fair hike there."

———

The first light of dawn had broken by the time they reached Milton's ranch. From the road they could see lights in the barn and cows waiting at the corral gate.

"We could go in," Eva said. "I'm sure Dub would take us to town."

"And admit that we are trespassers? I think not."

Milton's dog trotted from the yard with its nose in the air and watched them for some time before turning back to the house.

By the time they reached the river access, daybreak shimmered on the river. They took off their shoes, tied the strings together, and hung them about their necks.

"This is my last break-in, " Eva said, rolling up her jeans.

They hooked their arms together and waded into the river. The smell of moss and mud rose up from the bottom, and their toes curled in the cold water. The current tugged at their legs, and they shivered as it deepened. At about midpoint, Eva suddenly stopped and squeezed his arm.

"Look, Jim," she said.

Water swirled in a muddy vortex about the windows of a car, and weeds gathered on the antenna.

"Come on," Eva said. "We'll get help in town."

"But there might be someone in there."

"You can't go out there, Jim. There are holes and whirlpools— it isn't safe."

"Someone could still be trapped," he said. "I'm going out."

"Jim," she said, clasping his arm. "Be careful."

He lowered himself off the side. The water rose to his waist, and the current tugged at his legs. Pushing off, he swam toward the car, drifting at an angle in the current. As he swept by, he grabbed an open window and pulled himself over.

Gooseflesh tingled up his back when he looked inside, and the hair on his neck prickled. Earl Celf, slumped over the steering wheel, stared back at him. A Styrofoam coffee cup circled about him in the muddy water. Items from the dig kit and a cigar butt slopped against the windshield. Earl's ears and the end of his nose were gone, cropped, most likely by turtles, and his bloated face bobbed with each undulation of the water. His birthmark had darkened to a deep purple against the white death pallor.

Jim leaned in and could see a hole the size of a man's fist blown out of the back of Earl's head. He took a deep breath, turned, and swam back toward the low-water bridge. Eva reached for him and pulled him up onto solid footing.

Trembling with cold, he wiped water from his face.

"What is it, Jim?" she asked.

"It's Earl Celf," he said. "He's dead."

Eva covered her mouth with her hands. "Oh, god." Tears filled her eyes. "Dead?"

"It looks as if someone shot him while he crossed the river."

"What are we going to do?"

Jim looked out at the car. "First thing, we get out of this river," he said. "And then we'll decide. It's too late for Earl in any case."

———

Back at Eva's house, they showered and changed clothes. Neither spoke of what they had seen or what it might mean. They drank cups of hot coffee, and then they talked, their voices low and hushed.

Who could have killed Earl? Why? What was he doing out there in the first place? Why did he have his dig kit with him after having shut down the site?

"We have to turn this in to the authorities," Eva said. "We should have already."

"I know," he said.

A knock came at the door, and they both jumped.

Eva opened it to find Stufflebaum standing there, his hair disheveled. His belt, having escaped its loop, hung down in front like a dog's tongue, and his mustache, usually long and scraggly, had been clipped too short, and now looked like a smear of dirt over his lip.

"We're going to need you early at the museum, Eva," he said.

"Oh?"

"They found Earl Celf's car out in the river with him in it. He's been shot. He's dead as a carp."

Eva glanced back at Jim. "Do they know who did it?" she asked.

"I don't know, but Sheriff Nabson brought in Old Man Milton, handcuffed and swearing revenge."

21

The reality of Earl's death came home when they dragged his car down Freddie Street and stacked it among the other heaps at Reese Metal Salvage. Earl had been subjected to the indignities of an autopsy at the hands of the state pathologist, who proclaimed him dead as a result of a gunshot wound to the back of the head. "No shit," Stufflebaum said.

Milton was being investigated for murder, and Eva was assigned interim director of the museum. She agreed for Jim to stay on at the shop until he could make other arrangements.

He hadn't the courage to call home and tell them that he'd failed yet one more time. Without the field experience, his chances of employment hadn't changed, so he hung on in hopes that he could somehow reclaim the summer.

Several days passed before Earl's property came up for auction. Jim went to see it sell. In three hours of bidding and yelping and bad jokes, buyers reduced Earl's collection to two-dozen black trash bags that were destined for the dump.

Afterward, Jim walked back to the museum. As he passed the genealogy library, he overheard Pete and Auntie arguing, Auntie allowing that illegitimate children should be counted as part of one's family tree, even if the records failed to reflect it.

Jim went on to find Eva in the office, absorbed in her work.

"How did the auction go?" she asked, looking up.

"Like a food fight," he said. "A man's life can be settled up pretty fast.

"Listen, could I talk to you for a minute?"

She laid down her pen. "What is it?"

"It doesn't look like things are going to work out for me here. I think it's time for me to move on. I just wanted you to know that even though we didn't hit it off exactly . . . I mean, I just wanted to say thanks for letting me stay on for a while."

"And what will you do?"

"Go home and get Sara. I can take a job of some sort to get by. The archeology thing can wait."

Eva came around and sat on the edge of her desk. "There's something I've been wanting to say to you, actually. You remember that day in the river when you swam out to Earl's car?"

"I'll never forget it."

Eva clicked her pen against her teeth. "Not everyone would have done that."

Jim's face warmed. "It scared me spitless."

"But you did it anyway."

Through the window, he could see Pete and Auntie entering notes in their journal. The question of illegitimacy had apparently been tabled.

Eva opened a folder from the desk.

"There's something else," she said. "I met with the council this morning to go over the situation here at the museum. The thing is, they've made me permanent director."

"That's great, Eva. You'll make a good director. It's in your blood."

"I pointed out to them that with Earl gone, we were now short-handed and that, in spite of Earl's claims to the contrary, we had a surplus in our budget."

"Earl liked a margin," he said.

"And that since we had an expert in our midst—that would be you—we should take advantage of your expertise to straighten out the collection. That would be Earl's storage room."

"What are you saying?"

"They've agreed to hire you. It's temporary, but in the meantime, maybe we can get the dig back on track. Would you be interested?"

"Are you kidding?"

"The pay is minimal, but then I don't see why you couldn't stay on in the shop if you wish."

"When do I start?"

"You're already on the payroll. One other item of business came up at the council that I forgot to tell you about. They changed the name of Sixth Street to Earl Street."

"Earl would have hated that."

"I know. Here's the key to the storage room. Good luck. I think you're going to need it."

———

As Jim passed the soddy display on his way down to storage, he suddenly stopped. There sat the late Precious on the porch railing, her cobalt eyes locked on whoever passed. For a moment, he thought he saw her move.

"Nice, ain't she?" Stufflebaum said from behind.

"No offense, but it gives me the creeps. It's a soddy exhibit, Stufflebaum."

"Wouldn't it be special to have ol' Earl sitting right up there on that porch with her, what with his feet propped up on the railing, reading the paper and chewing on his cigar. Keeps me awake nights just thinking on it."

"Me, too. But Earl's safely in his grave." Turning, he looked at Stufflebaum. "Isn't he?"

"After that autopsy, all the king's horses and all the king's . . ." He shook his strawberry hair and added, "Hear you been hired on."

"Word travels fast around here."

"You'll be cleaning up the place like before?"

"Mining the storage room, organizing, cataloging. I've been hired as a real-live expert, my friend."

"I'd as soon organize a volcano, while it's still exploding," he said. "There is one thing."

"You can't stuff Earl and that's final."

"I can accept that, shortsighted though it may be."

"So what is it?"

"Earl built on that storage room near twenty years back. He started packing in junk on that far south wall and never let up. An organizing man like yourself should start at that back wall and work north. That room's already laid out in a fashion, you might say, given Earl never changed direction nor habit in all them years."

———————

Stufflebaum's chronology theory turned out to be the only logical thing in all of Earl's storage room. Like an archeological dig, the further back into the piles he went, the older the items. Other than that, Earl had failed to catalog or organize or file anything in any systematic fashion whatsoever.

For the remainder of the afternoon, Jim worked at orienting himself, making decisions about where to start and how to record what he found. When he looked up, it was nearly closing time.

He helped Eva finish out the day's receipts, then double-checked the doors while she turned out the lights. As they exited the building, they saw a man walking up the drive.

"Sorry. We're closed," Jim said.

Eva recognized Dub Milton and said "Dub, I'm so sorry about your father."

Dub shoved his hands in his back pockets. "He didn't do it, Eva. He had no reason to shoot Earl. They bickered on and off over the years, but it didn't mean nothing. They played a game, you know. Everybody knew that."

"I'm sorry, Dub. I'm sure things are going to work out."

"Sheriff Nabson said Dad shot Earl with his deer rifle, but there weren't no casings or shells found. Anybody could have shot him. But they ain't looking, figuring they got their man and that's that."

"Your father said things, Dub."

"I know, but he couldn't hit nothing with that rifle, Eva. A horse kicked him in the head when he was a kid, and it threw off his sight. He can't pour a cup of coffee without spilling it in your lap."

"Could we do something for you, Dub?" Jim asked.

Taking out his billfold, Dub counted off some bills and handed them to Eva.

"This here's the money we took from Earl for that dig site. I figure it's only right you get it back."

Eva glanced over at Jim. "Look, Dub, Earl cancelled that dig for whatever reason. But it's still an important site for us, and you'll be needing the money more than ever now. Why don't we just proceed as planned?"

Dub shook his head. "I'd like that fine, Eva, but thing is, it ain't mine to give no more."

"What do you mean?" Jim asked.

"Getting lawyered-up took everything we got. In the end we had to sell the place."

"Oh, Dub, you sold your farm?" Eva asked.

"Even now I don't know if we got enough to get through the trial. Luke's working down at the elevator, and I'm pumping gas just to pay the rent." He looked away. "Had to shoot my dog. He wouldn't understand being tied up in town."

"I'm so sorry, Dub."

"Who bought your land?" Jim asked.

"Evan Kingston offered the cash and with no questions asked," he said.

Jim and Eva watched Dub walk away, his shoulders slumped.

"That farm was all they had," Eva said. "And now it's gone."

"Not gone," Jim said.

Earl was dead, Milton arrested, and now Kingston owned Milton's land. But the land went on. Time has changed everything but nothing. Jim's quest remained the same. Like Coronado before him so many centuries ago, he looked forward to whatever treasures awaited.

22

Their bellies full of buffalo, the conquistadors teased and taunted each other, and laughter returned to the camp.

Coronado worked at his letters, keeping to his tent. The chances of posting were slim, but prudence dictated their writing. More than once fate had intervened, and posting had become available. He found it best to be prepared.

With food and rest, Coronado's health had improved, and his thoughts turned once again to the treasure that awaited.

The conquistadors now found much time to quarrel. Some turned to gaming in the night, which Coronado had forbidden, and so were chained near the dogs to remind them of their transgressions.

Angered by a passing remark, Saldivar set fire to Cherino's bed as he slept in it. Prayer and a lashing of some severity, administered under Friar Padilla's guidance, purged both Saldivar's conscience and his soul.

Isopete, whose language had much improved, protested the Turk's favor at every opportunity, charging him with theft and treachery, and complaining of the Turk's superior mount.

Each sunrise, Isopete faced northward to shake his finger in scorn and to shout out in the Turk's manner, "Quivira, Quivira, a few leagues more." If admonished, Isopete would curse, as if madcapped, and call for misfortune to fall upon the Turk.

Coronado, tiring of Isopete's rant, ordered him to take the count, causing Isopete to fall silent at last. Coronado proceeded then into the plains, while Isopete, having ceased his mewling, tallied each day the leagues and entered them into the journal.

The meat, having dwindled with the passing days, now sustained only thin soups. At evening the men talked longingly of the great kill at the ravine and of how their bellies ached once again with emptiness.

With summer's heat upon them, the water grew scarce—only an occasional wallow, the vile stink of which drifted in on the winds. The puddles, alive with larvae, caused even the horses to rattle their bridles in discomfort.

One day as the column took up its rest, Isopete's horse, having weakened from lack of pasturage, dropped to its knees in exhaustion, whereby the men fell upon it, dispatching it with a broadax so that they might eat of its flesh, but the meat—being unsavory and much depleted—was then discarded by them.

His mount gone, Isopete joined Friar Padilla in his trek afoot through the plains. The soldiers, much taken by these circumstances, laughed at the strange pair trudging through the dust. Even Coronado, who often lacked such humor, spoke of the holy and unholy walking hand in hand in search of glory.

On this day, Coronado called in his captains for council.

Alvarado, as was his way, folded his arms over his chest, "East or north, my general?"

"East," Coronado said.

"We follow the Turk, though the men are much fatigued and the way never ends?"

"As I have commanded," Coronado said.

"Isopete has said that the Turk deceives Coronado, that he leads him astray to suffer misfortune in the wilderness."

"Who is one to believe—the Turk, who found the buffalo as he promised, or Isopete, whose scorn is known by all?"

"The Turk is clever but with great duplicity," Alvarado said.

"Our numbers are few, and our food is scarce. We must follow the Turk or be lost," Coronado said.

"Perhaps the Turk leads only with words and empty promises," Alvarado said.

Coronado looked over at Friar Padilla, who had cast his head down in thought.

"And what does the friar say? Do we now follow empty words or a madman to our deaths?"

Friar Padilla pulled at his beard and thumbed the cross that hung from his waist.

"As a soldier of many years, I sinned much, from which I must now atone. I put my faith in God, for it is He who decides Coronado's fate. I will follow."

Coronado looked out into the prairie and then back at Alvarado.

"Isopete is small and grudging and lacks valor. Such a man is weak of character and cannot be charged with the lives of my men. We follow the Turk. But this I swear: the Turk shall be tested at every turn, and justice exacted without mercy, though the deception be slight."

23

As explorers, Jim and Eva were at an impasse. Circumstances had thrown them off course, and they had to somehow find their way back. In the end, like all explorers, they could only rely on themselves for solutions. They sat down on the steps of the museum after Dub had gone.

"This whole thing has turned crazy," Eva said.

"With Kingston owning the property, we may never get another chance at that site," Jim said. "Kingston doesn't strike me as the sharing kind. He certainly doesn't need the money."

"Do you think that Milton shot Earl? I find it unlikely myself."

"Old man Milton didn't have a motive as far as I can tell."

"He and Earl had never been friends," she said.

"Friends enough to strike a deal on that site."

"People do what they have to for money sometimes."

Jim stretched his legs out in front of him and hooked his elbows on the step.

"And what about Earl's wound?" he asked.

Eva shuddered. "What do you mean? Didn't you find the autopsy clear on that?"

"Think about it," he said. "Earl had driven into the river going toward the Milton farm at the time. Whoever shot him, shot him from behind. Why would Milton cross the river to shoot Earl from behind?"

"Maybe he wanted people to think someone else did it?"

"And according to Dub, the old man's depth perception wasn't what it should be. That shot had to be taken halfway across the river."

"And why did Earl cancel the dig in the first place?" she said. "Everything had been decided. Why did he lie about not having enough funds, and why did Kingston buy the Milton place? He already owns half the county."

Jim stood and helped Eva to her feet. "I'm thinking we should send those artifacts from the canyon in for analysis.

"Of course, iron can't be carbon dated, so it's difficult to identify the age. But sometimes inferences can be drawn through association, even though the evidence is only relative."

"I can't help but wonder what's going to happen to the Miltons. Their lives have been turned upside down."

"My bet is that, as far as the law is concerned, they have their man."

"And Kingston has the Milton place."

"And we're up a creek without a site," he said.

———

The next morning Jim left Eva in the museum office, took a deep breath, and went downstairs to mine the storage room. Walking by the soddy display, he was dismayed to see the omnipresent Precious under the porch. He confronted Stufflebaum and ordered the stuffed cat removed before the museum opened.

"Archeologists sure don't have much of a sense of humor," he said.

———

In the storage room, Jim scrubbed the two pieces of iron with carbonate of soda and water. After that, he dried them, numbered them, and wrapped them in paper. The bone he packed in a different container, exercising care to cushion it against damage while in transit.

Then he wrote out a lab report explaining how the artifacts had been recovered, the strata, the positions of the pieces relative to each other and to the site in general. In addition, he requested the age and identity of everything, as well as any other information that might be pertinent to their interpretation.

When done, he secured the whole sample in a mailing container, addressed it to the chief archeologist at the Historic Preservation Office, and gave it to Stufflebaum to mail.

After lunch, he returned to face the task of putting the storage room in some kind of order. Prudence dictated that he first organize items by subject matter.

Still grumbling, Stufflebaum rounded up a dozen cardboard boxes, on which Jim wrote general subject categories with a black Magic Marker. He planned to subdivide each one into more and more specificity until it could no longer be logically divided.

Of course, analyses had to be made and a numbering system established. Only then could the artifacts be understood and displayed in an intelligent manner. The sites had not been recorded, strata had not been identified, and no discernible relationships could be established. In fact, archeology would have been better off if Earl Celf had recovered nothing at all.

To top it off, many of the artifacts had yet to be cleaned and properly preserved. Already, a number of the lithics had peeled and sloughed away, while several of the wood objects had disintegrated altogether.

"Earl," he said, tossing a rusty mule shoe into the first box, "wherever you are, I hope your ears are hot."

By mid afternoon, he'd allocated relics to every subject content. It occurred to him while going through the box of iron artifacts that the location of Dub's iron piece had never been fully verified.

Both his and Dub's material looked to be identical, and he'd assumed they derived from the same site, but such assumptions should never be made by a good archeologist.

Establishing the age of his find through association with the bone would be shaky science, especially if the two pieces of iron had come from different locations. He needed to talk to Dub Milton.

Before locking up the storage room, he located the schemata he'd drawn of the Wichita site. It might help Dub remember the location of his finds. As he headed up the stairs to tell Eva of his plans, he met Pete and Auntie just coming out of the genealogy library.

"Why, hello, Mr. Hunt," Pete said.

"Hi, Pete. Auntie."

Auntie smiled and shuffled her feet.

"Still researching, I see."

"Turns out Auntie's illegitimate just like I always suspected. She's a stray, I guess you could say," Pete announced.

"It doesn't count," Auntie said.

Jim edged up the stairs. "Got to run. Nice seeing the both of you."

Pete said, "Been researching Henry's tree. You remember Henry, the cook down at The Westerner?"

"Oh, sure. Henry."

"Henry traded out two weeks of ham and eggs if Auntie and me would track down his line. Turns out Henry comes from a long line of horse thieves, don't he, Auntie?"

Smiling, Auntie said, "As far back as the beginning of time."

"Except for that one double great-great-aunt they hanged for witchery."

"Comes down through the blood," Auntie said.

"Now Henry refuses to own up to the deal," Pete said. "Claims all this genealogy is just shit. Says Jesus sent a thief to heaven faster than Churchill ever got there anyway, and we can just pay for our ham and eggs like everybody else."

Jim edged up another step. "You two are getting pretty good at the research."

"Oh, yes sir," Pete said. "We can take her back a good long ways. You want us to search you out?"

Jim hesitated. "Ah, no. I don't think so. Some things a man's better off not knowing."

"Yes, sir. That's a fact. Well, anytime."

Jim had reached the top of the stairs, when Pete called up to him.

"Say, Mr. Hunt, did you see a cat under the soddy porch this morning?"

"No, no I didn't."

"Big as a cougar and covering up its hole. Liked to have scared Auntie out of her underwear, didn't it, Auntie?"

"I never seen a cat so occupied," Auntie said. "It didn't move a muscle the whole of the time."

"I'll see you later," Jim said, ducking through the door.

He dropped by to tell Eva his plans before heading for the fire department. Maybe Sheriff Nabson could tell him how to contact Dub.

He found Nabson asleep in his office. The place reeked of cigarettes and burned coffee. Nabson had his feet propped up on his desk and his hat pulled down over his eyes. A wad of gum had stuck to the bottom of his boot.

Jim stepped in close. "So," he said.

Nabson's arms flew up, and his chair nearly flipped over backwards.

"Goddang it, Hunt," he said. "What the hell you sneaking up on a man for?"

"Sorry, Sheriff, I didn't realize you were asleep."

"Who's sleeping?"

"I'm needing some information about the Milton site and hoped to talk to the old man personally."

Jim started to sit.

"This is a place of business," the sheriff said.

"Sorry." Jim slid the chair back. "I thought you might tell me how I could reach him."

"Will it get you out of here?"

"It's a promise, Sheriff."

"They rented the old Jensen house down on the creek. It's a flood area. Ain't no one but a fool would live there."

"Thanks for the cooperation," Jim said.

The Jensen house didn't sit near the creek but in it, and debris still hung in the yard fence. By the looks of it, the old building had suffered through more than its share of floodwater.

Dressed in overalls, and with no shirt on, Old Man Milton answered the door. He stared at Jim through the screen.

"I don't have more to say to the law," he said.

"Wait, Mr. Milton. I'm Jim Hunt. I came out with Eva Manor to your house one day to lay out the Wichita site."

"The city boy?"

"Could I talk with you?"

Squinting, Milton examined him through the screen. "What is it you want?"

"I'm needing information about the artifacts Dub brought to the museum."

"Dub won't be home for another hour."

"Perhaps you could help?"

"I been charged with killing a man. You sure you want to come in?"

"I'm sure."

Jim followed him into the kitchen, which smelled of mildew and mud, and the wallpaper sagged from the ceiling.

"Sit," he said. "Coffee?"

"Yes, please."

Milton adjusted his overalls strap over his shoulder and set the pot on the stove. He looked old and frail, and his skin folded over his elbows.

"They say I shot Earl Celf," he said, lighting the stove. "Can't say I never considered it, but I didn't shoot him."

"Do you know anyone who would want to kill Earl?"

"Anyone who ever met him," he said.

"I know what you mean," Jim said.

"Had to sell my place to get out of jail. At my age it don't matter much, but it's hard on my boys."

"I'm sure it's going to work out, Mr. Milton."

"Toughest part, selling out to Kingston."

"Did he take advantage of your situation?"

"He wrote the check out for asking price and stuck it in Dub's shirt pocket."

"What happens now, Mr. Milton?"

"The lawyer figures it will take everything we got to fight the murder rap.

"The problem is that my boys don't know nothing but farming, and now that's gone. Working for another man eats up your spirit after a while. Pretty soon there ain't nothing left but regret."

"There's always hope, Mr. Milton."

He poured Jim's coffee, missing the rim of the cup and spilling some on the table.

"Sorry," he said. "Now, what is it you're needing to know?"

"Has there ever been another site on your place? Have you ever found artifacts anywhere else?"

"Can't say that I have. That old Indian camp has been there long as I can remember. As a kid, I used to pick up points there."

"Did you ever find iron?"

"Buried tools. Never know a farmer who didn't plow one under from time to time."

"Is there any other way to cross over the river besides the low-water bridge?"

"If another crossing existed, I'd have used it, wouldn't I? But that ended when the river changed."

Jim took a sip of coffee. "When the river changed?"

"Any fool can see that channel used to be deep and narrow. There's sinks and canyons where there ought not be and then she spreads out all shallow and wide—then there's places where that river runs fast and narrow again."

"I don't understand."

"It's a mystery all right. They tried putting in a bridge but couldn't find bedrock, so the WPA put in that low-water pass instead—cheap and fast, you know, and not worth the doing. Make-work that kept folks out of the breadline and Roosevelt in office, I guess."

"But earthquakes are virtually unknown in this area, aren't they?"

"I never knew of one, and I been here a good long while," he said.

The front door opened, and Dub, his hands black with grease, came into the kitchen. He smelled of gasoline.

"Mr. Hunt," he said. "What are you doing here?"

"This boy wants to know everything about everything," the old man said.

"Sorry to bother you, Dub, but I'm trying to organize artifacts at the museum. I realized that the location of that piece of iron you brought in had not been established. Could you tell me where you found it?"

Dub took out his handkerchief and rubbed the grime from his hands. "I can't remember exactly, Mr. Hunt."

"I've brought the schemata I drew of the site. If you could just point out the approximate location, it would help us get things in order. I'm sure Eva would appreciate the help."

Dub glanced over at the old man and then poured himself a cup of coffee.

"I guess I could take a shot at it."

Jim unrolled the schemata and set the cups on the edges to hold it in place. Dub sipped at his coffee and studied the map.

"I found most of that stuff right there on the north edge," he said.

"Of the site?"

"Right there," he said, pointing.

"And the iron, too?"

"Not so much the iron," he said, glancing over at the old man.

"Tell him where you found it, boy," Milton said.

Dub looked at the map and pointed again. "There."

"In the canyon?"

"No. There."

Jim studied the map, looking over at the old man and then back at Dub.

"But that's on the Kingston place."

"Yes," Dub said. "I know."

24

Eva listened to Jim from the other side of the counter.
"Dub found his piece of iron on Kingston," he said.
"We found the other in the Milton canyon."

"But you can still establish a carbon date from the bone, can't you?" she asked, turning up her hands.

"And sometimes other things as well, but now it's not going to tell us much about the iron. The site's been disturbed, so we can't be certain when the iron artifact was laid down. The original location could be on Kingston, or it could be on Milton. It could have been dropped from an airplane for all we know. In other words, it cuts the assumptions made with the relative dating process to zip."

"Maybe they will be able to identify it at the lab as a specific type of object."

"You've seen it. It's a piece of wadded-up rust."

"What do we do now?"

"What we do best," he said. "We wait."

―――――――

The light in the storage room shined yellow, and the air smelled of old papers and dust. Jim left the door open to let in fresh air.

Busy, he failed to notice that someone had entered the room. When he looked up, Sheriff Nabson stood at the door with a box in his arms.

Jim dusted off his hands. "It isn't visiting hours, Sheriff. This is a place of business."

Nabson set the box down. "Don't get smart, Hunt."

"Is there something in particular you want, Sheriff?"

"I've got Earl Celf's belongings from the medical examiner's office."

"What's in it?"

"Might be Earl hisself for all I know."

"Shouldn't it be given to his kin?"

"He didn't have no kin. This is Earl's museum, and this where I'm leaving it. See it's disposed of. Give it to charity or something."

"Fine," Jim said, turning back to his work. "Leave it. I'll get to it later."

He found Eva arranging the water fowl specimens Stufflebaum had finished up that week. She'd tied her hair up in a bandanna, exposing a smudge of dirt that had smeared across her forehead. After getting Cokes out of the vending machine, he told her about Nabson's visit.

"Far as I know Earl didn't have any living relatives," she said.

He set the Coke can between his legs. "I've been wondering about something Old Man Milton told me."

"What?"

"Have you ever heard that the river out there has changed its course over time?"

"That's what the old-timers say," she said. "It's wider both north and south from town. You can really see the difference at Pawnee Rock, an old landmark west of here. But then most rivers do change, don't they? Why do you ask?"

Jim shrugged. "Just curious. Perhaps it accounts for Milton's land being so inaccessible."

"I suppose there are tributaries and such that could have changed."

"I've read about that rock and would like to see it—maybe tomorrow."

Eva took off her bandanna and threaded out her hair with her fingers.

"We could drive over to it tomorrow. It's not that far."

"But tomorrow is your day off."

"As if you didn't know," she said.

———

Eva picked him up at the shop. She put her coffee on the dash and slid her arm through the wheel, watching him as he got in the car.

"You look nice," she said, glancing at his Pendleton tee shirt and denim shorts.

"Yeah?"

She smiled, and the slightest dimples materialized, vanishing as quickly as they had come.

"So do you," he said.

Within an hour, they were driving parallel to the river. The land stretched out like a tabletop before them, and had it not been for the trees growing from the bank, the river would have disappeared in the expanse like brush strokes in a painting.

Soon Eva pointed to where the river made a wide sweep. "There," she said. "Pawnee Rock."

It bore up from the prairie floor with singularity, like a beacon on a distant shore. Eva turned in, following the winding road to its base. Layers of rock jutted up from the soil like black stone tablets.

They parked in the shade of an old elm and walked around the rock in silence. Messages and names—some merely initials— had been etched on every available space, many dating back to trail days. There were love notes, inscriptions of devotion, and advice to passing travelers. Some told of the loneliness of the trail or of sickness and despair.

At the highest point, a cross had been carved into the surface of the rock. The initials scratched beneath had been obliterated by the years. Jim traced the cross with his fingers. He'd read that Friar Juan Padilla had a penchant for carving crosses. But that had been centuries ago. Anyone could have done it.

They ate the sandwiches Eva had brought and fed the crumbs to the crows which flew down from the rocks. Jim held his hand over his eyes against the sun and scanned the valley.

"I've forgotten why they call it Pawnee Rock," he said.

"Kit Carson camped here when just a kid. While on guard duty one night, he thought he heard a Pawnee Indian. He shot into the darkness and killed his own mule—thus Pawnee Rock."

"You make that up?" he asked.

"That's the story."

"See how the river takes a bend north toward Kingston and then back south again?" Jim said.

Eva nodded, holding her hand over her eyes. "It eventually empties into the Mississippi," she said. "This was the most dangerous spot on the Santa Fe Trail, they say. The Indians could see the wagon trains coming from miles away, so they would lay in wait."

"And those messages scratched into the rocks, like they are talking to us from out of the past," he said. "Come on. Let's hike over to the river."

———————

They crawled under the fence and struck out across the pasture. At the river, they dropped down on the bank to catch their breaths. Pawnee Rock loomed into the sky behind them. They dug their toes into the cool sand, and Jim pitched a stick into the water, watching as it drifted toward a rock overhang on the opposite side.

"There's a crosscurrent here. Let's swim over and see where it's coming from. Last one in is a Stufflebaum mummy," he said, taking off his shirt.

"I don't think so, Jim. The river's pretty fast."

"You wait then. I'll be right back," he said, wading into the water.

The bottom fell away quickly, and the water cooled as he swam toward the overhang. The current tugged at him, and he struggled to keep from drifting off course. He waved back at Eva when he got there. She had waded into the river up to her knees.

He ducked under the overhang, holding his hands above his head to keep from bumping it on the rock. The water swirled in eddies and lapped at his chin, and moss clung to the ledge in blankets of green.

Taking a deep breath, he dove beneath the water.

When he broke the surface, Eva waved her hands and called out to him. He swam toward her, the current sweeping him in a diagonal trajectory to shore.

Eva waited for him. "Are you okay?"

"For a minute I thought I might be headed for the Mississippi," he said.

"Don't do that anymore. It scares me."

"There's water coming up from under that ledge and feeding into the river."

"What do you mean?"

"There's a fissure down there," he said, wiping at his face.

"Where does it come from?" she asked.

"I don't know. From upstream somewhere, I suppose. If only I could track it back to its source."

They waded to shore. Eva held on to his arm while she rolled down the cuffs of her pants.

"That's Kingston land now," she said. "What chance of getting permission from *him*?"

Jim looked up the river where it led into Kingston's property.

"I don't know," he said. "I've never asked him, but that's exactly what I intend to do."

25

Jim drove past the monastery and saw the monks hoeing the rows of melon plants that had sprouted in the lush soil. They lifted each of the tentacles to loosen the crust beneath. Columns of wooden crosses stretched across the cemetery behind them.

The mausoleum's marble walls shimmered in the sun, and the smell of roses wafted through Jim's open window. One of the residents leaned on his hoe handle and watched Jim pass before turning back to his work.

Eva had not come along because of her responsibilities at the museum. Jim figured her coming would only complicate matters in any event. Visiting Kingston without an invitation was like dropping in on the queen for a cup of tea. But he needed access to that site, and Kingston held the key.

He rehearsed his pitch as he turned into the drive: "Think of the contribution you could make, Mr. Kingston, in furthering the understanding of our history. Consider your position in the community, Mr. Kingston. All of us will be indebted to you. I understand that the site is on private land, but we share a common heritage. All of us must contribute where we can."

In the end, Jim couldn't think of a single reason why Kingston would give a damn about any of it.

As he made the last curve, he could see that Kingston's gate had been chained and padlocked. He drove back down the drive, and as he came upon the monastery again, the same monk looked up from his work. Jim pulled in.

The monk, dressed in a brown robe, cinched a white rope up about his waist. He had a full beard, and his nose had peeled from sunburn. Dust gathered on his shoes, and his fingers stuck through the holes in his gloves.

He slipped off a glove and held out his hand. "I'm Brother Bill. May I help you?" His handshake shot a pain up Jim's arm.

"Jim Hunt. I'm looking for Mr. Kingston. I thought perhaps you might know where he is."

Brother Bill said, "He came to the mausoleum about sundown yesterday, which is not unusual for Mr. Kingston. His visits to the mausoleum are frequent."

"Have you seen him today by chance?"

"His car went by early this morning."

"It's rather important that I find him. Do you happen to know where he might have been going?"

Brother Bill dabbed at his forehead with his sleeve. "Mr. Kingston often takes a short business trip about this time each year. Perhaps that's where he has gone."

"Oh? Do you know how I could reach him?"

Brother Bill slipped his glove on and hoed around a plant before answering. "As you can see, we are neighbors. Mr. Kingston permits us our privacy and we his."

"Of course."

"He's rarely gone more than a week, if that is of help to you, Mr. Hunt," he said, looking up.

"Yes. Thank you. Nice meeting you. By the way, your garden is beautiful."

Brother Bill smiled. "It's nearly lunch time, Mr. Hunt. Would you care to join us?"

Jim hesitated. "Lunch?"

"It's simple fare, but delicious, though I do miss my rare steaks. We'd be pleased to have you as our guest."

"Well, I don't know. I'm not Catholic."

"But you do eat?"

"Regularly."

"Conversion is not a prerequisite for lunch, Mr. Hunt."

"Well. Sure. I'd be pleased."

The monastery chapel, with its wooden floor, harkened to a more austere time, but the altar, a structure made of Carrara marble, had an elaborate ancient crucifix above it. In contrast, the dining hall had been painted white, a bare room absent of even the most humble accoutrements. A wooden table encircled by straight-backed chairs stretched the length of the room.

Brother Bill delivered the prayer, which fell just short of a full-fledged sermon. Afterward, they ate in silence. The fare was indeed delicious, though the modest servings left Jim longing for more. The home-baked bread had too quickly been whisked back to the kitchen, and Jim had watched it go with disappointment.

After lunch, Brother Bill escorted him about the grounds to show him the bee colony and the bakery. They sat on a stone bench near the grotto and talked.

"It's peaceful here," Jim said.

"Someday you might like to take advantage of our retreat."

"Retreat?"

"We keep a few rooms available on the weekends for those wishing to get away from the world for a bit. The absence of conscious striving can be the most direct route to the spirit. Don't you find that to be true, Mr. Hunt?"

"I'm sure you're a better judge of such things, Brother Bill."

"The rooms are available, and you would be welcome. Donations are appreciated but not required."

"Thank you for the offer. I'll keep it in mind," Jim said.

Brother Bill then embarked on a narration about the Franciscan order. When the sun broke through the trees, he looked up into the sky.

"Oh, dear, I've gone on too long. I'm the historian for the order and sometimes forget that not everyone is so interested."

"How far back does the order go?" Jim asked.

"We are descendants of Saint Francis of Assisi, which dates us to the thirteenth century. What most people don't realize is that we Franciscans came into *this* part of the country very early as well. Friar Juan Padilla pioneered a mission in the area back in the 1540's. He was one of the first Christian martyrs in the U.S."

"So I've read."

"In fact, a memorial to him has been erected not far from here, though one can't be certain of exactly where he was killed."

"Time has a way of masking things, as any archeologist will tell you," said Jim.

"The monastic life is very old and has its rewards. But it's not for everyone, as you might imagine. Is it something you have ever contemplated?"

"Me?"

"You strike me as a reflective man, Mr. Hunt."

"It's piety I lack, Brother Bill, and discipline."

"The requirements are rigorous as you might suspect—six months as a postulant, two years as a novice, and after that a lifetime of not looking back.

"Then there's these confining robes," he said, pulling at his sleeve, "and a good deal of time on one's knees. In addition we all have our jobs. There's bread to be made and then the summer garden. But in the end, that's what makes it all of value."

"I think I'll stick with archeology."

"Do not forget to step back from it from time to time, my friend. The past can swallow a man."

From there, Jim had a clear view of the mausoleum and its carved marble columns.

"And has the monastery been here for a long time as well?"

Brother Bill walked over to the grotto, his back to Jim.

"Yes, though not always as you see it now. The exact date of its founding is uncertain, but we believe that this has been holy ground for hundreds of years."

"And how is it that Kingston's mausoleum came to be in such a holy place?"

Brother Bill turned. "The mausoleum doesn't sit on holy ground. It's on monastery property but is not part of the cemetery, though many assume otherwise. The site is quite rocky and unsuitable for graves. The Indians, or perhaps travelers along the trail, hauled in hundreds of stones and stacked them there."

"Stones?"

"Presumably a marker so that others might find their way, or perhaps a primitive shrine. Whatever the structure, it has long-since deteriorated. Digging graves there turned out to be quite impossible, so the monastery never sanctified the ground in that particular part."

Jim walked to the edge of the trees where he could get a better view. Brother Bill joined him at his side, towering over him.

"The stones didn't deter Kingston, I gather?" Jim said.

"The stones made a suitable foundation for a mausoleum, I should think," he said.

"And with all his land, he wanted it there?"

"Yes, atop the hill. Evan Kingston's persistence is as persuasive as his generosity. He built the mausoleum of marble, and then donated some of the marble for our rectory, Carrara, and of the highest quality. I believe it had been salvaged from a church in Italy, actually."

Jim smiled. "He has no shortage of charm, does he?"

"Mr. Kingston does manage to get his way."

"I understand his wife is buried there."

Brother Bill threaded his hands into his sleeves and nodded. "Hardly a night passes that he doesn't visit her tomb. Such a lonely man. He comes and goes at odd hours. We all could learn from such dedication."

"Did you know her?"

"Mr. Kingman placed her there without public ceremony. As far as I know, no one has ever been in the mausoleum except Mr. Kingston." He paused. "Perhaps his caretaker."

"Mitch Keeper?"

"All and all, an unhappy man."

"Well," Jim said. "I must be going. Thank you for the lunch and for taking time to show me around."

"Do stop in for a melon, Mr. Hunt. They are the sweetest in the hottest of summer."

———

Jim spent the next few days buried in the museum storage.

By the end of the week, he'd received his first paycheck and managed to clear a spot for a table in Earl's collection.

He considered it a breakthrough, and with money in his pocket, he thought about asking Eva out to dinner. But the council had scheduled a meeting she had to attend, and he'd been caught up in unraveling Earl's record-keeping. On top of that, Eva and Stufflebaum had embarked on building a new series of displays. And truth be known, he couldn't be certain about her answer or even his own feelings in the matter.

In the end, he didn't ask, and when Friday came, he found himself standing at Evan Kingston's open door. Kingston still had his hat on, and luggage sat on the foyer floor.

"Jim Hunt, Mr. Kingston. I wonder if I might speak with you?"

"How is it you are still in town, Mr. Hunt?"

"I've been retained to catalog the artifacts in the museum storage. It's temporary, of course."

Kingston looked at his watch. "I see. Perhaps this could wait. I've just returned from a trip."

"It won't take long."

"If you'll make it brief, Mr. Hunt. I have pressing matters."

Jim followed him into the study. A letter lay open on the table by the door. Jim glanced at the letterhead. Printed in bold typeface, it read: Richmond Institute of Antiquities.

Kingston removed his hat and took a cigar from the box on the mantel.

"Now, what is it that you find so urgent, Mr. Hunt?"

"It's my understanding that you have purchased the Milton property?"

Kingston walked to the window and looked out on the compound.

"Yes. The Miltons needed the money, and I paid them a good price for marginal land."

"As you know, Earl Celf had arranged for the museum to open an archeological dig on Milton's place this summer."

"If you are seeking a refund, I suggest you contact the Miltons. They struck the agreement."

"The thing is, we would like to proceed with the dig as planned."

Kingston turned and lifted his chin. "I'm afraid that's impossible."

"If it's a matter of money, we have located funds in the museum budget."

Kingston smiled. "The museum's budget is of little interest to me."

"This is an important site, Mr. Kingston, and should not be abandoned. The canyons are easily flooded, and critical information might be lost."

"Don't presume me ignorant, Mr. Hunt. A few more flint points and potsherds could hardly be called critical information."

"We would conduct the dig in a professional manner. There would be little disturbance."

"Indeed. Someone should have told Earl Celf that."

Jim took a deep breath. "We can't be held responsible for Earl Celf's death."

Kingston examined the end of his cigar. "I'm sorry, but the answer must be no. Perhaps a contribution to the museum will allow you to look elsewhere for your points. I'll send a check. Now if you'll excuse me, I have much to do."

Jim paused at the door, "You once told me that you explored this area for oil deposits."

"That's correct."

"Did you use seismology as part of that exploration?"

"Seismographic tests are standard procedure. Why do you ask?"

"Archeological sites are often disturbed in geologically unstable areas. Did you find anything to suggest such instability in the formations here?"

Kingston looked at him through a cloud of smoke.

"The formations in this area are not only solid but quite impermeable—and absent of oil, Mr. Hunt. Good day to you."

———

Jim spent Monday morning in storage but without much progress. He couldn't get Kingston out of his mind. So much of what he said didn't make sense. The artifacts from the canyon had been scattered and disturbed. And what about the sinks, the shifting of the strata? Maybe he didn't understand, but none of it fit with Kingston's conclusion of a solid, impermeable formation.

He finished sorting one of the boxes and slid it next to the worktable. At this rate he would soon have a path dredged from the storeroom door to the bathroom.

But things slowed with the process of identifying and dating artifacts. The collection, much of it trash, made the cataloguing difficult indeed. To make matters worse, he had poor reference materials, no computer, no access to archeological journals, and no chance of escape from Earl's archival hell.

He made his way up the stairs to find Eva and met Pete and Auntie coming out of genealogy. Pete had his foot hiked up on the step to tie his shoe. Auntie waited, her arms loaded with books.

"Why if it ain't Mr. Hunt," Pete said, looking up.

Auntie peeked at Jim from around her books.

"What are we researching today?" Jim asked.

Pete fished his knife out of his pocket. "Auntie's people," he said. "Turns out they're all hillbillies. All begat in the same holler by the same sire."

Auntie narrowed her eyes. "Not if you'd tally in that one's related to the queen."

"We already settled that, Auntie. Bastardly don't count. Auntie objects to being a hillbilly, cause it ain't sophisticated."

"I think Auntie is plenty sophisticated," Jim said.

Auntie smiled and shifted her books.

Pete worked at a fingernail, folded up his knife, and dropped it back into his pocket.

"Now that we're finished with Auntie, be glad to search out your kin on the computer, Mr. Hunt. Can't tell what will turn up."

"Thanks. I think not." Jim turned to leave, then hesitated. "You can trace anyone's background, can you, Pete?"

"Sure, if he ain't bastardly or a spy."

"Even someone like Evan Kingston?"

"Unlikely he's a spy," Pete said.

"See what you can come up with, will you? And Pete?"

"Yes sir?"

"Keep it to yourself. I wouldn't want Kingston to know we were checking his pedigree."

Archeology, genealogy—Jim thought of Brother Bill's warning about being consumed by the past. Here he was snooping into Kingston's. Had he gotten off track in his search for Coronado's leavings?

26

Coronado arose to the breaking of camp. He could smell rain in the air. The men saddled their horses and wadded grass under their cinches to lessen the horses' sores. The horses tossed their heads and flared their nostrils in protest.

Coronado summoned the Turk, as was his custom each morning before breaking camp. The questions had not changed: How many leagues must we yet travel to the land of Quivira? Does the gold await, as the Turk has said?

And each morning the Turk, his black hair loose about his shoulders, would mount his horse and point. "Just beyond the horizon, my general," he would say, riding off into the plain.

Coronado and his men would follow, their mounts much fatigued, while Friar Padilla and Isopete walked somewhere behind them in the dust.

This day all rode with heads bent. The plain stretched into the sun, a trek so endless as to strike fear into the heart of the most valiant conquistador. Soon the men staggered under the great heat, their lips cracking, dust gathering in their throats. Their horses, now too weak to be ridden, stumbled at the ends of their reins. Throughout the day the men and horses suffered much, trudging on in silence as the sun bore upon their shoulders.

That night they made camp, finding no water, and Coronado ordered food prepared, spare though the measure. Even so, without water, the men could not partake and soon turned away.

Wisps of clouds skimmed overhead, though no man dared hope for rain. Thunderheads soon churned upward, reaching into the heavens, but none spoke of it. But when lightning crackled and thunder rumbled across the prairie, the men rose up, lifting their hands, praying that God deliver them from their great thirst.

Raindrops smacked about them, and the sweet smell of dust and moisture rode in on the wind. When it faded, the men held their breaths in vigilance. And then it fell once more in windswept sheets, and the men danced and shivered in celebration.

Puddles gathered in the wallows, and they sucked the muddy water from their hands. Their caked lips bled once more with life.

The Turk took up his horse and walked to the edge of camp. There he stood looking eastward as the rain fell, his arms folded over his chest.

Friar Padilla, his beard clotted with mud, searched out Coronado and lifted his arms in praise. "God has delivered us," he said.

Coronado wiped the rain from his face and looked out at the Turk, who now sat on the ground with his legs folded. The sky blackened, and lightning shimmered deep within it.

"And where is Isopete?" Coronado asked.

"He comes behind as though an old man. I've taught him words for a thousand leagues, but he speaks no more than Alvarado's horse."

Coronado smiled. "He is to become a friar, then?"

"As shall Alvarado's horse," Padilla said.

An icy wind swept over them, and Friar Padilla gathered up his robe.

Coronado rubbed his arms against the sting. "The storm deepens even now."

No sooner had he spoken when small hail commenced popping about them. Clipped on the nose, Friar Padilla cursed and danced about, his nose scarlet red.

"May God purge me of cursing," he said. "It comes unheeded from the past."

Men from all over the camp stood and looked up into the sky. Horses, much frightened, pulled at their reins, their eyes wide.

"It is best to find cover, for the clouds darken even more," Coronado said.

Friar Padilla looked about but could see not a tree, not a bush, not even a rock under which to hide.

"But where, my general, for the land is barren?"

Lightning struck, and thunder pealed. A roar swelled from out of the sky, and great stones fell from the blackness. Men, suffering much from the stones, dropped to their knees and covered their heads.

Coronado and Padilla, knowing this misfortune also, fell to the earth. Horses circled in panic, their ears limp and broken and their backs bloodied.

The hail then passed as it had come, in a moment, and the cries of the wounded resounded across the plain. Men, battered by the stones, rose up from the grass like broken spirits.

Coronado looked about at the men. One soldier, having lost his helmet, lay bleeding from a large stone that hit his head. The Turk, who waited beyond, had escaped from the stones entirely, though all about him men suffered greatly from the pounding.

That night sleep did not come for the conquistadors, the camp being damp with rain and the men's backs tender with welts. Coronado lay listening to their suffering and wondered if they should ever know the sweetness of home again.

At sunrise, Coronado ordered an assembly and summoned the Turk and Isopete to his tent. The Turk, who found Isopete's presence disagreeable, refused to look upon him and stood with his jaw locked and arms crossed. Alvarado, having known their feud for many days and having grown impatient with it, drew his sword.

Coronado said, "We have followed the Turk eastward, investing him with our trust, even as Isopete counseled a northward course to Quivira."

Coronado turned and looked at the men. "It is my belief that the Turk has deceived us. Having summed the count this day, two hundred and fifty leagues have been logged. Though great hardships and hunger have been endured, there is yet no gold. Would I know with certainty of the Turk's trickery, the dogs would have their turn."

"Quivira is to the east, my general," the Turk said. "Death lies to the north."

"Do not speak, Turk, for Coronado listens not," Isopete said.

The Turk shifted his feet and stared into the prairie.

Coronado paced before his tent, a hailstone bruise visible on his neck.

"Place the Turk in chains," he said. "From this day forward, Coronado follows Isopete to Quivira."

Isopete glanced over at the Turk, who had grown sullen and quiet.

Coronado said, "Thirty skilled horsemen will proceed north by the needle to Quivira. Don Tristan de Arellano shall return with the army to Tiguex and await word of our journey."

Arellano, who stood nearby, said, "The army wishes to stay with Coronado, for great danger exists with so few men at his side."

"And what of winter?" Alvarado asked.

"Only God knows the seasons. I have made my decision, Captain."

"But so few men will surely be put upon by the enemy," Alvarado said.

"The column shall move quickly, as do the Indians. Quarrels shall be set aside until a more gainful time. After the gold has been found, Don Tristan de Arellano and the conquistadors shall join us to make claim of Spain's bounty."

Next morning, as the sun rose a lance high, Coronado and his band of thirty rode due north. Isopete, mounted on the Turk's horse, assumed the lead. Friar Padilla, who had grown accustomed to his place, bought up the rear of the column, while next to him, bound in chains and on the back of a Spanish mule, rode the Turk.

27

Being bound in chains and being confined to Earl's storage room had much in common, Jim reflected. He sorted through piles like a treasure hunter at a huge rummage sale. With all his effort, the process of analysis and identification had made little progress. His trash can overflowed with empty cardboard boxes, mildewed newspapers, and a huge sack of green yarn.

He lugged the can up the basement steps to the dumpster, cursing Earl's penchant for hoarding. When he flipped the dumpster lid open, he saw Precious, half-buried in the refuse, looking up at him. Pieces of foil dangled from her fur like Christmas-tree ornaments, and one of her ears had been knocked down. Her eyes gleamed like diamonds.

"Damn it," he said, taking her out. "Come on, Precious. Let's go find Stufflebaum."

Stufflebaum, busy stitching up the belly of a dead dog, looked up from his work.

"If it ain't Lazarus come back from the grave," he said.

Jim set Precious on the bench and adjusted her ear. "I nearly had a heart attack when I found her in the trash bin."

"You're the one who wanted her gone," he said.

"Come on, Stufflebaum, you had her perched over a hole in the soddy display."

Stufflebaum grinned. "There's a suds in the fridge."

Jim searched through the refrigerator, pushing aside a container with something unidentifiable growing on top of it.

"Want one?" he asked.

"Sure," Stufflebaum said, snipping the string with his teeth. "Just like new, ain't he?"

"That's revolting, Stufflebaum. What are you going to do with a dead dog?"

He washed his hands, took a beer, and sat down on the bunk.

"Displays ain't just about dinosaurs, Mr. Archeologist. Domestic animals have been the partners of man since the beginning of time. One cannot fully display human events without the participation of man's best friend."

Jim looked up. "Where did you get that idea?"

"Television," he said, wiping off his mustache.

The mustache, having grown back from its cropping, had been darkened with a heavy layer of mascara. With his strawberry hair hanging in strands under his ball cap, Stufflebaum looked Halloweenish.

Jim turned to leave, pausing at Stufflebaum's workbench. All four of the dog's feet were sticking in the air. Its lips were pulled up in a snarl, and its teeth shined paper-white. There was something familiar about it.

"Where did you get this thing?"

"Found it," he said. "Somebody shot it through the head. I plugged the hole with a wine cork. Can't even tell, can you?"

Jim leaned over for a better look. "Wait a minute. This is Old Man Milton's dog. Where the hell did you get Milton's dog?"

Stufflebaum unfolded from the bunk. "Found it on the river bank out to Milton's place."

Jim narrowed his eyes. "Hold on. That's Kingston's property. How did you get past Mitch Keeper?"

Stufflebaum checked the stitching again. "I've been hunting Milton's place for a good long while. I keep to the river mostly. Do my hunting at night, late at night, you might say. Guess maybe none of them knows?"

"But how do you get in?"

Stufflebaum took off his cap and ran his fingers through his hair.

"I cross the bridge at Overton. From there I go afoot, south down the riverbank. There's no better hunting in the state."

"No, no. Eva said the river flows up against the cliffs, and there's no way through."

"The river shifted several years ago. I guess no one's bothered to look. But as long as the water's not up, a man can walk through."

Jim looked at the dog and then at Stufflebaum.

"You're telling me there's another way into Milton's place?"

Stufflebaum screwed his hat back on his head. "You're a slow learn, ain't you?"

Jim walked to the door. "Could you get me in there without being detected?"

"Oh, sure," he said. "If I took the notion."

———

Eva scooted her chair back and slipped her pencil behind her ear. "Stufflebaum has the new displays almost built," she said. "I'm going to advertise in the paper. Maybe we can get some of the locals back."

"I'm stuck with analyzing the artifacts," Jim said. "Frankly, the research materials are grim. Without good references, it's going to be tough to identify some of that stuff."

"Like what kind of references?" she asked.

"Like, I don't know—like *American Antiquity, American Journal of Archeology,* like a computer, for example, and there's a dozen other books, just the basic tools. It's going to take some work to make it a collection."

Eva crossed her legs, and he could see the half-moon scar there beneath her tan.

"We could update, I suppose," she said. "There's enough funds, and it could be a good long-term investment for the museum."

"That would be great, but I would need some time in a decent library to put together a list."

"Oklahoma City?"

"Yeah, probably."

"Do you think Kingston will change his mind about the site?"

"It's hard to bribe a rich man," he said. "Did I tell you that I stopped by the monastery?"

"Oh."

"They told me that Kingston takes a trip at this time every year."

"Lots of people take trips."

"To the Richmond Institute of Antiquities in Oklahoma City?"

Eva thought for a moment. "I've heard of it. It's an organization that procures relics for museums and private collectors. They buy antiquities and resell them. They may even have investors."

"Are they legitimate?"

"Is anything legitimate in the world of antiquities?"

"High-dollar?" he asked.

"Let's put it this way, the Celf Museum hasn't bought anything from them lately."

"I saw it on a letterhead at Kingston's," Jim said. "I think that's where he had been."

"Maybe he buys art," Eva said. "He can certainly afford it."

"Not only that. Kingston told me he first came here exploring for oil. He said they used seismology in that particular search."

"What's your point, Jim?"

"He told me that the formations in this area are solid and impermeable. I'm not a geologist, but solid and impermeable doesn't explain caves and springs and water gushing out of fissures."

"Oil can be very deep, I think. Anyway, why would he lie about something like that?"

"I don't know. Maybe he just doesn't want us poking around."

"Kingston is an eccentric, a rich one. It's probably no more than that."

Jim stood up, pushing his chair under the desk. "About those reference materials?"

"A trip like that would have to be cleared with the council first," she said. "You'll know when I know."

On his way back to storage, he spotted Pete and Auntie in the genealogy library. Auntie thumbed through a book, while Pete slept in his chair with both feet on the table.

Auntie smiled up at him and nudged Pete awake.

"Why if it ain't Jim Hunt," Pete said, rubbing at his face.

"Having a little nap, Pete?"

"Serious thinking heats up the brain. I have to shut her down to cool off the machinery."

"You ever think about going into the blackmailing business with all this information?"

"Considered it," he said. "But Auntie can't keep a secret. First thing, I'd be down there in Nabson's jail, and Auntie would be riding her Harley off with a motorcycle gang."

"You find out anything about Kingston?"

"Did search out a little, didn't we, Auntie?"

Auntie nodded, pushing her glasses back up on her nose. One of the stems had been spliced with fishing line and glue.

"Like what?"

"Like Kingston ain't got a wife."

"I know, Pete. She died."

"Not exactly."

"What do you mean?"

"He never married."

Jim walked around the table and sat down. He drummed his fingers and studied Pete.

"Anything else?"

"According to the state records, Kingston is a bona fide petroleum engineer."

"I know that. He made his fortune in natural gas back in west Texas."

"He had a gas exploration business in west Texas all right, but he found bankruptcy, not a fortune."

All that afternoon Jim turned over what Pete had said. If Kingston didn't have a wife, who wound up buried in the mausoleum? If Kingston had gone bankrupt in the gas business, where did he acquire all his money? The only thing he knew for sure, was that up until now, Kingston had lied about everything.

———————

A week later he and Eva left for the city just as the sun rose over Lyons. Eva drove while Jim sipped at his coffee and looked out the window.

As they passed the cemetery, he could see the mausoleum as it caught first light. Its windows glowed with the colors of dawn, and he spotted Mitch Keeper's vehicle parked near the gate with someone sitting behind the wheel.

Kingston's mansion loomed on the horizon like a bulwark against a storm, and in the valley, the monks congregated for the day's work.

Thoughts of Sara pressed in on Jim as they drove on. First Sara had lost her mother and then him as well. He knew he should visit her on this trip, but his future hung in the balance. Better no more goodbyes for now.

Soon, they crossed the bridge into Overton. The river ran deep and fast, and where it curved south, high cliffs bordered it on the west. For a millennium life had assembled on the banks of this river, the same river that separated Milton from his land and Earl Celf from his life. The same river whose environs might yield Spanish articles dating from Coronado's time.

28

L ed by Isopete, Coronado's band drove northward at a fast pace for many days. It happened that a great herd of buffalo cows also followed a northerly route, providing fresh meat for evening camp. Isopete, keen with his bow, killed lingering calves or weakened cows, and with little disturbance to the herd.

Francisco Martin, the butcher, began building dung fires, as he had seen the Indians do, greatly improving the comfort of the nightly camp. Though some protested, finding the practice unsanitary, they soon came to its blue flame, its steady and clean heat, with much pleasure.

All men, suspecting the Turk's trickery, avoided his person, a shunning much encouraged by Isopete. He taunted the Turk, who posed little danger, having been secured in chains.

One evening the officers of most import approached Coronado to speak to him of the Turk's perfidy. Coronado considered their plan, finding it unacceptable. Later, after all slept, he summoned Alvarado to his tent.

"Secure the Turk from the others," he said. "His presence agitates them, no more so than at evening camp where his chains rattle as he moves about."

"But where would you have me secure him, my general? Better I should run him through, which can be done with discretion."

"I place him in your charge, Alvarado. Let him sleep in your tent, for I fear for his life."

"But, my general . . ."

"To execute the Turk could cause much grief, for the way ahead is unclear. Perhaps Isopete deceives us, and not the Turk, and we are so far from home and with so few men. The Turk must not come to harm until we have seen how things stand at Quivira with our own eyes."

That night, as the general had ordered, the Turk slept in Alvarado's tent. Alvarado, complaining of the Turk's smell, ordered him cleansed with fat and salt and then chained to the tent pole. Even so, knowing the Turk's great strength, Alvarado slept only lightly thereafter and with his sword at the ready.

Coronado, too, lay awake in the darkness, thinking of the gold that awaited in Quivira, knowing its weight and substance in his mind. Such thoughts in the past had invigorated and encouraged his search, caused him to rise each day with renewed resolve. The Turk, too, with his certitude and well-spoken stories, had fueled Coronado's ambitions, had given hope when hope no longer lived.

Now, his band of men, small and impotent against the enemy, crawled through the wilderness as a line of ants, not knowing from whence they came nor the way ahead, their fate resting with Isopete, a warrior of questionable valor. Such had been the severity of the Turk's deception to Coronado, a man favored with his heart.

He rose and watched the last of the butcher's fire sputter in the night. His thoughts turned to Doña Beatríz, of frigid nights as she lay warm in her feathers, smelling of soaps and perfumes, of her sounds in rare moments, and of her touch in the darkness.

On the fourth week of their trek, the band gathered on the bank of a dry creek bed. Streaks of salt struck through the red earth, and mica glinted in the sunlight.

An Indian stood with his hand held in the air, and at his back, a dozen warriors with their women and children at their sides. The Indians' dogs snarled and whined and lifted their legs.

"They look of a fierce nature," Alvarado said. "Even the women and children are disagreeable."

"But their leader makes signs of peace," Coronado said. "Perhaps they desire commerce, and the conquistadors are well received. Even now our horses falter with lack of maize and good pasturage. Send Isopete to parley, since he is much practiced in their manner, and will profit us the most."

"Does a blind man profit from light?" Alvarado said, motioning for Isopete to proceed.

Upon Isopete's return, he said, "These people will trade maize, enough for many days, for two horses to be given in return, for they have none such as these, and must walk, even when the way is stony and rough."

"The chief," Isopete continued, holding up five fingers, "gives these many pelts for the one with hair on her chin, who wears the squaw's dress, for he has heard of these squaw men, though none is of his tribe."

Friar Padilla looked at Isopete. "I vow to have Isopete carry water to the Turk and know his wrath each day."

Coronado held up his hand. "Isopete, tell the chief that the Spaniards cannot trade the horses, though the maize is in much need by the horses, that we will trade gifts of mirrors and knives, that are most pleasing, and will give his people great power over their enemies. Tell him that the conquistadors' horses cannot be traded, though the conquistadors wish it so, because the Spanish horse has come from many leagues away and cannot be found in this land. Tell him also that the one with the hairy chin, though wearing a squaw's dress, was once a mighty warrior and feared by many."

Padilla tugged at his beard and rolled his eyes.

When Isopete returned with the message, he said, "The chief says to bring mirrors and knives, and also the squaw man, whose spirit has been broken by much war."

That night all gathered about a great fire at the Indians' camp, which smelled of hides and teemed with yapping curs.

Coronado sat next to the chief, who was tattooed and carried a club made of bone, and next to him sat Isopete, while

Alvarado and the friar sat cross-legged on the outskirts of the fire. The horses, having been fed maize on sheets of hide, stomped their feet at heel flies as they ate. The Indian children watched the horses with great curiosity, as they had not seen them before.

Soon, buffalo paunches filled with curdled blood were brought forward by the squaws for each man to draw his share. Buffalo tongue, and hump, much desired by the Indians, followed, and were served on sticks of sage. When all had eaten their fill, a pipe of tobacco was passed around and the fire rekindled.

The fire blazed, and the drums commenced. From out of the darkness, squaws appeared, dancing as cranes into the light. One maiden, of different character, having pale skin and curly hair, stood out from the others. With hands clasped, the squaws bobbed and moved in a circle as they danced to the beat of the drums. Raven black hair hung to their hips, shimmering in the firelight, and slashes of red adorned their chins.

The chief spoke to Isopete while pointing to the young maiden with pale skin.

"What does he say?" Coronado asked.

"If the general favors the maiden, he would have her," Isopete said.

"And what does he require in return?"

"The red horse, which stands beyond the fire."

"Such a price cannot be paid, as I have said."

The chief, having spoken to the other warriors, summoned Isopete, who then reported to Coronado.

"The chief, who is most strong among his people, will fight the squaw man for the red horse. If the squaw man is a powerful warrior, as the general has said, and defeats the chief, then Coronado may take the maiden to his tent."

The friar looked up through his brows at Coronado and shook his head.

"I am a man of God and have given up such things, my general."

"Tell him the friar is a shaman, a man of God," Coronado said, "and cannot fight, for it is against his spirit."

For several moments the chief studied the friar. Rising, he lifted Padilla's robe with his war club and looked underneath. Red crawled up the friar's neck and settled in his cheeks.

Isopete repeated the chief's words. "He says that under the friar's robe, he is like the Spaniard's horse, but has the heart of a squaw."

Friar Padilla's jaw clenched. "Tell the chief if I thrash him, though it cause me much distress, I shall claim the girl *and* his best dog."

The chief paused, grunting his approval, and dropped his war club to the ground.

With his eyes locked on the friar, the chief circled the fire. The muscles in his arms quivered, and sweat glistened on his body. Padilla, having wrestled much in his day as a soldier, hiked his robe, tucked it in his sash, and spit into his hands. The muscles in his legs rippled with much strength, an attribute of birth, and from walking, as required of all friars.

The chief, agile and quick, stepped in to clinch his hands behind the friar's neck. Friar Padilla countered, weaving his arms through the chief's as they moved in tandem about the fire.

The chief, slipping the hold, grabbed the friar's beard and jerked his head down into his knee. The friar, dazed, groaned and sank to the ground. Blood oozed from his nose and into the thick of his beard.

Alvarado stepped forward to intervene, but Coronado held up his hand. "Wait, Alvarado," he said. "You would underestimate the friar's skills."

The friar, shaking his head, rose to engage the chief. When the chief moved in, Padilla, sidestepping, swept his legs from under him, spilling him into the ashes. Much excited, the dogs howled and lunged at their ropes.

Diving to the ground, Padilla locked his legs about the chief's center. His clutch tightened about the chief's middle, and the chief, frightened and short of breath, dug at Padilla's legs with his fingers.

Soon, drool spilled from the chief's mouth, his eyes bulged, and his legs flopped in the ashes. His tongue sprouted from between his teeth, and spots of blood gathered in his nostrils.

When his eyes rolled white, and he lolled to the side uncon-
scious, the friar released him.

The chief wormed about on the ground, his lungs sucking for
air. Padilla stood and brushed away the dirt from his gown. The
chief rose, teetering and uncertain. The friar looked about for
the girl and motioned for her to join the band. She obeyed and
moved to Coronado's elbow.

Friar Padilla picked up the chief's war club and pointed to his
dog. "That one, which is tied by the neck," he said.

The chief's eyes blazed, and the other warriors churned about
and lifted their weapons in a threatening manner.

Alvarado said, "That is the chief's dog. Let it be, Friar, or
we'll all lose our skin."

"The dog has been won fairly in God's eyes, Alvarado. Has it
not?"

"Surely. Padilla has prevailed by his strength and courage,
but a cur is poor commerce for one's life."

The friar narrowed his eyes. "That one, as I have said."

The chief looked about at the other warriors, who had drawn
back in fear, before commanding that the dog be surrendered to
the friar.

The dog cowered and shrank at the friar's feet. Padilla loosed
the rope from its neck. It stood motionless as if appraising circumstances, and then broke away into the prairie.

A gasp passed from the squaws who had been watching from
the safety of the tents. The chief, having witnessed the loss of
his dog, turned away from them and did not return.

That night Coronado ordered the horses secured at a distance
from the camp. He then summoned the maiden, who came without resistance to his tent. Though he questioned her about her
appearance and the paleness of her skin, she did not respond.
Afterward, when Coronado had finished of her, he slept soundly.

He awoke in the night to find the girl had fled, as had the
other Indians, and naught was left in the camp but dying coals
and the smell of smoke. Loneliness set in as he thought of home.

29

Home with Sara would have been better, but the Skirvin Hotel was a grand old establishment in Oklahoma City. After Jim and Eva checked in, they went to the library. Eva read magazines while Jim compiled his list of reference materials.

At the hotel, they agreed to meet for dinner and work out the details for the next day. Jim sat on the edge of his bed and looked at the telephone. Finally, he picked it up and dialed home. The phone rang several times, and as he started to hang up, a man answered.

"Who's this?" Jim asked.

"Don't you recognize your own brother?"

"Jesse, is everything all right?"

"No one's sick, if that's what you mean," he said. "We flew in this morning. Mom and the others are out shopping. It's Sara's birthday."

"Oh, Christ, I forgot. Things have been pretty crazy the last few weeks."

"Mom said you'd gone off on some geology thing."

"Archeology, Jesse. I needed the field experience."

"You have a responsibility here, you know," he said.

"I'm just in town long enough to pick up some reference materials. There are people with me."

Jim could hear Jesse breathing on the other end. "Gloria called," he said.

"What did she want?"

"Living alone didn't turn out so well for her. I guess she figured she could get you back."

"I'm not that crazy, Jesse. Tell Sara I'm sorry I missed her birthday."

"Listen, Jim, I might be able to get you on at the plant. It's assembly work, but the pay's pretty good."

"Thanks for the vote of confidence, Jesse. I'll keep in touch."

Eva arrived at dinner wearing an evening dress, heels, and a single strand of pearls.

Jim stared until she said, "I rarely get a chance to dress."

"Sorry. I didn't mean to gape," he said.

He ordered steaks and a bottle of Merlot. "Here's to the new director of the Celf Museum," he said, lifting his glass.

Eva sipped her wine. "You do know the council won't pick up the bar tab?"

"And do we care?" he said.

They finished eating and ordered coffee.

"I'd like to stop by the Richmond Institute of Antiquities before we go back," he said.

"Because why?"

"I confess to having asked Pete and Auntie to run a check on Kingston for me. Turns out he lied about being married, and he didn't make his fortune in the gas business. His story doesn't add up. I'm curious as to what this Richmond Institute is all about."

Eva lowered her glass. "Never married?"

"Apparently not."

"Then what's all that business with the mausoleum?"

"There are lots of unanswered questions." He stirred his coffee and fell silent.

"Is everything all right with you?" she asked.

"Sorry. I'm a little preoccupied. I talked to my brother. Turns out I missed Sara's birthday."

"Oh, I'm sorry, but you've been pretty busy, you know."

He reached over and touched her fingers. "Eva, I've been thinking."

Eva dropped her hand to her lap. "Before you go on, there's something I need to say."

Jim sat back. "All right."

"It's been pretty clear what's happening between us, and I think we should deal with it openly."

"Go on," he said.

"First, I'm not certain that I want a relationship with anyone at this point in my life. You are a nice guy, and I find you attractive. But in my experience even the best unions don't make for much happiness. Second, you have a daughter who needs you. Another woman in her life would only complicate things for her, for you, and for me. Third, you have your career to think about, and I have my own ambitions. Fourth, when the time comes, you're going to leave Lyons and me behind, and you will have forgotten this whole business before the year is out. In short, it's best we stop this before it begins."

Jim folded his napkin. "You tell it pretty straight."

"You can see how impossible it would be."

"Maybe you're right," he said, standing. "I certainly haven't done so well managing my own life. Why should I screw up yours?"

Jim lay awake listening to the sounds. He'd grown accustomed to the quiet and order of the prairie. The noise of the city clattered about in his head like static.

Eva had been right of course. Both his life and his feelings were confused. He had no business involving her or anyone else. He would wind up Earl's collection and come back home, maybe take Jesse up on his offer. Maybe he could salvage something yet.

He slept then, a disturbed sleep, and awakened in the night to something at his door. The knock came again. He sat up on the edge of his bed and then the knock came again, louder and more urgent. He slipped on his robe, making his way through the darkness.

"Yes? Who is it?"

"It's me," Eva said.

He opened the door, and she stepped in, closing it behind her. She smelled of talc and soap, and he could feel her heat in the darkness.

"Jim," she said. "You remember all those reasons I gave why this would never work?"

"Yes," he said.

"I failed to give the one reason why it would."

"And that would be?"

"Because I'm in love with you," she said. As she fell into his arms, the passion for treasure and for the secrets of the past was borne away by the moment.

30

One day as the sun shone overhead, the conquistadors advanced upon a great rock rising from out of the prairie, a river meandering to its north.

Isopete lifted his hand, signaling the column to halt. Suddenly, Indian squaws scrambled from out of the grass, pulling their children behind them. At seeing the Spaniards' horses, the children hopped about at the ends of their mothers' arms. The squaws, also frightened by the conquistadors, raced to where warriors gathered along the bank of the river.

When the warriors saw this, they sought cover among the trees, where they notched their arrows in preparation for battle.

Isopete, much pleased at seeing them, rode out in that direction, his bow raised above his head, while the conquistadors, who were alarmed at the numbers of enemy, waited for Coronado's orders.

Isopete, his hands remaining in the air, called out his own name to the Indians. One by one, the warriors, having recognized his name, lowered their bows and called back to him.

Much delighted at his welcome, Isopete dropped from his horse and approached them. The warriors, who now knew him with certainty, clapped him on his back, while the squaws greeted him with nods of their heads. Even the children, having seen his welcome, rushed forward to touch him.

Isopete signaled for the conquistadors to advance toward them. Alvarado and Coronado, uncertain as to their safety, moved forward with caution. With weapons at the ready, the conquistadors followed behind.

"Quivira is at hand," Isopete said to them as they approached. "These are my people who have greeted me with much affection."

Securing the Turk in a stand of trees so as not to frighten the others with his chains, the conquistadors followed Isopete and the Indians to their camp. Coronado, standing in his stirrups to rub his carbuncle, saw neither gold nor fortune nor a grand and marvelous city but huts of grass and racks of stinking hides. Placed at the doors throughout the camp were pots made of clay and baskets made of woven grass, filled with nuts and maize. Pits, having been dug from the ground, preserved many squashes and melons from the prairie heat.

Camp dogs circled about the conquistadors, sniffing their boots and kicking dirt into the air with their feet. The warriors, too, gathered close in to admire the horses, which were strange to them, and to observe the Spaniards' pikes and swords.

As Coronado waited for the chief to be brought to meet him, he looked about the camp. "There is no gold," he said to Alvarado, "nor silver, nor turquoise, as the Turk has said."

"Perhaps it is hidden from foreigners," Alvarado said. "Such treasure could be easily taken."

Isopete came and presented the chief, an old Indian wearing breechclout, moccasins, and a copper amulet tied about his neck. Coronado, having recognized the metal, glanced at Alvarado.

The chief, his face much wrinkled, walked around Alvarado's horse. He nodded his head and grunted. In halting Spanish, Isopete interpreted the chief's welcome: The Spaniards could camp where the river bends, where the wood and water were plentiful and, because a fresh kill had only recently been made, much buffalo meat would be shared among them.

When Isopete had finished, Coronado said, "Have the friar bring forward the *Requerimiento,* and summon the Turk."

Isopete's face clouded. "The Turk is unwelcome among my people," he said.

"Bring him forth," Coronado said, repeating the order.

The friar arrived first to present the *Requerimiento*, which he did with much authority, speaking of St. Peter, a man of superior quality over all of mankind, and saying that all men hearing these words were forever subject to the yoke of the church. Afterwards he crossed himself, as all the conquistadors did, and Isopete also crossed himself for the Indians to witness.

Isopete then explained how the friar, a medicine man of great power, made the sign of the cross to ward off evil spirits.

Having turned to his people, the chief also crossed himself as he had seen Isopete do. The warriors, seeing this, crossed themselves, while dancing and yelping like coyotes, as was their custom. Soon all in the camp, even the young children, crossed themselves, for none liked evil spirits to be among them.

This they did until Isopete charged them to cross themselves only once, or only when they ate of the buffalo, or when the friar commanded it be done.

After this discourse, the chief, much frightened of the friar's medicine, removed the copper amulet and hung it about the friar's neck.

When Alvarado arrived with the Turk, the people fell back. Having been secured by chains for many days, the Turk suffered sores about his body, and he smelled of filth from the trail. The slackness of his face, caused by poor rations, deepened the scar on his cheek

Isopete found his presence disagreeable and circled him as a cur might another. The Turk narrowed his eyes and glared back at Isopete and clenched his fists.

Coronado said, "This warrior, known as the Turk among us, has sworn that the people of Quivira drink from cups of silver and cook in pots of gold, that golden bells hang from the trees, and the birds' craws are filled with grains of gold."

The chief said to Isopete, "We know nothing of this Turk or of the things he speaks. The people drink from the buffalo's stomach. This is best in the drought, for it carries its own water. The trees do not hang with bells but with nuts, which are good to eat in the winter, except the walnut, which has a thick shell and little meat."

Coronado walked to the Turk's side and pointed to his chains. "These must be worn by those who do not speak the truth to Coronado. Perhaps the people have forgotten where the gold and silver is hidden?"

After the chief had spoken again, Isopete interpreted his words: "There is no gold or silver in this village, though it has been told that villages to the north have much gold. They are called the Guaes and are the enemies of our people. It is said by many that gold is hidden there."

Coronado walked over to the friar and lifted the amulet that hung from his neck.

"In all our journey, no people have worn metal such as this."

Isopete listened to the chief speak and then related the story of a god who had dropped the amulet on the prairie floor to be found by the people's chief. Among other things, the chief knew it had brought Isopete back to his people unharmed. Now he wished it be given to Coronado's medicine man so that Coronado, having its spirit with him, no longer would require Isopete to guide him.

Coronado looked at Isopete. "This is what the chief has told you?"

Isopete nodded. "The path to the Guaes is north, my general, and easily followed."

"Then so be it." Coronado turned to Alvarado. "Take the Turk to the bend of the river. Chain him there. We shall eat here, as has been offered, before making camp at the river."

After having their fill of meat, Coronado bade farewell to the chief, saying it was necessary that they ride on without delay.

Pleased with Isopete, Coronado presented him, as a rare gift, the horse he'd been riding. Much elated, Isopete paraded the horse about the camp for all to see and admire.

The conquistadors then returned to the river, where they pitched their tents against the night.

When the camp slept, Coronado stole to Alvarado's tent.

Alvarado stirred and sat up in his bed. "What is it, my general?"

"Is the Turk chained as I ordered, Captain?"

"Yes, my general," he said, rubbing his face, "to a log where the river bends."

"And is he so far away as not to be heard?"

"Yes, my general."

"Lead me to him."

The Turk, who huddled against the dampness of the river, stood at the sound of footsteps. The moonlight lit his shoulders and shined in the blackness of his eyes.

Coronado said, "I have come, Turk, for no longer do lies sustain you. You have misled the conquistadors and placed them in harm's way with your duplicity."

The chained Turk, much angered, pitched his chin high and said, "The people of Tiguex asked it of me, to avenge the Spaniards' plunder, to rid them from this land forever, and I have done so. The Spaniards are like children in the wilderness, who—without Isopete—would have their bones shined by buzzards."

"And so you acknowledge your deception, Turk?" Coronado said.

Turning his back, the Turk said no more.

Coronado and Alvarado worked their way along the bank of the river, the rush of the current whispering beside them.

Pausing, Coronado said, "The time has come, Alvarado."

"Yes, my general."

"Slay him, but do not alert the others."

"The Turk is strong and will resist even in his chains," Alvarado said.

"Summon the butcher, Francisco Martin, who is himself sturdy and skilled at killing. Dispose of the Turk in the river sands so that nothing is left behind."

"As you wish, my general."

Alvarado waited in the darkness for Coronado's footsteps to fade before searching out Francisco Martin, who slept in his bed. Alvarado knelt at his side, breathing the smell of butchery in his tent and clothes.

"Come with me, Francisco, but with stealth," he said, whispering.

"Who summons me at such an hour?" he asked, rubbing the sleep from his face.

"It is Alvarado. Meet me at the river's edge, and do not disturb the others." He paused. "Fetch your rope, Francisco, for the prey is large and perilous."

Together, they slipped through the darkness, swinging wide at the bend so as to come in from behind where the Turk had been chained. Francisco, having cut a length of oak, secured it in his belt.

The Turk slept, his knees pulled into his arms, and with his head bent. His hair fell about his face, and the moonlight glinted from his chains. His breathing came deep and steady as in sleep.

Francisco and Alvarado crept forward. Sweeping in from the river, the breeze smelled of fish and moss. The moment Francisco dropped the rope about the Turk's neck, the Turk stood, his fierce strength lifting Francisco off the ground as he lunged forward, coming to the end of his chains, and falling upon the ground.

Francisco, recovering and seizing the moment, fixed the stick into the loop and twisted the rope with his powerful arms. The Turk struggled to stand. Having fallen upon him, Alvarado held him and covered his mouth with his hands so that he might not call out in distress.

Francisco, his muscles trembling, tightened the garrote about the Turk's throat. The Turk's arms flailed, and his chains rattled as he struggled for breath. Francisco twisted the rope until the Turk's throat crushed beneath it, and he stilled.

Afterward, they dragged the Turk by his chains to the bend of the river where the sands had gathered in waves. There they dug a hole with their hands and pulled him in. Under the moonlight, they covered him and then returned to their beds.

Across camp, Coronado lay awake in his tent and listened, but could hear no sound, save for the beat of his heart.

31

I t is done?" Coronado asked.

Alvarado said, "The Turk has met his appointed time, my general, but not without difficulty, for his vast strength tried even his chains."

Coronado warmed his hands at the fire. With each league north, the cold nights seeped deeper into his bones.

"And what of Francisco, the butcher?"

"An oath of silence, my general."

"But all know of the Turk's absence, do they not, Captain?"

"Yes, my general. The log that secured the Turk rotted beneath the ground, and he escaped into the night."

"An unfortunate circumstance," Coronado said.

Alvarado scraped the sand from his boots. "Yes, though Alvarado shall sleep more soundly. What now is our course, my general?"

Coronado turned his back to the fire. Several moments passed before he answered. "It is said by the Indians that the gold may be hidden with the Guaes to the north."

"We have heard these things from others, my general. The gold is forever ahead, like eternity."

Coronado watched the men as they climbed from their beds. They spoke little as they saddled their horses. Each day they rose as from the dead to face what might yet befall them.

"Our numbers have grown small even as the natives have increased. Our lives now depend on the good will of our adversaries."

"A danger for the conquistadors, my general, who have known little fear."

Coronado paced, clasping his hands behind his back. "Perhaps the gold lies just there on the horizon. Perhaps the prairie is awash with gold."

"Perhaps it's a land without end, my general, and all the gold is but sand."

Coronado walked to where he could see the river below. "The dead are scattered behind like leaves in the wind. We have come far and paid dearly."

"What then would you have us do, my general?"

Coronado lowered his head and then said, "Go to Isopete. Take a mare and a horse in exchange for guides appointed by him."

"We go to the north as before?"

"Yes. It is not finished, Alvarado."

———————

On the fourth day, they came upon a small Indian camp. It overlooked a valley breached by a deep canyon. From their vantage, they could see the meander of the river. A few camp dogs stretched out in the sun, and the squaws worked at the drying racks.

Old men sat about the camp, which had been emptied of young warriors. They slept in the shade or sat cross-legged on buffalo hides to work flint points and arrow shafts. One old man, whose belly lay in folds, laughed and slapped at his leg as he talked to another in the camp.

"The Guaes, the enemies of Isopete's people," Coronado said.

"Perhaps the gold lies within their huts," Alvarado said.

"And do our guides yet await us behind, Alvarado, or have they, too, deserted us?"

"At the river as ordered, God willing."

Coronado rested his head in his hands. His arms had thinned, and a tremor jerked in them. He set his jaw and looked up at Alvarado.

"There is maize for our horses in this camp, and the warriors are few, the young ones having left."

"And so the gold has left with them, my general, for I do not see it."

"Perhaps they have been alerted and have secured it. We shall call our men to formation and enter the camp."

Alvarado looked down into the valley. "I pray they fear the Spanish horse, for our numbers have waned and can no more be feared."

"Friar Padilla, in his manner, shall prepare the reading of the *Requerimiento*. The heathen souls saved this day shall warrant him a place at God's hand."

————

The conquistadors entered the camp, mounted and carrying arms, causing a great flurry among the natives. Bewildered by the approaching band, the old men circled about in confusion, while the squaws hurried their children away into the trees.

Coronado advanced from the column. The old warrior, his muscles slacked with age, held up his hand, gesturing while speaking, making it known that they had entered the camp of the Guaes and, though their warriors were away, they were close by and soon to return.

Coronado took from his pocket a gold coin, showing it to the old man, who motioned that he knew nothing of this object. The others murmured and shrugged their shoulders.

To show the strength of the conquistadors, Coronado ordered a musket fired, the ball passing through the old man's head. A commotion went up as the old warriors formed a line of defense between the conquistadors and the squaws, who had taken refuge in the trees.

Coronado said, "Alvarado, bring forward the friar to have the *Requerimiento* read."

"But, my general, the heathens prepare for battle."

"They are old and much in need of salvation. I am sworn to execute these things for the mother church and the king of Spain. Let the Guaes now hear God's promise so that they may pledge their oath."

Alvarado turned in his saddle and ordered the friar forward.

The old warriors flourished their weapons in alarm and circled out to guard their flanks.

Friar Padilla, his feet black with dust and his robe bristling with burrs, came forward as ordered to read the *Requerimiento*. He held out his hands to convert them, but a wizened old man seized the *Requerimiento* and tossed it into the fire.

A cry went up from Padilla, as though his heart had been pierced, and he fell to his knees.

"This day the *Requerimiento* is burned," he said. "Their salvation is lost and mine to bear."

Alvarado, alarmed at these circumstances, brought about his mount.

"Withdraw, my general. The saving of souls must wait until a more gainful time."

His jaw tense, Coronado leaned forward in his saddle, a madness in his eyes that had not been seen before.

"Until the morrow then and no longer," he said, kicking his horse about.

As they rode away, the old men jeered and pitched rocks after them.

Coronado dispatched Alvarado to scout ahead for a campsite. He returned to meet the column at dusk, reporting that he'd found both water and wood in a canyon a few leagues away.

"But a canyon?" Coronado said. "Is there no alternative?"

"None that can be reached before dark, my general. The canyon has but a single ingress and egress. Guards could be posted to alert the general of approaching danger, though I saw no evidence of the Guaes hunting party.

"We are in much need of water," Coronado said. "We will camp in the canyon."

Juan Rodriguez, while gathering firewood in the canyon, came upon a cave and summoned Coronado and Alvarado, who climbed to him with great effort. Large enough for only three, the cave ended without warning. They leaned against the wall to regain their wind.

"Suitable for rodents and scorpions, Rodriguez," Coronado said. "Have you taken leave of your senses?"

"But, my general, listen to the waters."

"What does he cluck about?" Alvarado asked.

"It's the sound of water," Rodriguez said. "I hear it from the depths even now."

"Rodriguez is possessed and hears what others cannot," Alvarado said.

"But listen closely, my general. It comes from the heart of the earth."

Coronado cupped his ear into the darkness and did not speak. Turning, he said, "Perhaps Rodriguez is not mad, for I, too, hear it."

"A spring, which is common in such places," Alvarado said.

Coronado nodded his head. "It flows with much force like a river."

"Perchance a sign from God," Rodriguez said.

"Or Satan's den," Alvarado said.

Coronado dusted himself off. "Summon Friar Padilla to build a cross to mark this spot. Inscribe a stone, placing on it the name of Francisco Vasquez de Coronado. Having achieved our purpose, we shall return and build a shrine, for this is a place of sacred waters."

After being dispatched to the cave, Friar Padilla constructed the cross and inscribed it as directed.

As night fell, Coronado ordered a fire built and guards posted at each end of the canyon.

"Send Luis and Gonzales, for they have bickered too long," Coronado said to Alvarado. "Post one at the canyon's ingress and the other at the egress. Perhaps a night alone in the darkness will sweeten their temperaments."

"Yes, my general."

"Tomorrow we return to the Guaes, and Coronado shall not be turned away again."

As the moon rose over the canyon, Luis dozed, though he shivered in the cold, and his chain mail chafed his neck. The smell of smoke drifted from the camp's fire, and the distant cry of a coyote rose up into the night.

Disturbed by a sound from the darkness, Luis stood. When the blow shattered his skull, his sword, half-drawn by his hand, clattered into the rocks.

Having returned from the hunt, the Guaes warriors fell upon Luis, splintering his extremities with grinding stones, as was their manner, so that he could not rise from the dead to do them harm.

At the ingress, Gonzales, too, lay splayed among the rocks, his arms and legs also crushed and broken.

———

When dawn broke into the canyon, the conquistadors rose from their beds. Above them at the rim, the Guaes warriors, with bows drawn, gathered in great numbers. The morning sun highlighted their war paint as they waited in silence.

Having seen the warriors, Coronado joined Alvarado, who stood with sword readied.

"Their numbers are great," Coronado said. "We surely will suffer and die at their hands."

"They did not kill us in the night, my general, for they fear our horses."

"So they shall let us pass unharmed, Alvarado?"

"If it be God's will," he said.

Half-dressed, the conquistadors mounted their horses and moved with deliberation through the canyon. The horses' hooves clopped in the rocks, and the shadows of the warriors above them loomed in the morning sun. And as the men drew near the egress, they passed the bloodied remains of Luis. Each man held council with God, for at his back, a hundred bows were drawn.

Being afoot and last of the column to pass, Friar Padilla paused to make the sign of the cross and to whisper words from the Last Rite. Taking the copper amulet from his neck, he laid it on poor Luis's remains.

The drums of the Guaes rose behind them like the heartbeats of giants. The conquistadors did not stop until they had reached the camp of the guides, who had been left behind.

There they retold their stories, though all had been at hand, though they stood barefoot with their shirts in their arms. Afterward, they built a great fire and drew in close against the wilderness.

In much distress, Coronado made his way alone to the river. He knelt in the sand, his shoulders bent, and watched the current slipping southward.

The sun had lowered in the west by the time he returned to camp and summoned the conquistadors together. With eyes vacant, like candles snuffed away, he spoke to them:

"We have swum into the river and have found the current swift. We can swim no farther but must return to shore. Our numbers are few. The winter descends upon us. It is time to return to Tiguex. Isopete's guides will show the way."

Friar Padilla said, "My work is not ended, my general, but begun."

"My duty is to my men and my king, Friar."

"And what of the salvation of souls? Is there no duty to God?"

"God does not intervene, Friar, though it is in His power."

Alvarado sheathed his sword. "And what of the gold, my general? Is it also to be left behind?"

Coronado paused, looking northward into the prairie. "This I know with my heart: The gold lies out there but not for Coronado. It is not to be."

"And what of honor?" Alvarado asked.

Coronado lowered his head. "Nor honor as well, my captain."

Soon he would face the displeasure of the viceroy and loss of reputation. He could not have imagined the riches accruing to his name in the far future—for historians, archeologists, antiquarians, keepers of the cultural repository.

32

Jim and Eva located the Richmond Institute of Antiquities six blocks from the Skirvin. Made of limestone and marble, the building covered half the block. A black Mercedes sat in the parking lot, and a wrought-iron fence encircled the grounds, though the gates remained opened. Water spilled over a granite sphere, and the smell of roses filled the air.

Jim rang the bell. Eva glanced up at him and smiled, and their night together flashed in Jim's mind, a collage of searing images.

"Not to worry," he said. "We'll play this by ear."

The woman who opened the door appeared to have stepped out of a Bela Lugosi movie. Her hair had been pulled into a bun, stretching her eyes into exotic slants. A lace shawl draped over her shoulders, and a diamond broach effigy, part-human and part-lizard, adorned her dress.

"Yes?" she asked, adjusting her shawl. Nicotine stained her fingers, and her breath was stale.

"It's our understanding you deal in antiquities. We're in hopes of procuring something special for our museum," Jim said.

"Do you have an appointment with Mr. Richmond?"

"We haven't much time," Eva said. "We are on our way to Los Angeles, actually, and are looking to fill out our collection."

172

"I'm sorry, but Mr. Richmond requires an appointment."

"The opportunity presented itself," Eva said. "And the Institute's reputation is well-known. But we can buy elsewhere. Please don't bother if it's inconvenient."

"Well," she said. "I guess I could speak with him."

The woman left, and Jim whispered, "Boy, are you good."

Eva smiled and adjusted her purse on her shoulder.

A man clad in a black suit, crimson tie, and an egg-shell white shirt came to the door. Such men might have been born fully dressed. Freakishly tall, he peered down at them like some well-groomed giraffe. His hair disappeared in the front and cropped up elsewhere like a thicket row.

"Jim Hunt, and this is my associate, Eva Manor. We thought you might help us with our collection, Mr. Richmond."

"I usually work only through recommendations. Our clientele is quite select."

Eva smiled up at him. "It's just that a patron has left our museum an endowment, and we are anxious to complete our collection. This has all happened rather suddenly, and we are on our way to the coast."

"Yes," he said, dipping his head for a closer look at Eva. "Come with me, then. Perhaps we can be of some help."

They followed Mr. Richmond down a dim hall and into his office. A lead-paned window rose from floor to ceiling, and in front of it stood a large mahogany desk adorned with an ivory pen set, a rolodex, and a small crystal clock. A solitary golden bell sat on a marble pedestal next to the fireplace.

Mr. Richmond took up his place and invited them to sit in the high-back chairs that had been arranged at an awkward distance from his desk. He leaned forward on his elbows and folded his hands.

"Now," he said. "What is it we can do for you?"

Eva set her purse next to her chair. "As we have said, our museum has received an endowment. Since we were in town, we thought to stop in and see if the institute would be interested in procuring items for our collection."

"I see. And what kinds of items did you have in mind?"

"Pottery," Jim said.

Richmond donned his glasses and pulled a leather-bound notebook from his desk.

"Yes," he said, nodding. "We have some fine examples in our inventory. Have you dealt with the Richmond Institute before?"

"No," Eva said. "We have only recently received the endowment."

"I see. You do understand that the Richmond Institute deals strictly in cash?"

"Cash?" Jim said, glancing over at Eva.

"We exercise great care in establishing the provenance of each of our relics, and you can be assured of the authenticity of your purchase. But the antiquities business is fraught with opportunists willing to lay claim to what they do not own. We have found it best for both the institute and our clientele to conduct all transactions in cash."

"I think that could be arranged," Eva said.

"And may I ask what museum you represent?"

"The Celf Museum in Lyons, Kansas," Jim said.

"Lyons? I'm not familiar with it." Turning in his chair, he looked out the window for a moment. "Come to think of it, I believe we shipped some Italian marble to a monastery in a Lyons."

"The Franciscan monastery?" Jim said.

"Quite so. Antique Carrara, I believe. Your museum must be rather small?"

"Though the endowment is not," Eva said.

"Yes, well. Perhaps you could be more precise as to the kind of pottery you are looking for?"

"Native American," Jim said.

Mr. Richmond rose from his chair. "I'm sorry, but I'm afraid you have come to the wrong place. We don't deal in Native American artifacts. The paperwork is quite impossible. Our inventory is almost exclusively in primitives—Aztec, Inca, some Asian as well."

"I see," Jim said, standing. "Well, please forgive our intrusion. I hope we haven't wasted too much of your time."

"Perhaps another day. I'll see you out."

Next morning, Jim, being familiar with the city, took the wheel, relaxing as he turned onto the crosstown boulevard. From the overpass they could see the red tile roof of the Richmond Institute of Antiquities. Eva watched it pass by her window.

"I wonder if Mr. Richmond has arisen from his coffin?" she said.

Jim smiled. "And what about that woman who answered the door? Did you see her unfold her wings and flap away?"

For some time Eva didn't say anything. "Richmond struck me as a little nervous, and he never once mentioned Kingston. Isn't that odd?"

"Or the correspondence between them," Jim said.

They turned onto Interstate 35, and Jim set the cruise. He opened the window and could smell sunflowers on the wind, and the road opened ahead like an airport runway.

Eva slid under his arm. "About last night," she said. "No regrets?"

"I've lots of regrets in my life, but last night isn't one of them."

"Me neither," she said, nuzzling against him. "No regrets."

By noon they came to the Overton bridge. Jim slowed down.

"Look how much water is in the river here," he said. "This *is* the same river that goes through the Milton place, isn't it?"

"The same," she said.

"And Milton's not that far from here?"

"If you don't count the bends in the river."

She pointed out the window. "See those cliffs? The river bends just there, and the water flows against that rock face."

"Tough luck for Milton," he said.

"He's having his share of that lately," Eva said.

"Are you sure there's no passage?"

Eva shrugged. "For as long as *I* can remember, there's no way through, unless you want to swim, I suppose."

The Lyons wheat elevator came into view, and Eva slid back to her side of the car. The afternoon sun blazed its way through the sky, and the mausoleum, looking like the Greek Parthenon, rose onto the horizon in front of them. They could smell the roses that thrived in the St. Francis of Assisi Cemetery.

Jim fell silent as they approached.

"What's the matter?" she asked.

"Nothing," he said, shaking it away. "It's this place, I guess.

"Look," he said. "It's Brother Bill over there in the garden. Come on, I'd like for you to meet him. He owes me a melon."

"Maybe we should get back, Jim. I've been worrying about what Stufflebaum may have gotten in to."

"Whatever Stufflebaum's been up to, it's too late to do anything about it now," he said, wheeling in.

Brother Bill, wearing a straw hat and carrying his gloves in one hand, walked to the car. Jim introduced him to Eva.

Brother Bill smiled. "At first I thought Jim had returned to join the Franciscans," he said, taking her hand. "But I see he has found something more inspiring than spiritual solitude."

"Nice meeting you," Eva said, her eyes dancing.

"In fact, had I known such loveliness abounded in Lyons, I might have reconsidered my own vows."

Eva blushed. "Jim failed to mention your charm and good taste."

"I suspect that he did," he said.

"I came for a melon, Brother Bill."

"Oh, yes, a melon. Come with me. We'll pick one that's nice and ripe."

"Your garden is glorious," Eva said.

"The labor is long, and the harvest is short," he said, thumping a large melon half-hidden in the vines. "Ah, here we are."

"How can you tell?" Eva asked.

He hefted it onto his shoulder. "The curl is spent, and the sound is flat like a thump on your cheek. Come now. I'll carry it to your car."

Jim glanced up at the sun. "Perhaps you would have time to share it with us?" he said.

Brother Bill looked back at the other monks, who were busy chopping the thistle sprouts just peeking through the soil.

"There is a time for labor and a time for rest. Follow me to the garden where it's cool." Brother Bill led them under the shade of an elm and motioned for them to sit. He cracked open the melon, offering them each a piece.

"To use a knife would be blasphemy," he said.

Jim could see the mausoleum from the courtyard, the Carrara marble as supple and transparent as beeswax.

"You mentioned once that Kingston donated the marble for the rectory, Brother Bill."

"A generous donation. Each time I pray at the altar, I'm thankful for his beautiful gift."

"Did he procure it from the Richmond Institute of Antiquities by chance?"

"Yes. I remember it well because they delivered the shipment here to the monastery, the institute's logo being stamped on each pallet. I thought it odd that my name had been placed on the bill of lading."

"Not Kingston's?"

"No. At first I thought there had been an error, but Mr. Kingston paid us for the order—in full, of course."

"And he's never asked for anything in return?"

"Only that he be alerted if someone were to desecrate his wife's tomb. It seemed a reasonable request."

Eva hooked her arm in Jim's. "Thank you for the melon, Brother Bill."

"Perhaps you'd like to take another with you?"

"I prefer having it with you. Perhaps sometime we could do it again here in this beautiful place?"

"You brighten our garden, Eva. Our retreat here is for all to enjoy. We shall await your return."

As they pulled away, Jim slowed at the cemetery gate and could see Kingston's all-terrain parked in the shade of the large cedar that grew adjacent to the mausoleum.

When he looked again in the rearview mirror, it had disappeared.

33

Pete sat on the front steps of the museum with his elbows propped on his knees and his chin in his hands. Auntie leaned against the building, her legs stretched out in front of her, her ankles bulging over the tops of her shoes.

"It's Churchill and the queen," Eva said. "I wonder what's happened."

"Hello, Pete," Jim said. "How goes it?"

Pete dabbed at his forehead with his bandanna.

"Thing is, Auntie and me were doing a little research on the computer when Stufflebaum shows up."

Eva glanced over at Jim. "What happened?" she asked.

"I told him about how I was related to Churchill on the maternal side, and how Auntie would have been related to the queen had there not been a bastardly deed—which didn't make her related at all 'cause no records could be followed to back it up. I says it's one thing to be related to the queen with papers, but without papers you might just as well be related to a goddang taxidermist."

"Oh, my," Eva said.

"So Stufflebaum gets all blowed up like a bullfrog and says he's an employee of the museum and that he's sick and tired of hearing all this shit—excuse me, ma'am—about Churchill and the queen and that we can just get on out of the museum."

"What happened then?" Jim asked.

"I says that this here museum is a public institution since being turned over to the council and that he's just a handyman and a damn poor one at that. I says Auntie and me can come in here any time we want and research out our tree."

"Go on," Eva said.

Auntie stood up, straightening her skirt. "That's when Stufflebaum said he thought we must have got it all mixed up 'cause I looked more like Churchill, and Pete could be a dead ringer for the queen. I told him I'd slap his face good if he ever said anything like that again and that's when he said it."

Eva sat down on the stoop. "Said what?"

"That he'd stuff both Pete and me and mount us on the wall between the buffalo and the elk and tell everyone how he'd dug us up in a Neanderthal cave."

"I'm sorry about this," Eva said.

Pete rolled his shoulders. "Then you'll have a talk with him?"

"First thing."

"And we can come use the library?"

"Of course you can."

"Stufflebaum's got no business talking that way," Pete said. "Especially to folks with standing. Come on, Auntie, we best get to The Westerner before all the ham and beans is gone."

After they left, Eva dug through her purse for the keys to the museum door.

"I wonder what else Stufflebaum has done?"

"Why don't we just find out in the morning after we've had a good night's sleep?"

"I better check the mail, Jim. I'm expecting bills to come in for those new displays."

Jim walked through the museum while Eva gathered up the mail. He shut out the lights and came back to find her at the front door talking to Sheriff Nabson.

Nabson watched Jim over Eva's shoulder. "Here's one for your friend, too," he said.

"What is it?" Jim asked.

Eva turned. "We've been subpoenaed."

"For what?"

"Witnesses for Milton's trial."

"This is crazy, Sheriff. We don't know anything about Earl's death."

"I've known the Miltons my whole life," Eva said. "They might be on the odd side, but they wouldn't kill anyone."

Nabson lit a cigarette and shrugged.

"If Milton didn't kill Earl, who did? Someone wanted him out of the way, that's certain, someone who could profit one way or another."

Jim's face went hot. "What are you implying, Sheriff?"

Nabson, his breath boozy and his eyes bloodshot, looked out from under his hat.

"Oh, I'm not implying nothing. Just make sure you two show up at court. You don't want me coming back with a warrant."

Back inside, they sat at Eva's desk and read over the subpoenas.

"I can't believe it," Eva said. "Why would they subpoena us? We have nothing to hide."

"Other than the fact that we took artifacts off the Milton place that night and that we found his body before anyone knew he'd been killed. And, that we didn't say anything about it to anyone."

"Well, other than that," she said. "Oh, god, Jim, what are we going to do?"

He walked to the window and watched Nabson's patrol car pull away. He rubbed at his temples, at the jackhammer in his head.

"But then no one knows, do they?" he said. "There's no reason for those questions to even come up."

"I hope you're right."

"Let's get out of here. I need a drink."

Eva reached for her purse. "Oh, wait a minute. That box over there came for you."

"What is it?"

"It's from the Historic Preservation office."

Jim set the box on the desk. "The artifacts I sent in for analysis."

"Aren't you going to look?"

Jim fished out the pieces of iron and bone fragment from the packing worms to find the report on the bottom. He read it and then read it again. Picking up the bone, he turned it in his hand.

"I'll be damned," he said.

"What is it?"

"The bone carbon dates to about five hundred years old."

"And the iron?"

"They think the construction of the fragments are consistent with mail."

"Mail?"

"Armor," he said. "Spanish mail armor."

34

Jim worked late into the evenings in the storage room. Eva, too, busied herself finishing up the new displays. The exhibits had rarely been rotated or changed in the past.

Eva said that the public school conducted a field day at the museum each spring. This had been going on for as long as she could remember. Hardly a person in town had escaped the annual trek to the museum.

In the past, she said, the children had been paraded through at breakneck speed, forbidden to go to the bathroom, ask questions, or demonstrate any human curiosity. After which, Earl herded them into a room and subjected them to a thirty-minute lecture about how things used to be on the trail. The end result: not a citizen in town would reenter the museum short of gunpoint.

Eva hoped that the new series of exhibits would revive the flagging interest of the citizenry. In support, Jim had waded through tons of overburden in search of artifacts worthy of display. The findings had been mediocre. They were not, as Eva once said, on the order of King Tut's tomb.

Pete and Auntie, who had returned to the museum to resume their research, burst into Eva's office where she and Jim had just finished morning coffee. Pete's hat sat crooked on his head, and his overall strap hung off his shoulder. Auntie clung to his arm, her face the color of a ripe cherry.

"What is it?" Eva asked. "Is something wrong?"

Pete threw his hat on the floor. "It's that crazy man you got working here," he said.

"Who would that be?" Eva asked, looking over at Jim.

"Hey," Jim said, standing.

Pete stuck his hat back on. "No, no, I'm talking about Stufflebaum. It ain't right, I tell you."

"What's he done now?" Eva asked.

"He's put a password on the computer. I can't even get on the Churchill site."

"And that ain't all," Auntie whispered, cupping her hand over her mouth.

Eva lifted her brows. "There's more?"

Auntie looked at them through her fingers. "There's a stuffed dog back there with his hind leg up like he's fixing to piddle," she said.

"And right on my Churchill material," Pete said.

Eva glanced over at Jim. "A stuffed dog?"

Jim rolled his eyes. "Old Man Milton's dog. Stufflebaum plugged the bullet hole in his head with a wine cork."

"My god, Jim, Milton's dog is in the genealogy library?"

"It would seem so."

"Pete, I'll take care of this. Don't worry about a thing," she said. "You go back, and I'll be there in a minute."

After they'd left, Eva collapsed in her chair. "It's like living in an insane asylum, Jim."

"Are you sure Stufflebaum is the only handyman available?"

Eva dropped her hand onto her forehead. "There's no one half as capable. This place would come to a stop without him. Anyway, what else could possibly go wrong?"

———————

That afternoon the wind commenced to blow and did not stop for nearly a week. The windows rattled in their moorings, and the dust penetrated every crack and cranny of the museum. The curtains lifted and fell, and the stovepipe on the soddy display howled like the whistle on a steam locomotive.

When it finally quit, a layer of dust had settled over the entire museum. They all stopped to help Eva clean the place up. Today she wore jeans, and her hair had been secured with a red bandana. Her denim shirttail was knotted under her breasts, exposing her trim midriff. Aware that Jim was staring as she dusted, she smiled at him.

Stufflebaum allowed that the dust gave a certain quality to the artifacts—a patina, he called it. Left untouched, it might stimulate a new trend in exhibition science. Eva suggested he spend more time cleaning and less time woolgathering.

That same night, Jim, exhausted from cleaning, slept so soundly that his leg went dead. When he got up in the night to use the bathroom, he pitched forward and cracked his head on Stufflebaum's workbench. In the morning, neither Eva nor Stufflebaum believed his story and accused him of being down at the pool hall fighting again.

Having been relieved of cleaning duty, Stufflebaum came down to storage to see what Jim had been up to. "Whoa," he said, looking around. "I had no idea the size of this room."

"It's like mining the Sierra Madres with a knitting needle," Jim said.

"You still interested in making that trip upriver?" he asked.

"Sure. When?"

"When you take the notion. Let me know. Well, I better get back. I'm mounting a sheep today, if I can get it to stand still," he said, grinning.

———

Jim checked his watch—two hours until closing time. So for the next hour he dug through three orange crates of telephone insulators, a cigar box of sewing thimbles, and a garbage bag stuffed with table linens. At the bottom of the bag he found a 1932 license plate and the jawbone of a cow.

When a knock came at the door, he jumped. But before he could get there to open it, Sheriff Nabson stepped in, his face bloated and red.

"Hunt, you in here?"

Jim stepped out. "We've already been served subpoenas, Sheriff."

Nabson walked back to where Jim stood. "Still digging through Earl's shit, are you, Hunt?"

Jim pushed a box to the side with his foot. "Is there something you need, Sheriff?"

Nabson took a pack of cigarettes out of his pocket and pulled one free with his lips.

"There's no smoking in the museum," Jim said.

Nabson's jaw tightened, and he worked the cigarette back into the pack.

"I've got a warrant for the arrest of Old Man Milton. He's jumped bail, along with his two imbecile sons."

"Milton isn't here," he said.

"Dub's been selling things off around town. I figure maybe you've seen him."

"Maybe they went to Old Mexico," Jim said. "I hear a man can live on the cheap down there."

"Just make sure you stay clean of it, Hunt. Protecting a fugitive is against the law."

Nabson turned for the door. Pausing, he looked at something from under his elbow.

"Is that Earl's belongings I brought here?"

"Oh, yeah. I forgot them."

"See they're disposed of. They ain't your personal property, Hunt."

As soon as the sheriff left, Jim retrieved Earl's box from under a stack of old picture frames and set it on the workbench. A vivid image of Earl leaning over the steering wheel with the back of his head blown away rushed back. He could still smell the mud and motor oil swirling about in the drowned car.

He laid the items one by one on the workbench: a pair of muddy overalls, suspenders, a shirt still caked with blood, shoes, socks, boxer shorts with a hole in them, a pair of glasses with one of the lenses cracked. In addition, he found a plastic penholder from The Westerner Cafe with two ink pens and a tire-pressure gauge in it.

About to put them back, he spotted something in the corner of the box. It looked like an ear of maize made of metal, green and tarnished like copper.

He turned on the workbench light and held it under the magnifying glass. Though oxidized and difficult to read, he could see writing on the back.

After cleaning it with carbonate of soda and a toothbrush, he looked again. A few of the symbols were just visible, enough to begin a search at least. He flipped open a reference book and soon lost track of time.

———————

"Jim, do you know what time it is?" Eva said from the doorway.

"Come here and take a look at this piece."

Eva examined the piece under the magnifying glass. "Where did you get this?" she asked.

"In Earl's belongings."

She leaned forward to look again. Her hair brushed his face, and he could smell her perfume.

"But what is it?"

Jim shook his head. "It's an amulet of some sort, and there's writing on the back."

"Maybe it's Spanish, like the chain mail?"

"Except it isn't Spanish."

Eva pushed her hair back and looked up at him. "What is it?"

"I thought I had seen it before in my studies, and I found it in here. It's Incan."

"Incan? What does it say?"

"Children of the Sun. That's how they referred to themselves."

Eva studied the piece again. "But why did Earl have it?"

"And why didn't he tell us?" he said.

Eva pinched her lip between her teeth. "Maybe he didn't want anyone to know. Maybe that's why he shut down the site so that no one would know he'd discovered something."

Jim put Earl's belongings back in the box. He turned to her. "But what if someone did know, Eva? What then?"

35

Jim walked to the window and turned the amulet in the light. "And where could Earl have gotten this?"

"I guess he took that little secret to the grave," she said.

Jim turned. "What if I told you I know how to get into Milton's property?"

"I would say you were crazy, unless you propose to walk in from the west. Of course it's a twenty-mile trek through snake-infested canyons. The last time we went into Milton's we wound up in the river with a dead man."

"Stufflebaum has been slipping in there to hunt critters. That's how he found Milton's old dog."

"But how?"

"The Overton bridge."

"Not without a boat," she said. "And how did he come back upstream? The current is powerful up there."

"Stufflebaum says that the river has shifted enough that he can hike in from the Overton bridge."

"Forget it, Jim," she said, looking at her watch. "Come on, it's closing time."

"He said he'd take me in."

"Look, Buster, don't think I'm going to wait around while you get yourself killed."

"I could slip in there after dark, take a look, and come back the next night. No one would ever know. Maybe Earl left some clues."

"Then I'm coming with you."

"But there would be no one to keep the museum open. It would raise suspicion."

That afternoon Eva relented after Jim promised that he would stay no longer than necessary. Even so, when he left to find Stufflebaum, she held him for several moments before turning back to her work.

He found Stufflebaum patching holes in the guttering over the outside doors. His hat had blown off and lay among the marigolds.

Stufflebaum looked down the ladder and said, "Meet me at the shop in a couple of hours. By the time we get to Overton, it ought be dark enough to go in."

"Are we taking *your* truck?"

"You buying the gas?"

"Looks that way."

"My truck. Hand me my hat. It's a good long hike, and you'll need supplies. Don't pack nothing you ain't willing to carry in and out."

"Got it."

"And we ain't likely to get back in time for work in the morning."

"It's taken care of," Jim said.

Jim packed up what he could find—a rock pick, a flashlight, a package of beef jerky he found in the fridge. He didn't get back to the shop until closing time. Once, he thought to stop by the office for a goodbye but then decided better of it. Eva had been unhappy about his going, and he didn't want to face that again.

Stufflebaum sat on the tailgate of his truck, waiting.

"I'm set," Jim said. He climbed in, slamming the door three times, only to have the glove compartment flop open and spill its contents onto the floor.

"Been meaning to clean it out anyway," Stufflebaum said, pumping the gas pedal and cranking over the engine.

Jim looked back at the museum as they drove off and could see the office light on.

Stufflebaum hooked his arm out the window and adjusted his mirror. As they pulled out on the highway, the sky darkened in the west, an ominous sign, and the smell of moisture rode in on the wind. They didn't speak until they passed the cemetery.

"Aren't you going to ask?" Jim said.

Stufflebaum pulled at his moustache. "All right. What's this all about, you needing to go to Milton's place?"

"An artifact I found in Earl's belongings. "

"Now, that makes sense, don't it?" Stufflebaum said.

Jim watched the clouds thicken on the horizon. A few drops of rain gathered on the windshield and then raced upwards.

"He had an amulet in his things, a talisman of some sort."

"Maybe them Indians had a visitor," Stufflebaum said.

Jim rolled up his window partway. "I think it might be Incan but then it's a long walk from Peru to Milton's canyon."

"And you think the answer is at the Milton place?"

Jim shrugged. "I think that's where I have to start."

The mausoleum came into sight. Spring foliage dappled the hillside, and the pinks and oranges of sunset danced in the crypt's marble facade. The evening air hung thick with humidity and the scent of roses.

A little farther on, Kingston's mansion emerged in all its grandeur, its windows momentarily aflame in the twilight. He could see Keeper's all-terrain parked in the drive, though there were no lights in the mansion or signs of life.

Soon clouds drifted over the last of the sunset, and a mist settled into the valley. Jim slipped on his jacket. Neither he nor Stufflebaum spoke as they motored north. Their lights were but dots, like fireflies in the darkness on the empty highway.

Stufflebaum pulled off the road at the Overton bridge and shut down. They waited for their eyes to adjust. The cab smelled of heat and gasoline, and the engine creaked under the hood.

Stufflebaum slid out and took a leak on the back tire before poking his head back in.

"Stay put. I'm going to lower the fence. You see anything, give me a whistle. If anyone asks, we got a heat-up and are letting her cool down. Got it?"

"Got it," Jim said.

When finished, Stufflebaum slid back in. "We'll park under the bridge. They'll think we are fishing mudcats upriver."

Jim held onto the dash as they bumped through the darkness. When at last they had parked under the bridge, he leaned back and took a deep breath.

"Now what?" he asked.

"From here we walk along the river," Stufflebaum said. "It's slow without a light. Once we get around the bend, we can use our flashlights, at least for a while."

Jim could smell the creosote pilings of the bridge and hear the whisper of the river as it slid along in the darkness. The mist had deepened into a drizzle.

At the cliffs, they knelt at the river's edge to gauge its expanse.

"Should be okay," Stufflebaum said. "But it don't take much of a rain to close off the passage."

"And what happens if it *really* rains?" Jim asked.

"For one thing my pickup would wind up in New Orleans."

Stufflebaum put on his jacket and turned up the collar. "Stay up close. You fall in the river, I can't swim."

"Some scout you turned out to be."

Stufflebaum struck out at a fast clip with Jim close behind. The night darkened, and the water rushed at their side. Soon rain fell, dampening their clothes and turning the path to grease. The smell of mud and fish drifted in from the river.

Stufflebaum stopped, and Jim fell in at his side, catching his breath.

"It's just ahead," Stufflebaum said. "Up there where the river sweeps against the cliff."

Jim stared into the blackness. "How much room is there between the cliff and the river?"

"Depends."

"Depends on what?"

"How high the water is."

"How much room is there normally?"

"Depends."

"Damn it, Stufflebaum."

Jim considered killing Stufflebaum, setting him adrift in the river, but then how would he ever get back?

"Somewheres between a foot or two of room. She runs deep and swift through there. You go in the drink, don't be hollering because I ain't jumping in the river for no archeologist."

"And what if you fall in?"

"I'm the only scout you got, Hunt. I figure you'll take good care of me."

Soon the path narrowed, and the cliff crowded in at their shoulders. At times no more than a few inches stood between them and the river, the water sloshing over the tops of their shoes.

Jim pressed against the coolness of the rock and prayed that Stufflebaum knew how the hell to get through. He could hear the murmur of the river's current and feel its force against his feet.

Stufflebaum stopped. "The water's a little high here," he said. "We might have to wade through. What do you want to do?"

Jim's pulse quickened at the thought of stepping into the river at night.

"You're the scout," he said.

"It ain't that much farther. Hand me your things."

"You sure?"

"Yeah," he said. "I figure to salvage something if you don't make it."

When Jim stepped in, the water rose up, and the current tugged at his legs. He thought of Earl, of his body swollen and bloated in the river.

When at last they were past the cliff and onto high ground, Stufflebaum clicked on his flashlight.

"It's a clear run from here," he said. "We'll soon enough be there."

As they approached, Stufflebaum shut off his light and motioned for Jim to come forward.

"We're coming up behind Kingston's now," he said. "Where is it you want to go?"

"The canyon and on up to the spring cave. We'll get a good look around come morning."

"Better not use the light from here. Mitch Keeper can take that all-terrain about anywhere he wants, and he can be an unwelcome sight."

As they traversed the bog and moved up the hill, the drizzle deepened. When they moved into the canyon, Jim thought he heard footsteps, whispers from high up on the canyon wall, and his scalp tightened. He glanced over his shoulder, but the whispers had ceased.

Stufflebaum turned. "What's the matter?"

"Thought I heard something."

"Like?"

Jim cleared his throat. "Nothing," he said. "Let's go on before I change my mind."

Shortly, they took shelter inside the cave. Jim remembered it as being smaller and the floor less covered with rubble. The spring now barely trickled, the air smelled dank, and the walls seeped with moisture. Under their lights, glassy-eyed crickets scrambled into the cracks.

"Maybe we should sleep outside," Jim said.

"It ain't raining in here," Stufflebaum said.

"A fire would be nice," Jim said, shivering.

"So would a big-breasted woman, though it ain't likely on this night."

"You're an inspiration, Stufflebaum."

"You sleep over there, and I'll sleep here by the entrance."

"Why can't I sleep there?"

"Go ahead, but I hope no cougar decides to make hisself at home."

"On second thought, I like it over here."

"You get up in the night, don't step on my head. I got a thing about that," Stufflebaum said.

Jim chewed on a piece of jerky that tasted as rank as the cave smelled. He drew his legs up against the chill.

"The answer's got to be here somewhere," he said.

Stufflebaum groaned. "What?"

"The answer. It's got to be here somewhere."

"Go to sleep, Hunt. We got all day tomorrow for searching out answers."

Sometime in the morning hours, Jim awoke. His bones ached from sleeping in the rocks, and he needed to go to the bathroom. Stufflebaum had blocked the entrance during the night. Jim repressed the urge and tried to go back to sleep, but the first light of dawn soon hit his eyes.

He listened for life. The world waited, as still and silent as the grave.

And then from somewhere deep in his bones, he felt a resonance, a tremble so distant and measured that at first he doubted its existence. He lay his head against the rock floor, and felt it again, ebbing and flowing, at times fading away altogether.

The morning sun broke over the horizon, and a column of light shot into the cave. The sun rays lit every crack and cranny. Jim studied the structure of the cave, the stones being jagged and ill-formed, having lacked the effects of erosion. He figured that at some point the whole thing had collapsed and narrowed.

Suddenly, he sat up, his heart pounding.

"Stufflebaum, wake up."

Stufflebaum opened an eye. "What is it?"

"I can hear something behind those rocks," he said.

Stufflebaum shook his head. "What?"

"I don't know what."

Stufflebaum sat up and pulled on his boots. He combed back his hair with his fingers.

"It ain't the first time you've heard things, you know, Hunt."

"It's more like a feel," Jim said.

"I feel hungry myself."

"Come on, Stufflebaum. There's something behind that slide, and we've got to find out what."

They carried rock from the cave as the sun climbed into the morning sky. Stufflebaum searched out a limb from the canyon to lever the final boulder loose.

"Stand aside," he said.

He pushed, and the stone released, teetering in its opening before falling to the floor with a thud. The sound of rushing water filled the cave.

"I'll be danged," Stufflebaum said. "Listen to that."

"Give me your flashlight," Jim said. "I'm going to take a look."

"Be careful. It might not be stable, you know."

Jim slipped his arms through the opening and worked in his shoulders. But once in, he had little room to maneuver. He clicked on his light and panned the area. Sometime in the past the crown had given way and mostly filled the space with rubble.

"What is it?" Stufflebaum called.

"I can't tell for certain."

"Can you get in?"

"It's collapsed."

He'd started to click off his light when he spotted two pieces of stone lying just within reach. They were rectangular and uniform in shape. He brushed them free of dirt. They'd been worked by someone's hand.

"You okay in there?" Stufflebaum called.

Jim pushed the stones through the opening. "Take these," he said. "I'm coming out."

They carried the tablets to the door of the cave for more light. Stufflebaum knelt at his side.

"What are they?" he asked.

"A marker of some sort, I think. It's broken in half." Laying the pieces end to end in the sunlight, he scraped away the grime with his pocketknife. "There's an inscription."

"What does it say?"

Jim looked up at Stufflebaum. "General Francisco Vasquez de Coronado," he said.

So, he reflected, the general had defied oblivion by inscribing his fleeting presence in stone. And Jim knew that, nearby to the west, Friar Padilla had carved his initials on a rock after separating from Coronado.

36

Coronado had turned in his quest for gold, but Friar Padilla forged ahead in his very different quest. Following him faithfully to the north were his longtime associates, Sebastian and Lucas. Under his tutelage, they had trained as *donados*, lay persons permitted particular duties within the church. Nowhere had this been more useful than in administering the Last Rites for Indians, whose rituals in death were less stringent than those for Spaniards.

Sebastian had requested to perform these rites. Padilla agreed, inasmuch as his own duties, since staying behind to save the multitude of lost souls, had become increasingly pressing. Though Sebastian's qualifications in matters of the church were unquestioned by the Indians, they—being newly catechized—often dispatched their dead with pagan ceremony after Sebastian had departed.

A zealot and much committed to the holy church, Sebastian would then return and administer the rites yet again, once climbing into a burial scaffold to replace an elk's tooth necklace with a crucifix. When asked by Lucas if such a deed had not come too late for the salvation of the Indian's soul, he bristled, saying that the administration of divine law could never come too late.

Friar Padilla loved both these servants of God but knew them to be of little assistance in the wilderness. Neither one hunted nor built a fire of consequence. The conquistadors, who often mocked their ineptness, said that without guides, a *donado* could find neither butt nor bed.

On the other hand, Padilla found the Portuguese, a gardener of great skill and a man apt at practical matters, to be most useful when making right what friars could not, though their prayers winged to heaven.

Padilla, now traveling in an opposing direction of Coronado, counted each day passed as two days removed from the king's protection, and soon they were much alone in the wilderness, save for Isopete's guides, in whom Padilla had little faith. At night Padilla often lay awake to grieve, for in his heart he knew that they would never see home again.

Though elk and buffalo at times were taken, not much could be carried on foot. Finding waste to his disliking, Padilla would have the meat smoked, buried, and marked with a wooden cross for those who might follow. It was, he said, the dividing of the loaves in God's way.

By the third week of travel, no game could be found, and the guides had not been seen for many days, which caused the men great distress. Desperate for food, Padilla ordered a mule dispatched, followed by yet others as they trudged northward over the prairie.

One day the Portuguese, having stopped to rest his feet, spotted a rabbit tied in the limbs of a tree. Though the hawks had gotten there before them, leaving little but head and feet, the men's spirits were much uplifted, because the guides yet marked the way.

————

The sun rose on a hot day, and a rock outcrop could be seen on the horizon, a singular formation high as a ship mast. Behind it, a storm darkened, and lightning cracked from out of the blackness. A cold wind soon advanced toward them, and dust spiraled into the sky.

"We shall camp at the rock and take shelter from the storm," Padilla said.

"Perhaps our guides have arrived before us, and there will be food," Sebastian said. "My hunger can no longer be driven from my mind."

But to their disappointment, no food had been left. Not easily discouraged, the Portuguese gathered buffalo chips that he found in quantity. Having built a hot fire on the leeward side of the rock, they gathered about it to warm themselves against the raging storm.

The morning brought with it clear skies. Robins stretched worms from the soil. Blue jays clashed in the tree tops, and the men were much encouraged.

Friar Padilla climbed to the summit of the rock, from where he could see the river as it swept eastward. On the far bank, rocks jutted over the water, and trees greened with the first buds of spring.

This sight, like a great cathedral, filled Padilla with the spirit. He gave thanks that this day and this holy place had been granted him to restore his faith.

He climbed to where the stone opened as if a tablet, and with a hand strong from war and the hardness of the trail, he carved a cross and etched in his initials, F.J.P. When others stood here hence, they would know that in this place Friar Juan Padilla had touched the hand of God.

———————

Soon, the gentleness of spring gave way to the heat of summer. The buzzards circled above them, sentinels of death, which was smelled on the wind. They hovered in the quivering heat, suspended as spirits waiting for the first faltering of life.

At night, each man, having despaired in the absence of the guides, drew to himself. Without guides to show the way, they faced the wasteland with naught but a poor friar to lead them.

Padilla, much discouraged too, rose one night in the darkness and walked to the river. There, he prayed for a miracle, not for himself—his own life being of slight consequence—but so that he might finish his mission. He prayed for a miracle so that he might give succor to the lost, that they might find the peace and sanctity of the church as he himself had done.

How long he prayed, he couldn't be certain. But when he looked up, the sky had cleared, and a full moon cast its light into the prairie.

At first he didn't see the eyes now watching from the shadows. But when he did, a coldness gathered inside him, for what must remain but the angel of death?

He closed his eyes and prayed for deliverance in that moment, repenting for the evil and violence of his life. But had he not made amends in the days allotted him? Had not his prayers been pure and more for others than for himself? If his faith could not bear him into death, then what good remained?

At first he thought his soul had ebbed away, and he dared not open his eyes, but when he did, he saw not the angel of death but a dog sidling into his arms.

Moments passed as Padilla considered the animal, which now leaned against him. Looping his arm about the dog's neck, he pulled him in close.

"I fought once for your freedom," he said. "And now you've come to see us through."

37

At night Padilla wandered alone into the prairie. There he would pray for their deliverance. Other times he would sit and watch the moon ride through the night sky. He often thought of Coronado, who would soon be facing creditors. Though Padilla suffered the wilderness in all its misery, he took comfort that he, unlike Coronado, would be spared the viceroy's wrath.

Each morning they rose to follow the dog. Friar Padilla dubbed him Moses and permitted him open range. At times Moses led out at a great distance, or lingered to sniff about, or dug holes in quest of badgers, but in the end, he tracked with skill—moving always in a single way.

On the occasions they took game, though it be meager, Padilla shared full measure with Moses, who never failed in his northerly course. Soon they all worked as one, Moses hunting the game, the Portuguese dispatching it, and Friar Padilla dispensing the shares, from which Sebastian and Lucas gladly partook.

Though Moses found organ meat to his liking, he refused the flesh of fish, having learned this from prior masters. The dog apparently found Padilla's prayers—which gave thanks for the sun, the wind, and even the smallest insects—much to his disliking. Relenting to Moses's demands, Padilla permitted the dog to forego grace, saying that, like the Indians, Moses did not require

the spiritual rigor of Spaniards. The Portuguese said that if,
God forbid, he should return in another life such as this, he
hoped to be a dog.

Each day the heat mounted, and each day the winds bore
upon them, drying their eyes and cracking their lips. Padilla,
whose modesty did not permit disrobing, would lower his shawl
from his shoulders. Lucas whispered that even the back of Moses had less fur upon it than the friar's.

One day Moses sprinted to the top of a hill, sniffed the wind,
and then lay down. Padilla approached to see what lay beyond
and fell to his knees in thanksgiving. The others, having witnessed this, ran to join him. Below them, grass huts bloomed
like wild daisies in the valley. Staked nearby were the mare and
horse Coronado had given Isopete, and at the mare's side, a colt,
black as night.

Friar Padilla took Moses into his arms and said, "With God's
blessings, you have delivered us to Quivira. Now for the work
that has been set before me."

They approached the camp, and Isopete came out to welcome
them.

"We rejoice in your presence," the friar said. "Though the way
has been grievous and never ending, we have been led by the
dog, Moses, and are now most pleased to see Isopete before us."

Isopete looked at Padilla. "You bring the spirit to shed His
blood for Isopete's people?"

"To catechize and baptize your people so they may be lifted
up by the divine hand of God and be well received into heaven."

"Isopete will give Padilla a squaw, of which there are many, to
hasten his salvation," he said.

Padilla's neck reddened. "No, no," he said. "It is not the way
of the order to bed with women."

The Portuguese stepped forward. "But Friar, I beseech you,
to refuse such an offer might bring insult."

"Is there nothing which brings shame to the Portuguese?"

"To live alone among men gives me great regret."

"It is *your* soul to lose, Portuguese."

"Yes, Friar, and to be forfeited with much sadness."

Through the heat of the summer, they lived among Isopete's people, Friar Padilla being venerated among them, for was he not Isopete's friend? Did he not give the people horses? Did he not make the sign of the cross to drive away evil spirits?

Sebastian, envious of the Portuguese, mocked his squaw, her corpulence and lack of teeth, and he warned the Portuguese of God's wrath for lying with women. The Portuguese did not take heed of Sebastian. Though he found the fires of hell most frightful, were they not preferable to the dreariness of perpetual holiness?

Lucas and Sebastian, who bedded in the same grass hut, caused much curiosity among the people, none more so than the squaws who gathered about the fire to wait for the *donados* to pass, when they lifted their skirts and snickered.

Having grown sullen over the weeks, Friar Padilla spoke now of the Guaes to the north, of how he had failed in their conversion, how he had forsaken them to Satan's hand, and how the burning of the *Requerimiento* had been his own error, from which he now suffered much.

At summer's peak, Padilla then summoned them together and told them of his plan to return to the Guaes, for in his heart he knew he had abandoned them in their hour of need.

Isopete, much distressed by this, spit upon the ground and shook his head. "The friar gives his spirit to the enemy of Isopete," he said.

Lucas and Sebastian reminded Padilla of poor Luis and Gonzales lying dead in the canyon with their arms and legs crushed.

"The Guaes will surely slay us," Lucas said. "And what of the lost souls in the camp of Isopete? Are they to be left behind?"

But the friar listened not. "My work is with the Guaes," he said. "I leave in the morrow though no man follow me."

At sunrise the friar stood at the edge of camp, Lucas and Sebastian at his side. The morning fell silent, as no one came from the huts to bid them farewell—not Isopete, not the Portuguese, nor any of the people.

They had not gone a league when Moses, in his manner, fell alongside them. Padilla knelt and drew him near as he so often did.

Soon they turned to the river, as Coronado also had turned before them, and for three days they walked northward to the Guaes. On the fourth day, the smoke from the Guaes' camp could be seen from the west of the great canyon.

"There is much danger among the Guaes," Lucas said, looking at the smoke that curled skyward. "And I have only begun my duties as a *donado*."

Padilla pulled Moses down beside them so that he would not range out and alert the camp dogs.

"Tonight we will bed in the canyon, where there is shelter in the cave and sweet water to drink. Tomorrow, when the sun rises, I will enter the camp of the Guaes."

"Have you forgotten the fate of Luis and Gonzales, Friar?" Sebastian asked.

"The Indians were angered because of the one killed by Coronado. I am but a simple friar called by God. I will go in peace, and they will embrace me."

"I fear for your life," Sebastian said. "To be left alone on the prairie with Lucas is more than I can bear, for he cannot kill a rabbit or make a fire."

"Come now. I charge you to seek courage from your Maker," Padilla said. "We must find the cave before darkness falls."

Though the trek to the cave had not changed as Padilla remembered it, the tablet with Coronado's proclamation had been broken and discarded.

Gathering the pieces into his arms, Padilla carried them into the cave, where he found a great slide had fallen. Covering the marker with rocks, he said, "Coronado has claimed this spring and so shall it be. None shall dishonor this marker."

"Nor find it in this place," Lucas said.

"Remember these waters, Lucas, for they are holy," the friar said.

Lucas turned up the palms of his hands. "Even with God's eyes, I should never find them again, Friar."

So as night fell, they huddled in the darkness of the cave, the smell of smoke from the Guaes' campfires drifting in on the fog.

Padilla said prayers and then divided the food among them. They curled upon the floor to wait for daybreak.

Columns of light shot through the morning mist and into the cave, awakening the men. Shivering, they joined the friar in morning prayers. With little food, they drank heavily from the spring to fill their stomachs.

"It is a thin soup," Lucas said, rubbing the chill from his arms.

"But then your day may be short," Sebastian said. "And God's bounty will not be wasted."

"Do not four men conquer the Guaes at daybreak?" Lucas asked.

Friar Padilla's eyes flashed. "I would stripe your legs with a rod for impertinence, had I time," he said.

Lucas lowered his head. "Sometimes God stands a league from my fears," he said.

"I am sorry, Lucas, for an old soldier's temper is not easily quieted."

Padilla looked down at what awaited them in the canyon. The sun fell warm on his face. By noon even the lizards would scurry for shade.

"We shall go to the canyon's end. There, you and Sebastian are to wait hidden in the rocks. I will go to the Guaes and tell them of our mission."

Lucas glanced over at Sebastian. "And if you should not be well received?" he asked.

"Have you no respect?" Sebastian said.

Padilla held up his hand. His beard had grown long and white and now reached almost to his waist.

"If so, then take your leave, Lucas, and return to Coronado."

"But even now we are lost, Friar," Lucas said.

"Follow the river to Isopete and tell him that horses will be returned to him upon your safe delivery to Coronado."

————————

Finding a suitable path, they made their way down the canyon. Moses, who had taken the lead, waited in the shade of the canyon wall for the men to follow. The cliffs towered up about them and shut away the breeze. Their voices echoed back as ghosts from the past. Each man remembered that day the Guaes had driven them into retreat, and now like Daniel into the den, they had returned.

As the egress came into view, a hill, capped with stone and barren of trees, rose up in front of them. A fracture rendered its summit, and the land about was sunken and disturbed and absent of life.

"Lucas and Sebastian, secrete yourselves in these rocks. I shall go to the summit to reconnoiter the route to the Guaes camp. If I am not returned by the noon sun, follow my instructions as I have ordered."

"And what of Moses?" Sebastian asked.

"Keep him with you, for no harm is to come to Moses. He has been our guiding star."

Sebastian and Lucas then hid in the rocks. Though Moses struggled to follow Padilla, they held him close and would not let him go. Near the summit, Padilla glanced back before commencing his climb.

As Padilla reached the breach, he knelt to peer into its depths. Suddenly, he rose up. "Coronado, Coronado," he called out. "Where are you now?" He trembled as Guaes warriors surrounded him with bows drawn. At first a single arrow pierced his chest and then many bristled from his body. Once, Padilla lifted his arms in prayer but then collapsed and did not move again.

The Guaes rejoiced as they dragged Friar Padilla's body into the breach, and through the heat; they covered him with many rocks. And when the breach had been filled, when there could be no more, the warriors fell away. Heat quivered up from the rocks of Padilla's tomb, and the day fell silent once more. On the summit, Moses lay curled by his master's tomb.

Lucas and Sebastian, fearing for their lives, stayed hidden in the rocks until darkness. As the moon rose, they could hear the Guaes' drums beat and see their fires licking the sky. Moses rejoined them, but soon stole away into the night. Finally, Lucas and Sebastian made their way back toward the river and the cave.

38

L ike Neanderthals, Jim and Stufflebaum sat hunched over
their monumental find at the mouth of the cave.
Stufflebaum scratched at his head. "But what does it
mean?"

Jim picked up one of the tablets and turned it in his hands.

"That Coronado must have been here."

"Is that possible?"

"Well, Coronado searched for the seven cities of gold here in
North America."

"Did he find them?"

"He found mud pueblos and a load of trouble."

"Maybe he made a little side trip and left his Kilroy here just
for the hell of it. Men been scratching their names in rocks for a
good long while when you think about it."

Jim looked down into the canyon. The morning mist had
lifted, and heat quivered up from the rocks.

"Earl's amulet is Incan. This is Spanish. It doesn't make
sense." He brushed the dirt from his knees. "But a lot can change
over time, over an eternity."

"I can't think that far off," Stufflebaum said.

"Eternity extends equally into the past and into the future,
you know."

Stufflebaum searched a piece of jerky out of his pocket and tore off a bite. "You got to stop," he said, chewing. "My head's going to explode."

Jim wrapped the tablets in his jacket and tucked them inside the cave.

"We've a few hours left before we go back. I want to search the canyon. Keep your eyes open for anything out of the usual."

Stufflebaum worked off another bite of jerky and grinned. "If you ask me, you're about as unusual as it gets, Hunt."

The search turned up nothing, though they walked the canyon from end to end. The sun lowered behind the canyon wall, and they headed back to the cave. They were nearly there when Stufflebaum motioned for him to come.

"Those are footprints," he said, "and they're fresh. Someone besides us has been up here."

Jim knelt and examined the prints. "Maybe they're Earl's."

"Maybe I can't tell eternity from backwards, but I know a *recent* track when I see it. Those prints are a damn sight fresher than Earl is. More than one person's been tromping through here, too. Far as I recall, Earl didn't have that many friends."

Jim glanced over at him. "How fresh?"

"I ain't *that* good," he said. "Come on. The sun will be down by the time we get packed."

Jim carried one tablet and Stufflebaum the other. As they passed behind Kingston's estate, car headlights swept the horizon and then disappeared. After that, Stufflebaum refused to use the flashlights, which delayed their arrival at the river.

To make matters worse, the water had risen even higher, and the path had been submerged. They picked their way through slowly, because a misstep could have sent them plunging to the bottom of the river.

Dawn broke just as they made it back to the Overton bridge. Jim, exhausted, scooted down against one of the piers to rest

while Stufflebaum loaded their belongings. A car passed overhead, and the vibration traveled down the piling, settling between his shoulder blades.

"We best be going," Stufflebaum said. "Carrying that rock
halfway across the country's given me a powerful appetite."

Jim groaned as he lifted himself up and leaned against the
pile. Creosote oozed from it like black teardrops, and splinters
from pole-climbing spurs prickled down its length. "How long's
this bridge been here?" he asked.

"A good long while," Stufflebaum said, scraping the mud
off his boots on the pickup bumper. "The WPA first figured
to build on Milton's but could find no bedrock. They had to
settle for that low-water pass, which ain't worth spit, as you
well know. They still needed a bridge, so they built it here
instead."

Jim looked out on the river. At each piling the current split
like the tail feathers of a bird. The water gurgled and danced in
the morning sun as it rejoined the main stream.

Jim said nothing as they pulled out on the highway. He
rolled down his window and surfed the wind with his hand.
His body ached, and his feet had turned to ice. But it had been
worth the effort. In the back of Stufflebaum's truck lay a couple of stones that could be a major contribution to archeological history.

"You say there's no bedrock on Milton?" he asked.

Preoccupied, Stufflebaum turned off his lights and checked
his gas gauge.

He pushed back his hat and said, "You going to fill my
tank?"

"First chance. But how would they know?"

"Know what?"

"How would they know that there's bedrock at Overton but
not on Milton?"

"Seismograph. No bedrock. No bridge."

Jim watched a flock of ducks lift off the river and circle back.
"Where would that kind of information be found?"

Stufflebaum shrugged. "Most likely in the county engineer's
office at the courthouse."

Jim clapped his hands together. "Of course. You are one smart taxidermist, Stufflebaum. Pull over there. I'm going to fill this wreck up."

"And a doughnut?"

"A doughnut, too."

"Make it a dozen?"

"All right, a dozen it is, you thief."

39

Jim searched for the phone. "Hello," he said, rubbing the sleep from his face as Eva came on.

"Why didn't you call? Are you okay?"

"We got back late, and I didn't want to wake you."

"Wake me?" she said. "I spent half the night thinking about us. So I took a shower. It didn't help because I got to thinking about how it would be in the shower—about soapy, slick bodies, about what it's really like."

"What's it really like?" he asked, his voice cracking.

"Like returning to the sea to spawn, like doing it in the sea."

"Jesus, Eva."

"I could hear you breathing in the dark. I could hear you sleeping next to me, you bastard, and you *didn't* call?"

"I'm sorry, Eva. You'll never know *how* sorry, but I've got something exciting to show you. Can you meet me in storage?"

Jim held the tablets under the water and scrubbed the lettering with an old toothbrush. Chisel marks appeared. "Look," he said.

"And you think this could have been left by Coronado?" Eva asked, leaning over his shoulder.

"Or anyone else. The concrete evidence of his being this far north is scanty. A diary survives describing his expedition, even the prairie landscape, but that covers a lot of area when you think about it."

"It would explain the mail armor," she said. "But why would the marker be buried in a cave? Isn't the point of a marker to let people know of your existence?"

"A lot can happen," he said.

"What do you mean?"

"Rivers shift. Landslides occur. Hills become valleys."

"I suppose we will never know."

Jim traced the lettering with his finger and checked his watch.

"Go to the courthouse with me," he said.

"Jim, the courthouse? Really? But Stufflebaum would have to open up."

"We could be back by noon."

"I don't know what to say," she said, running her hand through her hair.

He pulled her to him, dropping his hands about her waist. "I need to talk to the county engineer. This could be important, Eva."

"Oh," she said, glancing down. "I suppose I could get away, but you'll have to take responsibility for Stufflebaum."

"No problem," he said.

———————

The county engineer, a pencil stuck behind his ear and his shirt button one hole off, slid his glasses down on his nose and peered at Jim and Eva. On one side of his heavy desk, a water bottle sat on a stack of papers, and next to it perched a computer that hummed with impending old age.

"Yes, we do seismograph tests before building a bridge," he said.

Jim leaned forward. "In the Lyons area, for example?"

The engineer lifted his brows. "In any area, for example. Say, are you with the inspector's office or something?"

"No, no," Jim said. "This is Eva Manor, director of the Celf Museum. I'm Jim Hunt, her assistant. We are interested in conducting an archeological dig and need to be certain of the geological structure of the area before we start."

"And what area would that be?"

"Two areas actually, the Milton low-water pass and the Overton bridge."

"That goes clear back to the WPA. If we have the records, they would be in those file drawers. Most of those haven't been put on the computer."

"Could we have a look?" Jim asked.

The engineer took his pencil from behind his ear. The eraser had been crimped into a black smudge.

"Well, now, I don't know. I can't remember anyone but engineers and such asking before."

"I should think it a matter of public record," Jim said.

"Technically, I suppose it is. I guess it wouldn't hurt. Let me see if I can find them."

"We really appreciate this," Jim said.

They waited as the engineer worked his way through a file at the back.

"Here we go," he said, taking his chair. "You understand that the documents can't leave the office?"

Jim glanced over at Eva. "The problem is that we don't know how to read them anyway."

"I see. Well, what is it you are wanting to know?"

"If there are any surprises awaiting us. Having to move a site after it's committed costs money. It's a government thing. You know how the government is about paperwork?"

"Oh, hell yes," he said, taking the records from the folder. "I been putting up with those bastards for twenty-five years. Excuse my French, Miss."

Eva smiled. "Oh, we know bureaucracies."

The engineer unrolled the map and set his stapler on one end, his pocketknife on the other. Showing Jim the map, he said, "Take the Overton bridge for instance. She sits right there. You could build the Golden Gate on that bedrock. That structure sits on wooden piling, but she ain't going nowhere, I can tell you."

Jim examined the chart. Finding it incomprehensible, he turned it back around.

"And what about the Milton low-water pass?"

"Well, let's see now. That would be about here as I recall. Lots of fractures through there and a number of voids. Some of them are shallow, too. The area is just too damned unstable for bridge pilings."

"Could you elaborate on what you mean by voids?"

"Seismic reflection picks up underground spaces. Not much different than looking for oil."

"There's oil there?" Eva asked.

"Oh, hell no," he said, turning the chart around again. "See that?"

"Yes," Eva said.

"That's all halite deposit."

"Halite?" Jim asked.

"Sodium chloride, sea salt laid down in the lower Permian. She's shot through with voids."

Eva leaned over the chart, drawing her fingernail across the graph. "What's this?" she asked.

"Same thing. Just bigger, Miss. A damn sight bigger. Where she's close to the river like that, dissolution can occur. My guess is that sometime or another an underground river flowed through there. She left behind a damn big hole."

Jim's pulse ticked up. "And where is that, exactly?"

The engineer pushed his glasses up on his nose and studied the charts and then his map, marking the spot with a twist of his pencil.

"Well, sir," he said. "You know where that monastery sits just out of town?"

"Yes," Jim said.

"Then you know where that monk cemetery is?"

"That void is under the cemetery?"

"Not exactly under it. It starts at the west elevation and then trails off that way by the looks of it."

"But doesn't the river run across there?"

The engineer rolled up his map and leaned back in his chair.

"That halite deposit is a damn sight deeper than the riverbed. Fact is, in some places she's over a thousand feet below the surface." The engineer looked over his glasses. "You hadn't figured on digging a thousand feet deep, had you, son?"

"No sir," Jim said, shaking his hand. "We certainly hadn't."

40

Jim and Eva had just gotten back when Pete and Auntie knocked at the door.

Eva rolled her eyes. "They're all yours," she said to Jim. Jim motioned for them to come in.

The stitching on Pete's ball cap had loosened. A piece of the fabric hung down over his eye like a canopy, and food had dribbled on the front of Auntie's dress.

"Pete, Auntie," Jim said. "Have a seat."

Auntie's ample rear failed to fit between the arms of the chair until she molded it into place. She sighed and crossed her ankles. Pete scrunched down in the chair next to her, took out his pliers, and commenced pulling sandburs out of the cuffs of his overalls.

Jim, dreading the answer, said, "So, what can I do for you this morning?"

Pete stacked the burrs on the arm of his chair. "Well, sir, it's about Stufflebaum," he said. "Auntie and me ain't snitches, you understand, but sometimes you just have to do your duty."

"Stufflebaum has done something untoward?"

Pete dumped the burrs into the wastebasket. "It ain't that so much as him being just plain ol' annoying."

"I see," Jim said.

Eva cleared her throat and signaled for Pete to get on with it.

"Fact is, he's done it again," Auntie said, spotting the splotch on her bosom.

"Done what?" Jim asked.

Looking down her nose, she scratched at the soiled spot. "One of them felonies," she said.

"Excuse me?"

"He's been messing with the computer in the genealogy library again," Pete said.

"What has he been doing?"

"Making them obscenities," Auntie said.

Pete nodded his head in agreement.

"Stufflebaum's been making obscenities?" Jim asked.

"Sure as hell has," Pete said. "Every time I turn the computer on, there it is big as life."

From the side, Eva said, "I knew something like this would happen."

"What exactly is on the computer?" Jim asked.

"Winston Churchill."

Jim knitted his brow. "Winston Churchill is hardly an obscenity, Pete."

"Is if he's naked."

"Naked?"

"Makes my stomach pucker every time I see it," Auntie said.

"And Auntie ain't even a relative," Pete said.

"Churchill's naked on the computer?"

"Naked as a newborn," Pete said. "He's smoking a cigar and drinking brandy. And that ain't all."

Jim's heart sank. "There's more?"

"He's got the body of a woman."

"A naked woman," Auntie said, lowering her eyes.

"Oh my," Eva said.

"Maybe it's a little joke," Jim said. "You know how Stufflebaum likes to joke."

"Poking fun of a man's relatives ain't no joke," Pete said.

"No, of course not. You're right. We'll have a talk with him," Jim said. "It won't happen again."

Pete adjusted his hat. "I told Auntie you'd take care of it. Well, come on, Auntie. Time's a clicking."

After they'd gone, Jim and Eva sat for some time without speaking. Finally Eva tossed her pencil onto the desk.

"You said nothing could happen if we got back by noon."

"It's a little after noon," he said.

"So *you* can just talk to Stufflebaum this time."

Jim found Stufflebaum taking the spark plug out of the museum lawn mower. His tools were laid out in a row on the floor and a grease rag was sticking out of his back pocket. Stufflebaum took out his pocketknife and scraped at the carbon that had gathered on the plug. He held the plug up to the light.

"Why that's just a danged black lie. It ain't in my nature to be making obscenities."

"You weren't on the genealogy computer?"

"I didn't say that."

"Pete said Churchill's head had been placed on a naked woman's body."

Stufflebaum screwed in the plug, pushed the wire back on, and looked up at Jim over his shoulder.

"The hell it was?"

"You didn't do that?"

"Not that I recall."

"You didn't put photos on that computer?"

He unscrewed the filter cover, took out the filter and set it on top of the mower.

"I didn't say that."

"Then you did put photos in the computer?"

"I've been trying out that new scanner some."

Jim folded his arms across his chest. "And one of those pictures you scanned in might have been of Churchill?"

"It's possible."

"And a naked woman?"

Stufflebaum pulled at his chin. "By golly, I did scan in a woman."

"Naked?"

"No sir. I had on my overalls the whole time."

"Stufflebaum . . ."

"They must have gotten mixed together somehow. I'll be more careful in the future," he said, grinning. "Maybe read the manual."

———————

At quitting time, Eva came down to storage and found Jim staring at the amulet.

"Did you talk to Stufflebaum?" she asked.

"Yes," he said. "He swore he would never do it again."

She draped her arms over his shoulders. "He's sworn before. I have this feeling, Jim, and it's not good."

"What do you mean?"

"All this with the site, with Kingston. I think we're in over our heads. One man's dead, and another is under suspicion of murder. We've got no business trying to deal with this."

He took her hand. "No one knows we've been in there. No one knows about the amulet or the marker either. This could be a big find."

"I hope you're right, Jim, because our lives might depend on it."

"Eva, it's Friday, and there's no rush to get home, is there?"

"I suppose not."

"Would you mind driving by the monastery?"

"Jim Hunt, have you heard a word I've said? What are you up to?"

"Nothing. Really. I just want to look."

She put her hand on her waist. "Just this once, Buster, but no more."

———————

Freddie Street was deserted, and no cars sat in front of The Westerner. Jim and Eva turned onto the highway and headed north. The sun lowered, and the first evening shadows eased across the prairie.

The mausoleum came into view, and Jim directed Eva onto a dirt road that ended abruptly at an old farm site. Both the house and barn had been moved off, leaving little behind but a crumbling foundation and a storm cellar.

They walked to a grove of cottonwoods across from the cemetery. From there they had a clear view of the road leading up to the mausoleum.

Eva leaned into him. "What do you think you'll find out here, Jim?"

"Brother Bill said that each night Mitch Keeper unlocks the mausoleum and then relocks it at sunrise."

Eva threaded her fingers into his. "Unlocks it for what?"

"So that Kingston can visit his wife's crypt, a wife he never had."

The sun languished on the horizon, and the clouds churned with the reds and golds of dusk. The evening grew chill as they waited. Jim could see the lights in the monastery kitchen, and the silhouette of Kingston's mansion against the horizon.

"I'm freezing, Jim."

He pulled her into his arms. "We won't be long."

No sooner had he spoken when Mitch Keeper's all-terrain pulled up to the cemetery. He opened the front gate, swinging it back, and then drove up to the mausoleum. He unlocked the iron doors to the vault, walked back to his vehicle and stood at the door for a moment. The thump of his radio rose in the stillness.

"I think he's looking at us," Eva said, gripping Jim's hand.

"There's no way he can see us in all these trees," Jim whispered.

Keeper cleared his throat, got back in, and drove down the hill. At the front gate, he backed in behind some bushes and shut off his lights.

Eva, trembling with cold, said, "That's creepy. Let's get out of here."

"Not just yet."

The sun lowered below the horizon, and the first evening stars popped into the sky.

Eva looked at her watch. "We could be here all night."

"I don't think so," he said. "Look."

Headlights pulling down Kingston's driveway moved slowly. They went past the monastery, turned into the cemetery, and stopped at the mausoleum. The lights went out.

"Kingston?" Eva asked.

"Got to be."

"But what can he be doing?"

"And why at night?"

An hour passed, and then two, before the headlights flicked on again. Jim and Eva, both half asleep, jumped.

"It's Kingston," Eva said. "He's leaving."

Kingston's car moved down the hill. As it rounded the curve, its lights illuminated the rows of crosses. When the car stopped at the gate, Jim and Eva could hear voices and then Kingston drove away. Jim and Eva waited in the darkness for Keeper to leave. He never did.

———————

At two in the morning, they finally pulled into the shop. They had waited hours for Keeper to leave, finally resorting to driving back to the highway with their lights out so as not to be detected. Jim gave directions with the window down as they negotiated their way through the darkness.

Eva shut the motor off, and Jim said, "I have an idea. I think I know how to get into that mausoleum."

"Look, Jimbo, I've had about all the ideas I can stand for one night."

"From the time Kingston left, Keeper remained at his post by the front gate. Right?"

"Right."

"That would give us time to get into the mausoleum for a look before he comes back to lock things up."

Eva stared at him through the darkness. He could see her shaking her head.

"Seeing as how Keeper's parked at the gate, all we have to do is let a helicopter drop us in and then pick us up, right?"

"It's easier than that, Kiddo. All we have to do is go on a little spiritual retreat."

41

Jim put new batteries in the flashlight while he waited for Eva.

When she arrived, he opened the car door and said, "You didn't forget your gloves, did you?"

Eva rolled her eyes. "Oh, of course not. I've been looking forward all morning to hoeing someone else's garden."

"Brother Bill says work is good for the soul," he said, getting in.

Eva pulled out. "Does he also say it provides him free labor?"

"I don't remember that."

"Jim, are you sure about this?"

"You look great," he said.

"Stop blowing smoke up my skirt, Buster. I've already said I would go."

The morning sun rose as they drove through Lyons. They could see the old men gathered for their morning klatch at The Westerner.

"Stop and I'll get us a coffee," he said. "I think caffeine is against monastery rules."

"Swell," Eva said, pulling over. "What else is against the rules?"

"Well, we should have thought of that before we left."

Eva smiled. "Go get the coffee. Jim, look over there."

Nabson's patrol car had been backed into the alley. The lights were off and the windows rolled down. The flicker from a cigarette lighter went up—and then darkness.

"It's a little early to deal with Nabson," he said. "Let's get out of here."

———————

Wearing a hood, Brother Bill looked like a black vulture standing in the doorway.

"Welcome," he said. "You're as lovely as ever, Eva."

"Thank you. I'm looking forward to our retreat."

"I think you'll find it a blessing. I hope you've eaten. We have breakfast rather early around here."

"We're fine, Brother Bill," Jim said. "Exactly what is this retreat thing?"

"We have Mass each morning. You're welcome to attend, of course, but it's entirely up to you. Mostly, it's an opportunity to escape from life's pressures, to get in touch with one's self. The days have a way of stealing away our lives. Most of us never stop to live the moment."

"Great," Jim said. "Would it be possible to get rooms overlooking the cemetery? I find the view quite peaceful, actually."

"I think that could be arranged. Separate rooms are required for singles. There's no smoking and no liquor allowed. Other than that, there are very few rules. You are welcome to work in the garden but that, too, is voluntary."

Brother Bill showed them their rooms and left for the field. Eva's room was at the end of the hall, well away from his own room, which contained a small bathroom, a bunk, a wooden desk, and a straight-back chair.

But he had a clear view of the mausoleum and of the path along the back fence that led up the hill. Jim figured that Keeper, being preoccupied and a creature of habit, would never spot them from the front gate.

After lunch, he and Eva walked the grounds before joining Brother Bill and the others in the garden. The day turned warm and the job hard, but they both soon found themselves caught up in the esprit de corps of fieldwork.

That evening they had a simple dinner of fresh-caught fish, corn on the cob, and a slab of sourdough bread slathered with butter, topping the whole thing off with a pitcher of cold milk, which all shared.

After dinner, he and Eva sat in the courtyard and listened to the monks sing with their simple strong voices. The moon rose, and the crickets chirped from the cemetery.

When the lights flicked on and off in the rectory, Eva said, "That means it's time for bed. My mother used the same signal."

Jim sneaked a kiss at her door. "I'll knock on your window when it's time," he said. "Meet me outside."

He opened the curtain in the darkness of his room. The moon cast its light on the mausoleum. He took a shower, directing the hot water on the muscles in his shoulders, which had stiffened with fatigue. He lay down on the bunk to wait. Brother Bill had it right. Manual labor had its rewards, a bittersweet mingling of exhaustion and accomplishment.

When he awoke, the moon arched high over the mausoleum. "Damn it," he said, checking his watch. He'd been asleep for hours. He looked for Kingston's car, but it wasn't there. "Damn it," he said again, slipping the flashlight into his hip pocket.

He knocked on Eva's window and crouched in the shadows to wait. Within moments she joined him and knelt at his side.

"I didn't think you would ever come," she said in a whisper.

"I fell asleep."

"Jim Hunt, do you have any idea how tired I am?"

"I'm sorry."

She leaned into him, her body warm in the night air.

"Has Kingston left?"

"I don't know. I've been asleep, remember?"

"Terrific. Now what do we do?"

"He's bound to have come and gone by now. Let's take our chances."

The path to the mausoleum couldn't be seen from the front gate, but the moon, now full and bright, left them exposed as they dashed from shadow to shadow through the cemetery.

They found the mausoleum gate closed, and Jim's hopes vanished. But when he tried the bolt, it gave. Eva, her eyes lit in the moonshine, clutched his arm.

"Creepy," she said.

Jim turned on his flashlight, and they held hands as they made their way down the steps into the mausoleum. Providentially, the iron door leading into the tomb had been left ajar. He eased the door open, and the smell of dank and staleness spilled from the tomb. Two crypts lay side by side in the center, each covered with a six-inch-thick slab of marble.

Jim panned the vault with his flashlight, and a ray of light reflected from the corner, startling him. But then he recognized it as his old shaving mirror that had rolled down the steps weeks ago.

He examined the crypts. "Odd," he said. "No inscriptions."

"This one has been damaged," she said.

Jim put the light on the slab. "It has been moved."

Eva picked up an iron bar that lay on the floor next to the crypt. "Perhaps with this."

"Hold the light for me," he said. "I'm going to have a look inside."

Eva shuddered. "This is too ghoulish."

"We've got to see what's in there."

He positioned the bar under the slab of marble, inching it over, repeating the action until he could peek in.

"I wonder what the sentence is for body snatching?" Eva asked.

He shined his light into the crypt and looked up at her. "There's no sentence, because there's no body," he said.

42

"T"he crypt's full of rocks," Jim said. "But I can see a passageway through the floor of it and a ladder that's been secured at the top. Help me lever this slab over some more."

"We're going down there?"

Jim stopped to listen before answering. Silence reigned within the massive walls of the mausoleum.

"If we can move this enough to get in. Grab a hold of this bar."

Together, they scooted the slab a fraction of an inch, repeating the action again and again until they were winded.

Jim squeezed through, followed by Eva, who took a last look around before disappearing into and through the crypt.

The passageway narrowed, having been excavated through rubble. At times Jim had to raise an arm over his head to get past the rocks jutting into the opening. Eva managed with less difficulty.

At the end of the ladder, he called up to her. "Hold it. Let me check things out."

He directed the light between his feet. Below, he could see a ledge no more than a yard wide. Beyond that, the beam disappeared into the blackness of an abyss.

"Jim?" Eva called from above.

He worked his light into his pocket.

"A bit of a drop," he said. "I'm going down."

"Be careful, Jim."

He hung off the bottom rung to lessen the distance and waited for his body to stop swinging. Closing his eyes, he let go.

The moment he touched ground, he froze, fearing that he might plunge into the chasm. He clicked on his light and whistled, the ledge being even more narrow than he'd realized.

He called up to Eva to let herself down. He grabbed her legs and pulled her to safety on the ledge.

"There," he said. "Not so bad, huh?"

Eva peeked over the side and then pushed herself against the wall. "If we get out of this alive, I'm going to kill you," she said.

Jim shined his flashlight about. The beam danced and skittered as it refracted in the crystalline formations, and he could see where a breach opened into the ceiling. Swirls and bowls had been washed into the formation from ancient waters. He wet his finger and rubbed it on the wall, touching it to his tongue.

"Salt," he said. "And a lot of it. There's been water in here at some point, too, probably through that crevice. See where the eddies have eroded away the softer materials."

"Not lately, I hope."

"A few million years ago. Come on," he said, taking her hand. "These batteries are not going to last forever."

———

When they came upon a chamber at the end of the ledge, they both stopped, gasping at what lay before them. The room shimmered with treasure—golden heaps and stacks and piles that reached to the ceiling, some of it scattered about as if it had been tossed aside or discarded, some buried in salt and debris and green with corrosion. The caustic environment had tried but failed to diminish the splendor of the treasure that filled it.

Jim cleared his throat. "My god, Eva."

There were golden sun disks, hummingbirds, bells, ears of maize with silver leaves, golden turtles, spiders, masks, headdresses, and a raft carrying a king. He counted a dozen golden hawks, not to mention pumas, alpacas, and a deer the size of a small dog. Golden beakers encrusted with jewels lay everywhere. There were breastplates of gold, armlets, figurines, and a throne big enough for a child to sit in. Near the back he saw a golden cornice, probably taken from a temple.

They found jewels of every description: necklaces made of gold nuggets, pearl-encrusted ear caps, golden bracelets, strings of rock crystal and turquoise, earrings of shell, and golden deities with enormous phalluses. Buried in the debris were hundreds of stone bowls carved into the shapes of animals, dozens of bronze axes, and mace heads.

Wooden crates had been stacked by the entrance and plastic bags of packing materials, as well as hammers and nails and a length of rope coiled on the floor.

Eva reached for him, her fingers cool in his hand. She pointed to something lying on the floor at the back of the room. "Jim, is that what I think it is?"

He knelt to examine the salt-encrusted bundle.

"It's a body," he said. "It appears to have been dragged back here recently."

In the salt, the mummy's skin had dried to leather, and little remained of what had once been a man. Jim brushed away the salt and dirt and could see bits of coarse fabric. Flint points lay inside the chest cavity, and the appendages had been crushed and splintered.

"Indian?" Eva asked.

"The fabric is not, and then there's this," he said, holding up a small cross. My bet is that it has been down here a good long while, maybe for centuries.

He turned in a circle with his light. "My god, Eva, there's a fortune here in gold alone."

"Where could it have come from?"

"Look at the geometric shapes and the repetitive patterns on these artifacts. They've got to be Inca."

"Like Earl's amulet?"

"Yeah, like Earl's amulet."

"But wasn't the Incan treasure plundered hundreds of years ago?"

Jim picked up a golden sun disk and studied it.

"Have you ever heard of Atahualpa?"

"No."

"He was the emperor of the Incas, taken prisoner by Pizarro, a Spanish explorer. They killed Atahualpa, plundered his treasure, and melted the gold into bars and coins. Legend has it that the Incas hid some in the mountains of Ecuador before the Spanish could get to it. But none was ever found."

"And you think this may be Atahualpa's gold? And the gold that Coronado was searching for? But how did it end up in Kansas?"

"I know it's crazy, but maybe the Incas carried the treasure farther and farther northward because they were trying to increase the distance between themselves and the Spanish who were tailing them. Maybe the Indians found it instead, or maybe they were complicit in a plan. They had ever as much reason to hate the Spanish as did the Incas."

"And there's that stone marker with Coronado's name," she said. "He came so close to finding the gold. For five hundred years, it has just been waiting here for us," she said.

Jim shook his head. "Not for us, Eva. For Evan Kingston."

They both recognized the sound as that of someone dropping from the ladder onto the ledge. Jim motioned for Eva to hide. He cut his light and ducked behind the packing crates. In the absolute darkness, his head whirled, and he reached out for the wall to steady himself.

Then from the passageway came a flash of light, like heat lightning in a summer storm. Jim searched about for something to protect himself but could find nothing in the blackness.

The figure stepped into the chamber, and Jim knew by the wheeze of the man's lungs and the smell of him that Keeper had found them. Keeper's light swept the room, stopping on Eva, who crouched against the back wall.

"If it isn't Miss Eva Manor," Keeper said.

Jim rose to the attack, spilling the crates in the process. Keeper whirled about, entangling his foot in the coil of rope on the floor.

Jim delivered a blow across Keeper's ear. Keeper's light clattered onto the floor, and a howl filled the chamber.

Jim circled, positioning himself for the coup de grace, but he'd underestimated the speed of Keeper's recovery. Like a cougar, Keeper struck from out of the darkness and dragged Jim into his lair.

Jim, his ears ringing from Keeper's crushing hold, struggled to escape. Hauled to the edge, Jim could feel the cool and dampness rising up from the abyss. Behind him, Eva called out his name. He could see Keeper's flashlight lying on the floor next to her. She stood in the doorway of the chamber with a rope in her hands.

When she yanked, Keeper's foot slipped from under him. He stumbled forward, letting go of Jim as he attempted to recover his balance. He waved his arms in circles, staggered to the rim, and made only the smallest yelp as he plunged headfirst into the black depths of the chasm.

For several moments Jim and Eva held each other, staring into the void.

"Come on," he said. "We better get out of here while we can."

Back at the ladder, Eva took his arm. "Let me go first, Jim."

"But someone could be waiting up there."

"But who?"

"Maybe Kingston, or even the sheriff."

"Nabson?"

"You remember when we stopped for coffee, and Nabson was there. I think he's in Kingston's pocket, and he's been following us."

"And if they are there, we would both be stuck. I can negotiate that passage a lot faster than you."

"I don't know about this."

"It's the practical thing to do," she said, laying her hand against his cheek.

"You hear anything, get back down fast," he said.

Jim stood at the bottom while Eva climbed up the ladder. Her light disappeared, and all grew silent. His heart beat in his ears.

Several minutes passed as he waited, and suddenly he panicked. Should anything happen to Eva, his life would be at an end. He considered going up the ladder anyway, but if he blocked the passage, she would not be able to descend if necessary.

Then he spotted her light, and he wiped the sweat from his hands on his pant legs.

"Is it clear then?" he asked, helping her down.

Eva, trembling, locked her arms around him. "The crypt's closed," she said. "We've no way out."

43

They stood motionless in the blackness.

"You don't think we could move it?" Jim asked.

"Without the bar? Besides, only one person can get up there at a time."

"Maybe someone will come," he said.

"Inside a mausoleum?"

He turned on his light and scanned the area. "There's got to be a way."

His light fell on the fracture overhead, and he paused.

"What?" Eva asked.

"That's most likely where the water came in that carved out this cave."

"A million years ago you said."

"It came from somewhere. It has to lead to somewhere."

"We can't go in there."

"No," he said, shutting off the light. "I suppose you're right."

Several minutes passed as they sat in the stale tomb, the blackness like a shroud.

"Okay," she said.

"Okay what?"

"Okay, how do we get up there?"

"We stack up those sun disks until I can reach the channel. Once in, I'll pull you up."

"And when our lights go out?"

"Dark's dark," he said. "Down here or up there, it makes no difference."

They recovered Keeper's flashlight and carried sun disks to the ledge, stacking one upon the other until Jim could reach the rim of the channel.

He pulled himself up and in, determined to ignore the yawning gulf behind him. He could just clasp Eva's hands by lying on his stomach, and within moments, they were crawling along the ancient river canal.

At times it lowered, forcing them onto their stomachs, requiring them to worm their way along like moles in a burrow. Other times it opened into chambers big enough to stand, or twisted away in contorted loops, or dropped off in precipitous falls.

Salt stung their eyes and gathered in the cracks of their lips. They fought to breathe within the limits of the tunnel. Time ceased without the cadence and rhythm of life, but they struggled on to whatever might lie ahead.

Keeper's light failed first, and they left it behind. Jim's light too could fail at any moment.

They'd worked their way through a tight turn, when Jim lowered his head onto his arm to listen.

"Wait," he said.

"What is it, Jim?"

"Water," he said. "I hear water."

A few yards more and the channel opened onto a large chamber scoured from the salt. Jim climbed out, helping Eva onto her feet.

Rubble covered the floor and rose up the wall. Below, a stream of water entered the chamber, pooled against the rubble, and then disappeared beneath it.

"The channel's blocked," he said. "It's the end of the line."

"There's no way out?"

"The dome has collapsed and closed off the passage. It looks like the river diverted into a lower strata. I'm sorry, Eva. We should never have tried this."

Eva took his hand. "Do we go back?"

Jim turned his flashlight against the wall. The beam had dimmed to a pale yellow.

"Even if we made it, there's no way out."

He wedged the flashlight between two rocks and directed the beam onto the ceiling. He pulled Eva next to him and put his arm about her. She dropped her head against his shoulder. The light faded, and their shadows rose up the wall of the chamber as the blackness descended.

———

At first he thought it phantom light, the sort generated in the congenitally blind. But the spot did not waver, a pinpoint in the rocks.

His heart raced. "Eva," he said.

"I see it," she said.

"It must be sunrise, or we would have seen it before. I'm going to go up."

"Not without me you aren't."

He took off his belt, hitched it through a loop in his britches, and placed the tail in her hand.

"Hang on to this so we aren't separated."

They trained on the light as they inched through the blackness. The air, though scant of oxygen, had grown dense and thick with moisture. Now and again rock would loosen and tumble in a cascade to the floor below.

They pulled the last few feet to the top of the rubble, their hands bleeding. Jim pressed close to where the light seeped through. He could see nothing, but he could smell the sun and the earth.

"I'm going to dig," he said.

Eva's breath fell warm on his shoulder. "I'll help."

"Don't move. I can work faster if I know where you are."

He worked at the stones with his fingers, loosening each until it plummeted to the bottom. As the rocks gave way, both the light and their hopes grew larger.

"I'm going to try to get through," he said.

"I'm smaller. Let me."

"Not this time. We don't know what's out there. Stay close. Whoever blocked the crypt might know about this exit."

"Kingston?" she asked.

"Or his cronies."

Though a tight squeeze, he wiggled through the opening, leaving a shoe wedged in the rocks behind. But they soon worked their way through the breach and into the morning sunlight that streamed in upon them. They fell into each other's arms.

"Where are we?" Eva asked.

"It's Milton's cave," he said. "We must have passed under the river."

When Eva didn't answer, Jim turned to see Kingston standing in the entrance, his weapon leveled. Next to him stood Sheriff Nabson.

Kingston looked over at the breach and then at the rocks that had been shoved free onto the cave floor.

"Where's Keeper?" he asked.

"He took a long dive down a deep hole," Jim said.

Sheriff Nabson shook his head. "You done it this time, Hunt."

"You best hope he's dead," Kingston said. "Mitch can be altogether disagreeable about such things."

"I think Keeper's bullying days are over."

Kingston waved his gun. "Raise your hands and move on outside."

He propped his foot up on a rock, his shoe covered with dirt. "Hunt, you and your lady friend are trespassing on my property."

"It's a bit late for theatrics," Eva said. "Your little secret has been discovered."

"Indeed, but a fortune in Incan gold is not so little, Miss Manor, not to mention its value on the antiquities market."

"What gold?" Nabson said.

"How did you find it, Kingston?" Jim asked.

"By accident, actually, while conducting seismographic tests for oil. The void turned out to be quite large, too large. It piqued my interest, shall we say. I soon discovered a natural opening, though filled with surface rock. After considerable work, I found something remarkable inside."

"Why didn't you just take it, Kingston? You had Nabson here in your pocket."

"What gold are they talking about, Mr. Kingston?" Sheriff Nabson asked again.

"Unfortunately, the entrance turned out to be on monastery land. At that time the underground river made access from here impossible."

"So you built a mausoleum over the opening for your poor departed wife?" Jim said.

"Clever, wouldn't you say. This allowed me to sell off the artifacts a few at a time so as not to raise suspicion. I had every reason for frequent visits to the mausoleum to visit my wife. The monks found my dedication endearing."

"And so you struck a deal with the Richmond Institute of Antiquities?"

"I found the antiquities market to be discreet."

"But then Earl came along with his dig and made a discovery," Jim said.

"Unfortunate business that, but Earl was getting close to discovering the treasure. When he shut down the dig, I couldn't take the chance that he hadn't already."

Nabson shuffled his feet and looked about. "I ain't been told about no gold, Kingston. You were fixing to leave me out of things?"

"Go back to the car and wait, Sheriff."

"No one swindles me and gets by with it, not even you, Kingston. I'll see you pay for this."

Kingston turned and cocked the hammer. "I'm afraid not, Sheriff. You see, I have to sell the rest of my treasure and catch a plane."

Nabson instinctively covered his face with his arms, but the impact from the slug sent him sprawling head over heels into the canyon below.

Eva screamed, and Jim stepped in front of her, sweat trickling into his eyes. Kingston brought the weapon about, his hand steady and his smile slow.

"I do this with some regret, Mr. Hunt, but I've come too far to leave witnesses behind now."

Jim closed his eyes, and in the pending instant of the report, every muscle in his body convulsed. Eva screamed as he waited for the pain of shredded tissue and organs and bone, for the weakness, the palpitating heart, the rush of cold to his extremities. When none of it came, he opened his eyes.

Evan Kingston, with a purple hole the size of a nickel in his forehead, lay splayed against the rocks. Blood trickled down his cheek and pooled in the hollow of his neck.

Up on the rim of the canyon stood Old Man Milton with Dub at his side.

When they had worked their way down to the cave, Jim said, "Surely glad to see you Miltons. We thought you'd run off to Old Mexico."

Old Man Milton leaned the rifle against a rock. "Naw," he said. "The idea of leaving our place behind didn't set so well. Been living in this canyon and slipping up to the house come night. Keeper rarely made rounds after dark, you know."

"Those tracks were yours then?" Jim asked.

"Likely."

"But how did you shoot Kingston from up there? I thought your eyesight . . ."

"Oh, no, that was Dub here who had the pleasure. He seldom misses when it comes to killing skunks."

44

A squirrel scolded from high in the cedar, and the scent of faded roses steeped in the fall sun. Jim could see the monastery, and beyond that, Evan Kingston's mansion ascending from the hill like a deserted and ancient castle.

He leaned against the wrought-iron gate of the mausoleum to wait for his eyes to adjust to the darkness. Unlike the first time he stood here, the door was swung open, and no longer did he wonder who lay within. Down there lay the remains of an ancient friar and in the chasm, the body of Mitch Keeper.

The Celf Museum had shipped the treasure, some of the richest ever found, to the university for study, and he'd been personally welcomed back into the folds of academia. Years of work awaited.

Pete, Auntie, and Stufflebaum had sat on the steps of the museum waving goodbye with wide swings of their arms. Eva, smiling, had watched on from her office window.

Even though he'd return home to his studies and to Sara, he knew, as Coronado had known before him, that a great treasure would be waiting for him.

Notes

Chapter 3

15   *"The distances in this place . . ."* Now known as the Llano Estacado.

Chapter 7

31   *Soon they stood on the shore of a rolling river.* Canadian River.

Chapter 15

74   *The earth soon opened onto a rugged and numbing plain . . .* Approaching the Palo Duro Canyon country.

Chapter 22

116   *Coronado proceeded then into the plains . . .* They were now north of the current city of Amarillo, Texas.

Chapter 26

142   *"Thirty skilled horsemen will proceed north by the needle to Quivira."* The band turned northward in the Texas Panhandle, southeast of the present city of Amarillo.

Chapter 28

150   *Streaks of salt struck through the red earth, and mica glinted in the sunlight.* Near the Glass Mountains of northwest Oklahoma.

Chapter 30

159   *a great rock rising from out of the prairie, a river meandering to its north.* Known as Pawnee Rock, a historical landmark near the Arkansas River in Kansas.

159   *Suddenly, Indian squaws scrambled from out of the grass . . .* Most likely the Wichita tribe, which occupied much of this area.

162   *"They are called the Guaes . . ."* Thought to be the Kaws or Kansa.

Chapter 36

196   *a singular formation high as a ship mast* Pawnee Rock, located in central Kansas.

CPSIA information can be obtained at www.ICGtesting.com
Printed in the USA
LVOW04s0404120813

347386LV00002B/2/P